The Prosaist
and
The Unholy Ghost

ISBN-13: 978-1-7377620-0-3
ISBN-10: 1-7377620-0-5

First printing: October 2021

Edited by Angela K. Durden

Cover design by ThomasMax

Front cover photo by Bonni Newberry

Bloody dagger in photo provided by Rheylen Quinton and Tod Newberry.

Published by:

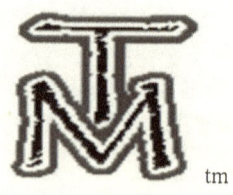
tm

ThomasMax Publishing
P.O. Box 250054
Atlanta, GA 30325
www.thomasmax.com

The Prosaist and
The Unholy Ghost

A. Shane Etter

ThomasMax

Your Publisher
For The 21st Century

ACKNOWLEDGMENTS

First of all, I would like to thank Lee Clevenger of Thomas Max Publishing for believing in *The Prosaist and The Unholy Ghost*. Thank you to my editor, Angela Durden, for your professionalism and genius. Jedwin Smith, my mentor, deserves all the credit for bringing me along for the eighth novel under your tutelage. To all the friends who have given me their support and encouragement during this literary journey, please forgive me for not mentioning you all by name. It would take more space than I have here. You all know how important you are to me. Thanks to my sister Amy Etter Mills, for your support and love.

And to Bonni Newberry, my primary and first reader, for everything.

All mistakes in settings or timing are completely my own and I take full responsibility for them.

The Prosaist and The Unholy Ghost is dedicated to Rheylen Quinton, the nine-year-old little boy who calls me "GrandMan" and never misses a chance to tell even virtual strangers, "He writes books."

When he gets older I think he should go into marketing. I'd hire him.

OTHER BOOKS
BY A. SHANE ETTER

Bottom Dwellers

Mind Dwellers

Trail Dwellers

A Brain in Third Person

A War in The Bronx

*A Brain in Third Person II
– The Return of The Bad Penny*

Devil's Sympathy

World of Rage

Chapter One

"Got a lot on my mind"

With more enthusiasm than the early hour merited, the quintessentially-dressed elderly gentleman from next door said, "Good morning, sport." Nobody used *sport* anymore unless they were a senior citizen from the Midwest. That made it seem almost normal for the twenty-first century.

Grayson recognized the flat Midwest non-accent. "Good morning. How're you this fine fall day?"

"Oh, just splendid, thank you. You certainly are more talkative than you were last night."

Or splendid, Grayson thought

"What? What are you talking about?"

"I work the late shift. You know I volunteer at the senior citizen's home over on Broadway? Answering the phone and doing paperwork and other somewhat less than pleasant mundane chores. Mostly involving cleaning up after little accidents, you know. That's the worst part of it. Anyways, got home a wee bit after midnight and you were leaving. Didn't seem to want to get into a conversation."

"Oh. Uh, sorry. Got a lot on my mind. The new book, you know." *What the hell is he talking about? I didn't go anywhere at midnight last night. I'd already been asleep at least an hour. He must have been drinking. I know he has a love affair with his gin, especially since his Blanche died. Or maybe it's dementia. He is getting up there. It can't possibly be easy for him since he lost his wife. Just him and those damn cats.*

"No problem. I know how it must be when you're a famous author. How's it going, by the way?"

"What's that?"

"The new book?"

"Not bad, thanks. Ready for release."

"Great. Good luck. I can't wait to read it. I'll want a signed copy. Anyway, have a splendid day."

"Thanks. You, too."

Chapter Two

"What do you want anyway?"

"Damn, how am I ever going to finish this chapter if people don't stop interrupting me," Grayson Cole said to the buzzing new iPhone lying face down on the rich walnut desk he'd found in one of his favorite antique shops on Manhattan's Lower East Side, the infamous Bowery area. He thought he'd hit the metaphorical jackpot when he spotted the redoubtable piece with its inlaid leather top and classic gold embossing. A most natural thought…and it only cost him an arm, not an arm and a leg. Even considering the financial success of his latest novels, he appreciated a bargain and didn't spend his fortune willy-nilly.

The walnut wood was the same color as the built-in bookshelves and trim on the study walls. That had been his good fortune. The biggest challenge to acquiring the piece was moving it from the previous-century house of antiquities in the Bowery to his Upper West Side brownstone. Not that it was that distant, it wasn't but two or three miles and not nearly as far as it seemed in the 1800s when the whole of Manhattan Island was hilly farmland. But this is New York City and such things are never easy.

The Bowery, now known for its pricy condominiums, and furniture, décor and design stores, was a far cry from its genesis as a district for drunks, prostitutes, and the homeless. It was now famous for being where the notorious mid-nineteenth century murderer Bill the Butcher had plied his bloody trade and made a truly menacing name for himself.

Only to keep it from annoying him with its incessant buzzing, he jerked up the smartphone and flipped it over.

"Oh, it's you," Grayson answered to the digital name of his literary agent, a necessary but nonetheless-as-annoying-as-the-buzzing important part of his life.

"'Oh, it's you?' Is that how you greet the most important person in your little life?"

"And who deemed you the most important person in my life?"

"You have, every time you finish a new manuscript that I can sell for a six-figure advance…and you will again say it — and I'll remind you of this conversation again."

They laughed and Grayson teased, "Good thing I've finished *Rapacious...* and starting on another. What do you want, anyway?"

"I'm setting up an interview for you on *Today*. Wanted to check your schedule. Their producer called. Apparently, because I do such good job of repping you, he heard about *Rapacious*."

"Don't break your arm patting yourself on the back. You like to think that without you I'd be nothing but an anonymuncule, but hey, you know me, anything for you." More laughter, then, "Let me check my calendar."

The first question interviewers always asked is "Where do you get your ideas?" He hated that question. *Hello? My head?* is what he wanted to say. The second was, "Is your name a pen name?" His ready answer was always, "No, I'm trying to sell books. I want people to know who I am."

He pulled up the calendar app in a different window on the iPad Pro he used for everything, including writing. It contained every detail vital to his existence. The parlor, repurposed as his study where he did all of his writing, faced east. The flirtatious morning sun tormented the old-world room like a puppy terrorizing an old dog, determined to make it look as it did when the townhouse was new in the early twentieth century.

It smelled of fresh coffee, ancient wood, leather, old books and, for the last year, a new cologne, the designer fragrance *Tom Ford Vanille Fatale* that blended well with the small fire burning in the grate. Even with his current obscene income, the fine cologne was one of the few indulgences he allowed himself. That and his monthly bottle of Blanton's small batch bourbon. Fortunately, a fifth could last him all month as long as he kept his head.

The entry to the room emerged through a wall of books. The built-in bookshelves, covering three walls, bent under the weight of heavy leather-bound tomes. Tools of his trade, some used for research, most there because of his love of reading. One of the positives of being a writer, he could read all he wanted and call it work. Books, even expensive leather collectors' editions were tax write-offs for an author, or at least that's what his accountant told him. She had said she could write off just about every penny he spent if he'd just let her.

Of course, she was a poker player, went down to AC almost every weekend. But she was playing with his money when she gambled with the IRS.

The only furniture besides his desk and a high-backed leather chair was an over-sized rich brown suede armchair sitting at an angle to a corner, lovingly caressed by an Old World Tiffany floor lamp, its cushion depressed from long hours spent there reading and musing about his works-in-progress.

Providing entry to the center of the co-op, a square enclosed cobblestone courtyard, was a high breezeway, also called an arcade, of the same shape that provided entrance to the one in the nearby Dakota under which John Lennon was assassinated. Homeowners could park their cars — if they kept one in the city — in the courtyard. Indeed a parking space in the city could cost as much as rent. Once upon a time the courtyard was a space reserved for horse-drawn brougham carriages and two-wheeled hansoms. It had once been strewn with hay filthy with horse shit. But, as the great Nobel prize-winning poet Bob Dylan had said, "The times, they are a changin'."

While he waited for the app to open, Grayson whistled a random tune and watched the pigeons entertain themselves on the dung-stained windowsill overlooking Central Park. The winged rats were the only reason he didn't leave the windows open on fresh autumn and spring days. That was a shame since the city always smelled fresh in the fall. He kept them undraped, however, so the morning sun bathed the east-facing room in brilliant yellow light. It wasn't like he would have peepers on the third floor.

He looked down on broad Central Park West, its busy sidewalks and verdant lawn painted orange and gold with fallen leaves except where interrupted by feral large schist boulders with crystallized layers, some as large as a car or a small dinosaur, bubbling up. Not wholly unlike the gneiss in the Bronx, both formed over four hundred fifty million years ago, vestigial reminders of the last ice age when dinosaurs stalked and flew over Manhattan. The boulders also served as witnesses in the nineteenth century when the whole of Manhattan was farmland, dotted with squatters' shacks, and, most recently, during the Great Depression of the twentieth century when the shanties joined to form Hoovervilles, unceremoniously credited to the president at the time.

But now, a playground for the masses, the wealthy and blue collar alike, as architect Frederick Law Olmsted intended when he designed it and, honestly and without the slightest hint of braggadocio, proclaimed it the greatest of his life's work. The trees of the city's playground, scarlet oak, red maple, and American elm, were at the peak of their yearly autumnal transformation from green to shades of crimson, gold, and orange. If he were on the ground, on the great lawn, he would smell the tang of the colors.

Beyond the Palisades, Central Park and New Jersey were ablaze with twinning kinetic color. Late morning and already children were playing tag while nannies and au pairs stood close watching protectively. Old men and young women, not only Chinese, practiced tai chi gracefully. Healthy shirtless young men ran and threw Frisbees while pretty young coeds sat on benches and blankets sunning and watching, watching and sunning, pretending they're interested in the game.

The rest of America doesn't understand the importance of Central Park, indeed all parks, to New Yorkers. In other cities and towns across the country, parks in the form of backyards, for barbecuing, running and jumping and outdoor living, are common. But not in Manhattan, Brooklyn, or the Bronx. That's why their parks are as much of a necessity as the police or fire departments to New Yorkers.

It wouldn't be long before winter's bitter cold would freeze the ponds. Grayson worried about the ducks and where they would go when the surfaces were frozen solid. He wished he had a place for them to go for the long winter.

He would have killed without consideration to have bought a townhouse on the Upper East Side in the coveted historic Sutton Place, but even given the success of his two most recent novels he didn't feel like he should, even if he could, shell out the eight figures it would require, so instead he settled for shelling out the seven figures the west side commanded. Maybe after his first movie, he kept telling himself. Like Brett Easton Ellis. In fact his writing was already being compared to that of the prolific author of *American Psycho* and the imminently successful film of the same name. At forty, and without arrogance, even he thought the comparisons between himself and the highly respected prosaist were justified.

Sometimes he even wished he'd been born a half a century or more earlier. The wish, proof that Grayson was truly a throwback to a different era. He would have loved to hang his square chin over a chilled martini or Manhattan, condensation clouding the sides of the icy glass, while sitting at the bar of El Morocco or The Stork Club, it opened by Oklahoma bootlegger Sherman Billingsley in the twenties and a society nightspot with a heavy 14-karat solid gold chain at its entrance through which patrons were allowed entry by a huge, swarthy, sour-faced but well-dressed doorman…but only if he recognized you as an A-Lister, or you were the guest of an A-Lister and looked the part by being eye-catchingly dressed.

The important man must have been paid well because he couldn't be bribed or inveigled for passage nor chicanery employed against his uncommon common sense.

It was a time of the elite and described by New York newspapermen as swanky; when movie stars, athletes, celebrities, swells, showgirls, and Mafia hoodlums all mixed in the club's VIP Room. Bob Hope, *New York Daily News* columnist Ed Sullivan, and Ol' Blue Eyes himself, Sinatra, along with prizefighter Max Baer, Elizabeth Taylor, and John Kennedy before he was president — all habitués of the Stork.

Joseph Cherney had been Grayson's agent since his second novel. He'd done a serviceable job of earning his keep, and enjoyed the ten percent commission from his authors' advances. In his sixties, he was a throwback — not exactly a dinosaur, but a reminder nonetheless — to what the book business had once been. Publishers, agents, publicists, acquisition editors were all Jewish. Now they were mostly goy, gentiles. All young enough to be the agent's grandchildren, highly-educated and attractive. Cherney had forgotten more about the book business than all of them knew, in total. He liked to tell people he sold Simon & Schuster the first book they ever published. It was a stretch of the truth, of course. He wasn't that old, but most of the young agents and editors he dealt with would never know that.

Cherney began to drum his fingers on his desk impatiently. The scarred brown wood work surface the only thing in the office that wasn't beige. It and the beige carpet with stains of various colors and hues. He knew he needed to relax — his internist, a young man half his age, had already warned him about his heart — but he had other clients and potential ones he needed to call on this Monday morning, even if they weren't as prolific or didn't make him as much money as Grayson, and a lunch meeting at the Carnegie Deli to which he couldn't be late. The fact that he loved the world-famous cheesecake the restaurant had invented, was almost irrelevant. He liked mountain-sized slices with cherry topping. Couldn't believe anybody would eat it with blueberries. A travesty like none other.

What his doctor didn't know wouldn't hurt him. He was considering retirement as the frenetic pace of a literary agent was finally beginning to wear on him. Still, actually working was better than sitting in his ancient threadbare one room office in Midtown all day. But he had to have somewhere to go to get out of the house and away from the screeching, stooped, old Jewish woman he'd wed over forty years before.

Older than Cherney, the bland old office could probably tell more tales than he. Only rising to the third floor of a mid-century concrete-colored aging skyscraper topped with real honest-to-God griffons and gargoyles, it didn't even offer a view of the sidewalks of 50th Street. Of the businessmen and women racing on important missions that couldn't wait. Couldn't wait another minute—

Grayson scrolled through his calendar. "I can free up early mornings almost any weekday. Make it happen."

"Don't I always? By the way, what do you think about the Unholy Ghost?"

"I don't."

"Then you must be the only one in the city who doesn't. The public is obsessed with him." The truth was New York hadn't been this terrified since David Berkowitz — Son of Sam and also known as the .44 Caliber Killer — was on his killing rampage during the summer of '76.

"I hope that's veridical and maybe they'll buy even more books about serial killers."

"And in that there is always hope. Well, for God's sake, you watch out for yourself. I'd hate to lose my biggest client."

"You watch out for yourself. I'll be standing by about the *Today* interview date and time." Grayson disconnected the call then, aloud to himself, said, "I think it's time for someone else's coffee."

Pushing up determinedly from the comfortable desk with both hands, his voice sounding hollow in his head and in the empty house, he closed his iPad. "Jesus H. Christ, talking to myself. The voices dissonant in my head must finally be getting to me. Oh well, comes with the territory, I guess. Only surprise is it's taken this long."

The bane of novelists, writers of fiction, they always wonder if they're mad, especially since everyone already thinks they are. It was part of the writer's life. But when madness becomes reality, and a friend who *is* mad says they aren't, do you believe them? Most likely one would be making reservations for their friend at the infamous Greystone Park Psychiatric Hospital in Morris Plains, New Jersey. Or chaining them in the basement, or behind a stone wall like in *The Cask Of Amontillado*, the terrifying timeless short story by the original author macabre, Edgar Allen Poe.

Furthermore, Grayson wasn't bothered by cognitive dissonance since as a fiction writer he wasn't bound by such outdated ideas. Likewise, no other norms, mores, or societal constructs could affect him.

If someone asked him what he likes about writing fiction, the first answer Grayson would think but couldn't tell is that people think everything he writes — every thought, every idea, every word — is untrue. So, he can get away with telling a true story or inserting pieces of truths because people think it false. Yet nearly every word he writes has a kernel of truth, of unvarnished honesty, to it. But he couldn't speak of what he told as fiction that others had done as fact. Also because it would be like a magician revealing his tricks, showing how the rabbit gets in the hat. Then the show, or in the case of the novelist, the story, would be over. The mystery, or the rabbit, disappeared.

Grayson wore regular-fit Wrangler jeans and a sweatshirt of dark blue with Yale emblazoned in stark white letters in a comfortable large arc across the chest. He pulled off the brown suede, fleece-lined, ankle-high slippers he wore around the house for warmth and left them where they fell under his desk. The warm sweat shirt wasn't an original from his time as an undergrad, although he still could've worn the old one at the same five ten and a buck-sixty he was twenty years before. His lean physique and the energy of a high school centerfielder made him appear younger than his years.

He grew up in Great Neck, out on Long Island. The burg, full of counter-culturists, was a typical early twentieth century progressive New York suburb of the nearly affluent. A short drive but a world away from the business capitol of the world called Manhattan. His parents were early hippies in the mostly liberal conclave. The whole bohemian, anti-establishment, free-thinker way of existence was probably a big influence on him becoming a writer. As it turned out, the two most influential forces in his life cared not that he wasn't interested in a nine to five, corporate-rat-running-the-maze job.

He swept a hand through his stylishly unkempt brown hair, still undefiled by gray at forty, giving it the perfect yet insouciant look of having just climbed out of bed. Even in casual attire, in no way would anyone think he appeared louche. Old-school and unstained, his canvas Nike sneakers with red vinyl swooshes replaced the slippers for a brisk hike down Broadway to the nearest shop. Owned by Latinos, he wasn't sure if they were Dominican or Haitian.

Wasn't sure it mattered since both countries shared the island of Hispanolia. *I wonder how many people know that obscure fact of geography?*

Funny the arcane bits of knowledge one picked up while doing research for writing fiction. But their coffee was good. Maybe they were Colombian. He chuckled softly to himself at his harmless little joke. But then a sign in the window said their specialty was Vietnamese coffee. Rich, dark, and full bodied. *Sounds like a woman I would like.*

He admired the owners though, immigrants who came to a strange country from their homeland and created something indispensable: a caffeine delivery system in the city that never sleeps. Helping it stay awake.

Funny. I'm on a roll today.

Lifting his ring of keys from the brass hook next to the door, Grayson stepped onto the small stoop, and used one of the brass keys to lock the door behind him. He cupped his hands around a cigarette to block the ever-present morning zephyr sweeping off the Hudson from blowing out the flame. He kept telling himself he was going to give up the disgusting habit, but it soothed his fears, the ones all authors experience, that they can never do it, or never do it again, when they wrote. The mid-morning air was bracing and surprisingly fresh, especially for New York.

Grayson bounded down the steps, the surprisingly cool temperature causing him to step up what was usually his more relaxed pace to the coffee shop. The piercing blue sky had never been more vivid. It would be a perfect October afternoon for a World Series game at Yankee Stadium. Alas, the Bronx Bombers sucked this year, languishing in the cellar of the AL East. Grayson was old-school, a fan of the New York football Giants and the Bronx boys of summer.

Although he was fond of their doughnuts, keeping an eye on his envious waistline, of which men ten years younger were jealous, he passed up the Dunkin', noting its name change to a new abbreviated version. The company's marketing geniuses must think it cooler. It shared a space wearing an artistically rendered BR in bright neon over the door. The same marketing geniuses must have thought that was hipper than Baskin-Robbins. Those signs were evidence that he could most likely make a living writing marketing copy if the fiction writing gig ever dried up. God help him if he ever had to do something as soul-sucking as that.

Grayson leaned on the door of West Side Trade Coffee Emporium that he knew from previous visits was annoyingly strident. Unless they'd applied a healthy dose of WD-40, not that it was likely since his last visit. It had been squeaking for as long as he could remember. He thought the riot bars over the windows were somewhat less than necessary in this neighborhood, too, especially since the loose door could be forced by any good-sized male. The shop smelled of fresh ground beans and spicy incense. Jasmin, frankincense, and myrrh. The shop's aroma a zeitgeist of pleasant but hazy memories. The incense reminded Grayson of the illegal effervescence of his freshman year dorm at Yale.

"You got any WD-40? I'll fix that noise for you," he said half jokingly.

"Thank you, but we like the squeak. No robbers, or nobody else, can sneak in on us," said the still-cute upper-middle-aged female who, along with her husband, owned the shop.

Grayson smiled understandingly, though this was known by most as one of the city's better neighborhoods. In fact, he knew Jerry Seinfeld lived nearby, even though he'd never met the man or even laid eyes on him. He had been to the studio and gallery of world-renowned artist Peter Max, no more than ten short blocks and a half-mile away. Met the man usually regarded as the greatest pop artist of all time when he happened to be in on that early morning. Peter wouldn't be caught dead in a less than reputable nabe.

Grayson decided it was a special day since *Rapacious* was being released, and ordered a nonfat latté in a heavy-sided off-white ceramic mug with a coffee bean brown WTC logo, instead of his usual coffee, regular, the way real New Yorkers drink it. And a bagel. He thought their bagels were the best in the city. Even better than those at H&H, famous for their taste and air and not far away on the Upper West Side. H&H was made even more famous on the comedy show Seinfeld as the employer from which Kramer, played by co-star Michael Richards, was on strike for the entire nine-season run of the legendary series.

Grayson liked West Side Coffee because the customers leaned closer to the *hoi polloi* than the bourgeois-like customer that coveted Starbucks, which it seemed was on every block in the city. The former offered him much more inspiration for his dark stories of the city. In a pinch, he even liked the original New York favorite, Chock full o' Nuts, which had closed its doors years before but whose stores were beginning to pop up again. *Of course, as I always say, coffee is what separates us from the animals.*

He sat at a small, scarred wood-topped table that could barely seat two. Probably acquired at a secondhand store, its surface was scratched with various curses, clever sayings, and random thoughts, none of which inspired him. On it were strewn previously-read newspapers, wrinkled and stale coffee-stained copies of the *Daily News* and *The New York Times*. He lighted a cigarette. *Second one of the morning. Son of a bitch.*

Retreated into his coffee. He didn't often smoke; only when the stress of writing was beginning to overtake him, but the coffee; he couldn't live without caffeine. He had more stories to write. Or read Tolstoy. It was a toss up. Tolstoy would make him feel better. Tolstoy always made him feel better. It was the realism. Of course life, his own realism, was beginning to worry him. He wasn't sure why. Why couldn't he be happy, or even accept, being a successful millionaire novelist, admired by many? Alas, he sighed, pondering that which was above him, or beneath him. It always depended on how one considered above or below. Or deep.

Grayson, though only forty, was a throwback. He loved newspapers, the important part of the word being paper. He didn't know what he'd do when they stopped the printing. It was inevitable; he just knew it. Digital-only was the future. He knew he could read them on his iPad, but it wasn't the same. He liked the tactile sensation of paper, the smell of ink.

He preferred the *Daily News*, in spite of its use of Old World terms, poor grammar, invented words, and uncommon abbreviations, all done to fit the allocated space, because of its gritty realistic style of writing, which, if one wanted to be kind, could work creative in there, also.

But he thought he should look at *The New York Times* in public because it was considered more intellectual, and if anyone recognized him at least it would be more apt for the well-crafted media image his manager, agent and publisher all worked so hard to cultivate.

Using a small plastic knife useless for anything else, he spread a popular brand of cream cheese, named for the historic city about ninety miles down the New Jersey turnpike, from an individual-sized plastic tub onto the toasted bagel, before stifling a yawn and wondering why he was sleepy. He'd gotten a solid seven hours the night before.

That's been happening more and more lately. Maybe I should see my doctor.

Done with the bagel, he snatched up the coffee-stained printed words. He usually enjoyed the unblemished smell of newsprint, but this one was newsprint mixed with stale coffee. The front-page headline announced that the Unholy Ghost had struck again over night. Although the killer's nickname sounded like something Steve Dunleavy of *The Post* would've come up with, probably while holding court sitting on his favorite stool at the bar at Langan's Irish Pub in Times Square, he had died the year before, surprisingly not sitting at Langan's bar and *not* from alcohol abuse, so the sobriquet must have been given by an earnest young news reporter obviously in quest of a Pulitzer, and hoping to become the heir-apparent to the Australian-born, world-renowned Dunleavy. Unless of course, he had really big dreams and aspired to be the next generational Damon Runyon.

But that was something one would never speak aloud. To even dream it might be considered too lofty.

The most recent slaying increased the total to twelve attributed to the gruesome serial killer with a blade, during the earth's most recent trip around the sun. The first one had been a beloved, white-collared parish priest, his beloved rosary missing — hence the religious/non-religious sobriquet of the killer — in an historic Irish Catholic Cathedral downtown, even more magnificent than the deconsecrated one that became infamous as the notorious seventies-era Limelight disco only a few blocks away.

A young woman leaving a Midtown dance club in the late evening was found in an alley with her chest cavity slashed open. She'd been nearly disemboweled.

The killer was especially sinister since he didn't seem to follow a pattern. Young, old, male, female, any race. It didn't seem to matter. As far as law enforcement could discover, none had connections to others, so it was hard to keep safe unless one stayed home. He knew it was a rhetorical question, but who was going to do that in the city that never sleeps? And different methods of killing, although a blade of some sort seemed to be his preferred method.

Grayson was focused on his reading, but the sound of the annoying door alerted him to someone entering. A young man in the current young people's style of tailored gray sweatpants and a dark hoodie. It covering all but the oval of his unremarkable face.

He must have been a regular as the proprietor knew his preferred libation and had it waiting for him by the time he reached the counter. The young man sat at a nearby table and cupped the mug in both hands and draped his face over it for the warmth it provided on a chilly morning. Grayson sat, trying to watch the young man without staring, and rubbed his face. That's when he realized he'd forgotten to shave…again. He'd been doing that more lately, too.

Back at home he was writing a murder a scene and the *Daily News* article he'd read gave him plenty of inspiration for an especially bloody killing he'd been pondering. He had thought *Rapacious* would be his darkest and most violent story to date. He was always trying to take it to the next level and still appeal to the book-buying masses, especially women who, according to Amazon demographics, seemed to read serial killer novels at a higher percentage than their male counterparts. To push the envelope and exceed the boundaries of good taste while still increasing book sales was his goal. But he was outdoing himself with his current as-yet-unnamed tome.

Chapter Three

"No one but you"

At least half of the horde, tourists. One could tell by the way they dressed, and how they stared open-mouthed at…everything.

It was crowded but not oppressively so where he sat at the bar in the Show Room at The Paradise Club on Seventh Avenue so he could talk to people. The newest nightclub gift to a rejuvenating Gotham from Ian Schrager of Studio 54 fame.

All for the *soi-disant* grandiloquent. The Soigné. The bougie. The artists, authors, actors, and musicians. Genuine or wannabes, they had one thing in common — scratching for their big break or keeping it going. One couldn't know if they were to the manner born, or pretended to be. Couldn't always tell the difference in the real and incredible. Isn't that always the way it is? Or should be. Then there were those who wanted to rub elegantly veiled shoulders. Practiced ersatz bonhomie.

There was nothing worn or antiquated in the modern stainless and glass club, and no old smell. Glass and steel have no odor. The only aromas were those of expensive perfumes and colognes, the amalgam *beau mondes* wore.

The ostentatious club was far different from Toots Shor's in more ways than the short two miles from its former site and three-quarters of a century. The people in this fancy nightspot would never have been allowed in Toots' place. It for constructionists, plumbers, anybody whose collar was blue and arms were short-sleeved red, and wanted to hang their chin over a heavy mug of beer; and not microbrews, the only hops you could get were those from PBR, Schlitz, or Old Milwaukee.

Smoking was graciously allowed, if not encouraged.

Gordon couldn't get into too much detail in an insouciant convo since his whole plan worked only if he maintained a fairly low profile and didn't draw undo attention to himself.

At the same time he couldn't just walk up to someone's table and start talking to them, as that would be too awkward. So, the bar was it.

Being very cool about it, from the pile of dirty dishes on the counter next to him he nonchalantly slipped a piece of unclean cutlery up the sleeve of his expensive but common-looking sport jacket, hoping no one would notice it was missing. Not for the first time, nor hopefully to him, the last, his plan was in place and had begun.

After a busser removed the dishes a moment later, he felt the air move on the back of his neck as someone passed behind him in response to an unspoken prayer. She was young, sallow-skinned, dark tressed, and in her early thirties, though dressed professionally in business wear rather than club clothes. "Is anyone sitting here?" she said, as if she expected to get a seat. She was attractive but not as attractive as she thought she was. But that confidence made her more attractive, so maybe her opinion of herself was warranted. Dressed as she was, she looked like she'd recently left the office. But it was too late for that.

"No one but you," he said.

"Thank you." He helped her shrug off a long black winter coat, protection from the nascent cold, and hung it on the back of the high-backed chair. Most New Yorkers wear black year-round, night or day, to camouflage the city's grime.

"You're very welcome."

"I'm Rachel."

"Gordon," he said, offering his hand, while sizing her up like a plump slice of Carnegie Deli cheesecake. "Pleased to make your acquaintance." He leaned closer, turning his head so his ear was closest to her lips as it was hard to hear over Snow Patrol's *Chasing Cars* playing on the loud, expensive sound system.

"Likewise," she nodded.

The recorded music would go on until the live show began, which would kick off in but a few minutes, at eleven p.m. He could smell the flowery bouquet of her perfume.

He hoped she would do all the talking, not asking anything of himself because he couldn't remember…or know anything of his past. That was the frightening part. If he didn't remember, that could be explained away: illness, injury, drugs. He could live with any of those. But not know? Why wouldn't he know?

All Gordon knew was killing. A side effect of not knowing or remembering, was that he was getting better at making shit up on the fly.

Not only was killing all he knew, it was all he thought about. It was part of his DNA, and consumed his very being.

He knew better than to ask the woman what she did for a living because she'd then think the polite thing to do, whether she cared or not, would be to return the favor, and then the dance would begin, the back and forth. What do you do? Where do you like to go? Where did you go to school? Where are you from? Not difficult to answer for the average person, but questions Gordon didn't know the answers to. He couldn't even make them up because of some reason unknown to him he wasn't even knowledgeable of things like those, his past nothing more than nebulous. Besides, it would slow him down from his deadly intent. Small talk bored the shit out of him. He was sure small talk would bore the shit out of shit.

Please start talking, so I don't have to ask you anything.

It was almost like she read his mind. She straightened her hair with a practiced stroke. "I work at the new World Trade Center," she said.

In the capacious dark room with the bright lights pulsing to the backbeat he could barely see her. "How nice. What do you do?"

"I work for an importer, anything from semiprecious trinkets to large goods, coming from Southeast Asia."

"Cool. How's business?"

"It's great, thank you. I'm paid fairly well and get to go to Southeast Asia from time to time."

"That's great. I love the pearls of the Orient."

"Oh, me, too. But I've never been here before." She waved a hand indicating the room. "Friends in the building I take lunch with have been after me to try it out. I thought they were going to be here. But I guess I got my nights mixed up."

"You aren't worried about the Unholy Ghost everyone's talking about?"

"Not if you don't remind me about him. But two glasses of wine is my limit. I like to keep my lucidity, so I should be okay."

"Well, he worries me. I'm not much of a fighter. Not one for getting fistic. I'm more of a lover. I hope they catch the worthless piece of shit soon and throw him in the tombs," he said.

The tombs was the better known and altogether unnerving moniker, also sometimes referred to by cops who think they're especially clever as the Gray Bar Hotel rather than its more dramatic and noble name The Halls of Justice. In the 1800s more than fifty prisoners had met their ends at temporary gallows set up in the street under the Bridge of Sighs.

"At least until they send him to a more permanent home up the river," Gordon continued with a chary look, using the euphemisms everybody knew for the violent and dark Rikers Island Jail where New York's Boldest — the army of more than eleven thousand uniformed officers who process and watch over more than one hundred thousand inmates each year — would make sure those inmates see the error of their ways. At least until he was transferred to the state prison, the latter given the phrase being sent up the river to the infamous Sing Sing, fashioned by criminals literally being sent up the broad Hudson. They also fashioning the well-known prison euphemisms The Big House and The Last Mile.

Gordon finished his drink in one go. "Excuse my French," he said.

"No problem. I speak a wee bit of the French, too," Rachel cleverly remarked before taking a last tipple of her Chardonnay and, seductively in the bartender's direction, waggled the glass now christened with a fresh, hot pink lipstick stain.

The veteran bartender responded immediately to the request from the comely customer and looked at Gordon. "How about you?"

"Thought you'd never ask." Even he thought it was risky when he said that, but no bartender ever got mad at him. At least not so it showed, except for maybe a rolling of eyes indicating it wasn't the first time they'd heard that one. Of course he tipped them well as their reward for laughing at his woeful stabs at humor, so it served them well to pretend they were amused.

"I like the way you think. I wish all my customers thought like you."

The mixologist returned with the glass of wine, and a moment later a Manhattan poured with a generous measure of rye. His spirits in the genteel stemmed martini glass and her large-globe Chardonnay glass, they tilted their drinks to each other in the way of two people trying to be cool and proper, and to impress. Sadly, it came across as rehearsed, or even nervous.

"Where do you live?"

"Meat Packing District," she said, referring to the much respected rapidly gentrifying former industrial warehouse neighborhood. In no more than a few blocks walk it would refashion itself from ultra-expensive flats to warehouses and back to pricey flats again. "You?"

"Nice. Upper West Side, the Seventies."

"Talk about nice. What do you do?"

Gordon took a swallow of his Manhattan and cleared his dry throat nervously before answering. He was more edgy than just somewhat. Attempted without much luck to put a smile on his face, to buy some time. This is where the conversation could get dicey. Giving too much information. Or the wrong information to the wrong person.

"Thanks, but it's not like CPW is Sutton Place. The New York Mercantile exchange. You know-NYMEX? On the trading floor."

He thought he saw Rachel cast a quick sideways glance toward the shiny mirrored disco ball suspended above the dance floor and the deejay's glass aerie on the opposite wall. An indication of boredom? He couldn't blame her if she were. This was the kind of small talk that bored the shit out of him.

"I feel like a dance before the show starts. How about you?"

"Sure."

Gordon couldn't remember a time when a girl had asked him to dance, but he didn't mind. 'Course there wasn't much he could remember except for the details of every murder he'd ever wrought. Those were embedded in the depths of his gray matter, never to escape, easy to recall when he desired a warm feeling. Like a man remembering all the sexual notches on his belt to give him inspiration for future conquests and keep him warm at night, why would he want to forget something that gave him so much pleasure?

After a turn around the floor to the latest hit from Bruno Mars, they returned to their seats. But Rachel was to call it a night. "I'd love to stay for the show but it is a school night, you understand."

"Can I see you to the station?"

"I shan't think you a gentleman if you left a lady wandering alone in the dark wilderness."

"That would be a tragedy unlike no other. Let me settle our tabs." He withdrew enough cash from his wallet to cover both tabs and provide a good, though not memorable, tip. He had credit cards but the name on them wasn't his. He couldn't risk someone noticing and asking him who Grayson was. He didn't know. He just knew he wasn't Grayson. Besides, it sounded like a pussy's name.

"I'm going to the ladies room. I'll see you in the lobby, Gordon."

He nodded happily. After his short wait in the plush lobby, Rachel returned. It wasn't a long walk to the nearest subway entrance but because the night air was chilly they didn't take their time. The air smelled fresh after the warmer conditioned air of the club. But it was too cold for small talk. The cold hurt one of his molars even through the thick skin of his cheek. He thought that must mean he was getting a cavity. He'd have to see a dentist, but he couldn't remember having one. Surely he did, though.

Gordon thought they'd made enough small talk already. If he found out too much about her or decided he liked her it might detract him from his mission. He'd learned many murders ago he had to be careful of that. Certainly, this wasn't his first rodeo.

The city was always loud. It didn't matter what time of day, or night, it was. A veritable auditory assault. The sidewalk was bright from the coruscation of New York neon, but a self-important moon hung in the limpid night sky refusing to be usurped and shone condescendingly on the vertiginous skyscraper canyons, they an essential part of the city's sprawl. The inspirational green lady of the harbor could be seen through those canyons keeping vigil over New York's waters, and the cargos, freighters, and liners plying them indefatigably, as she has for almost a century and a half. No living person had seen the gift from France in its original brown copper color before the elements turned it to its tarnished green.

Grayson thought the edge of the night beautiful; something to be enjoyed by those of means and the dispossessed, living in wealth and destitution side by side in close proximity in this, the greatest city on earth.

"Do you mind if I run in and get a paper?" Gordon asked, pointing at a brightly lit news store. "I'd like to find out the latest on the Unholy Ghost." He said insouciantly. Indeed, every paper's headline was about the infamous killer. But he chose one that mentioned the lead detective on the case. Salvatoré Rossi, an aging Italian with twenty-five plus years on the job. It wouldn't hurt for Gordon to find out all he could about the man whose life's quest it would be to stop him and send him to prison for the rest of his earthly existence.

"I'll wait right here."

"Don't wander off. It might not be safe," he said with feigned but believable concern.

Walking back outside and taking a deep breath of the nighttime chill and seeing the white cloud of condensation when he released it, Gordon said, "It looks like we're going to have an early winter." It seemed winter always arrived early in New York, with the season's first snowstorm to follow close on its tail as a mad, raving lunatic. Dumping beautiful but traffic-snarling, teeth rattling, unprovoked maliciousness on the vulnerable. Usually in young December. New and rarely waiting until the twenty-first of the month to make its presence felt, unlike more cooperative places.

"I so hope so. I love the way the city looks in the new snow."

"Come on, Rachel. Here's a shortcut," he said, taking her by the arm and somewhat less than gently pulling her toward a darkened maw. It was no more than a deserted alley, but it would serve his purpose, if she were trusting, and gullible.

"Are you sure?" she said, reluctant to leave the safety of the busy sidewalk.

"It'll get us out of this cold faster."

"I guess it's okay, then," she said, still hesitating.

"Let's go."

No more than a dozen paces in, panic on her face, Rachel said, "I think this was a mistake." She didn't mean entering the alley. She was beginning to realize her bigger mistake, leaving the safety of the club with this unknown man; even before that, sitting down next to the stranger at the bar. She would regret it for the rest of her soon to end short life. The look on her face made him uncomfortable. This was the only time he was ever bothered by what he did − right before he did it; when they both knew what was about to happen. But then he always got over it. As quickly as the feeling overcame him, it left, to be replaced by desire. He was only doing what anyone would do in an amoral society lacking a virtuous creed. At least he had one. That's what he told himself, anyway. That was the most exciting time, for him, at least. The feeling, sublime.

He wondered: when he killed one of those parasitic amoral organisms, did they feel relief at the end of their unenlightened existences?

How could they not? The only thing that bothered him was that he had no one, friends or acquaintances, since everyone he met he killed. That was the bitch of it all. But then he'd remember to ask himself the question because it made him comfortable with himself: Why should he desire a connection with one of those types? He would be unable to think of a reason. Besides, by killing them, their lives and souls were connected in the deepest way imaginable, forever.

"We all make mistakes," he replied unconcerned.

She tried to dart away but he grabbed her wrist, twisting it savagely with more strength than he appeared capable of having. He rotated his body behind her, his eyes glazed over and his mouth twisted into an angry snarl. Making him seem more feral than man. An evil, conscienceless creature of the night, on the dark streets that were, to him, where he belonged. At home in the concrete jungle.

Rachel — although he now thought of her as victim, no name — tried to scream, but twisting her around so her back was to his chest, he shoved a hand over her mouth, stifling her scream. With the other he pulled out the serrated-edged steak knife he had concealed up his sleeve, smelling of expensive house-made steak sauce. He stabbed her in the stomach, hara-kiri-style, halfway between what was most certainly an outie navel and the midpoint of her eye-catching cleavage, ripping the knife left to right. He had grown accustomed to the tearing sound it made. First the skin. Then the meatier parts containing fat, cartilage, and ligaments. Then a raspy sound that he felt more than heard, as it scraped on the breastbone before giving way to the hissing sound of air escaping the lungs. He was mostly protected from the spray of the somewhat more than small runnel of blood that soaked her clothing in a dark flow down her body.

He could smell it from behind her, it and the stink of entrails and what they contained. He let her drop.

A silent scream frozen on the victim's no longer attractive face, the Unholy Ghost straightened the lapels of his sport coat nattily, and the collar of his shirt, then waited for a group of people to pass before, in his signature move, he ducked his head and covered his face faking a soft sneeze, and exited insouciantly onto the busy sidewalk behind groups of late-night theatre goers dressed to the nines. If the world were in black and white, it would be a scene from the '40s.

In sharp contrast were the skimpily-dressed hookers displaying their wares even in the clear vesper chill. Rich and squalid side by side. Tight leather skirts and blingy scanty tops. Lean, lithe bodies with large man-made breasts, they had to be freezing in their tiny outfits. The darker of two ladies of the night glanced his way.

"Hey, good looking. You wanna get laid? Issa slow night. You can have both of us for the price of one. Chocolate and vanilla. For real. C'mon, whattayasay?"

He thought of the line from the soulful song by Simon &Garfunkel, *The Boxer*: "Just a come-on from the whores on Seventh Avenue." He was only a block away from the street of the popular song. But unlike the song, he didn't take some comfort there. He turned his face toward a shop window with a display of Big Apple souvenirs while trying to look sick and be forgettable.

"Whatsa matter? You shy? That's cute."

She carried on a nonstop, machine gun patter. He couldn't think of a clever retort because he felt sorry for her. Nothing that wouldn't come off like he was chiding her for her lack of morals, anyway. The irony of that canting thought eluded him. Him chiding anyone for a lack of morals.

After making his way a couple of blocks from the crime scene, he hopped a cab for the roughly thirty-five blocks home, less than a two mile ride, but in Manhattan, that was a world away. He preferred cabs to the subway anyway because the unsavory and dangerous element on the trains frightened him. And the inevitable foul-smelling homeless types, the worse-smelling winos, and those that were both, homeless winos smelling of filth and urine. Not only that, but the subway also didn't have near the magic it once did when the cars were covered with colorful urban graffiti by artists like Keith Haring or Jean-Michel Basquiat, the former before he became famous and rich before dying from AIDS at the age of thirty-one; the latter before he became famous and rich and before dying from an accidental heroin overdose at twenty-seven.

How do I know all this? Alone in his thoughts by the time he got home, Gordon decided that a wide-brimmed black hat of the type worn by Hasidic Jews would help to hide his face in future pernicious excursions. He could pick one up at any haberdasher's shop in Midtown.

Chapter Four

"You know the drill"

The body wasn't found until early morning in the still dark when a restaurant worker getting ready for a Jewish diner's breakfast rush went out the back door to throw some spoiled lox into the filthy dumpster in the bleak alley. A quick call to 911 and the place was a shit storm of police cars and black FBI sedans. Agents wore their dark blue parkas with the three large yellow letters emblazoned on the back. That was another reason Rossi didn't like them, every agent he'd ever met thought wrongly that their raid jackets were cooler, that plus the fact they weren't exactly known to have well-developed senses of humor, not to mention inapt. Staid or sober had probably been invented to describe them.

And they talked too much. Couldn't keep a secret about a case if it killed them. Rossi'd lost track of how many times he'd said fuck 'em if they can't take a joke, referring to an asshole agent. But the main thing he didn't like about them was that they didn't solve murders. They sent their CPAs and managers in after the fact to supervise murder scenes. Too late to get their hands dirty. They loved threatening real cops. Of course he had to admit that they had cool canines. To be honest, their German Shepherds were way cooler than the agents themselves.

A mobile forensic lab, EMT vehicles and, since they monitored police bands, news trucks with satellites complete with reporters filled the street. Much to the pleasure of all the males on site, the curvy blonde from ABC13 was there. Trying to win an Emmy, of course, already trying to set up near the mouth of the alley for the perfect remote angle to show off her cleavage...and the crime scene, of course.

The first officer to arrive had been a crisp-looking mounted policeman who was no more than a short block north when the call came in. Even in the heavy early morning traffic, the beautiful chestnut mare with the blonde mane was able to make her way nimbly through the congestion forthwith.

* * *

"It's probably the work of the Unholy Ghost, but get over there and confirm it," said the inscrutable lieutenant. "And I've got an idea. Why don't you catch that asshole motherfucker," he added as an afterthought, "or Captain's going to chew my ass. And you know what that means, don't you?"

"You're going to chew ours?"

"You know what they say about shit rolling downhill. The Commish chews the Chief's ass. The Chief chews the Assistant Chief's and he chews Captain's. Cap chews mine, and So Forth and So On. You are So Forth and your new partner is So On." The lieutenant thought that was an exceedingly clever line, but he'd forgotten he'd used it before. He was such a straight and narrow tight ass he probably got out of the shower to take a piss. At the same time, it also meant they didn't have any concerns about his probity.

They were housed in the 19th Precinct on the Upper East Side, one of Manhattan's more densely populated neighborhoods, although the detectives from the SID could work temporarily wherever they needed to. Everyone knew it to be one of the most ethical and professional precincts in the NYPD. The 19th looked the same as all the others, up to and including black and white photos of the current and all previous police commissioners, including Commissioner Theodore Roosevelt, future Governor of New York and President of the United States, hanging on the front entry wall. Alongside tributes to and memorabilia of those lost on 9/11. Unlike One Police Plaza, it of the Brutalist architecture, the 19th was a previous century building of decaying yellow brick, grayed by the soot, dirt, and grime of the city, topped by a U.S flag whipping in the stiff breeze, the sound unheeded in the noise that was the sine qua non of New York.

The structure wasn't exactly terrible, but it did house the jail and unless one was into BDSM, jail sucked. The building more dismal than a bar on Sunday morning. The smell of bodily odors and fear permeated its walls. The broad-shouldered structure itself an aging but menacing cop, still standing proudly, ready to do its duty for the world's largest police department.

The precinct extended from E 56th St. north to E 96th St., and from the FDR Parkway on the eastern edge of the island to Fifth Avenue on the east side of Central Park. Sounded larger than it is at less than four square miles.

The lieutenant hovered over Rossi's desk, his abundant stomach invading the space, a perpetual scowl painting his mardy face an enraged shade of crimson. He had recently cultivated a Fuller brush above his upper lip. He thought it made him look cool. Detectives in his command thought he should shave the damn thing off, forthwith. The wrinkles lining his heavy forehead were trending to folds and the hair of his head, going completely to gray, made him begin to dye it black. He'd decided the gray didn't look distinguished, just old, thus the dye job.

Rossi's new partner was in the breakroom getting coffee. He hoped the kid would bring him a large cup. It would go a long way toward making Rossi accept him. Maybe the heavy purple striated half-moons under his eyes would magically disappear with the first dose of caffeine of the early morning. Like that was going to happen. But there was always hope. He still hadn't gotten used to them. When the intrepid first grade detective glared at the image in the mirror he didn't recognize the face he saw staring harshly back at him. The lines, wrinkles, and the blue-black thick Italian hair going gray. At least it was still thick. To think when he was a new detective more than thirty years before, he'd grown a mustache to try and look older because the senior detectives — some now retired, some now dead—told him he looked like a baby. They wouldn't believe their eyes if they saw him now.

October, that time when summer gives release to early autumn, was usually a benign period for violent crime. It seemed that even the criminal element enjoyed the fresh new season. But with the Unholy Ghost on his rabid prowl, it was anything but new or fresh, and it was getting to everybody on the job, making all jumpy. Even so, crime was good for job security.

"I got it, Lou. Don't I always take care a' youse," Rossi said, knowing he was being churlish, but not caring, using the diminutive form of lieutenant accepted as normal by police departments just about everywhere; it still sometimes pissed off those to whom it was addressed. Rossi was hoping for that result now. And It worked; in spades.

"Smartass. You suck. I'm about to get tired of that mouth a'yours, ya know," said the lieutenant somewhat a little less than truculently. "Just because you've been here longer than me doesn't mean your arrogant old ass can talk to me any fuckin' way you want to. Besides, you're supposed to be setting a good example for the kid."

"Fuck him if he can't take a joke. Or as our Irish brothers in blue always say, joke him if he can't take a fuck! He can learn on his own like I did. It'll mean more to him that way. That's what my old man always told me." But Rossi really didn't mean it. He was just throwing shade at his boss. He liked to get him worked up early in the morning, before he had his coffee; it always made for an interesting day…and it had worked again this time.

"You aren't his fuckin' old man. You're his senior. You're supposed to train him up. Just get out there and find the fuckin' Unholy Ghost," he said, waving him off and turning his back on him. The only thing they could be sure of was that the Unholy Ghost wasn't in La Cosa Nostra — La Familia — because his first victim was a Father, a Monsignor, and the mob wouldn't want to go cross with God. Or the Holy Mother Church.

To His Imminence The High Lieutenant's back, Detective First Grade Salvatoré Rossi, said, "You know me. I'll coach him up right, but remember; I'm no fuckin' Lyceum." The lieutenant ignored the comment because he knew he'd pushed his man too far. And pissed him off. Detective Rossi was the most senior and most successful detective in the division, proving himself time after time after time, with the most collars. Like most Italians, he was anything but laconic, especially when it came to imparting wisdom to his children or, more importantly, his grandchildren…or even a junior partner. Not that he was avuncular on the job; in truth, he was anything but. He might be described as a living, breathing crucible.

But, to anyone that could benefit from his guidance and life experience, he was willing to share. His Christian name meant savior in Italian, as Jesus Christ was called. He was honored to follow all those Italianos that came before him who had been on the job since first passing through Ellis Island. Known for his volcanic temper, too explosive for him to be described as saturnine, other detectives thought him irascible. It wasn't that Rossi was innately sagacious, but in over thirty years on the job he had just about seen it all — and learned from it. Pity the poor medical examiner, forensic technician, or uniform patrolman who got in the way on one of his cases. Truth be known, on the job it was possible they were right in their opinion of him, but never with family.

He was still ruggedly attractive in a manly way, with a strong Romanesque nose, a handsomely furrowed forehead caused by the anxiety of too many years on the job, and warm, sensitive, dark eyes beneath a heavy brow, though wisps of silver were gaining domicile on his short dark hair, his once powerful physique was prevailing thicker with the years, and his face beginning to go doughy with his once taut neck beginning a slow but steady turn to wattle. He kept his hair short or it developed a curl. His wife liked the curls but his brothers in blue busted his balls if it got curly, and he couldn't abide that. He had a tattoo in Latin on his right forearm reading V*irtus et Honos*. Strength and Honor. Both important to him.

The other detectives got a kick out of telling him he looked like Steve Schirripa, the Italian actor best known for his portrayal of Bobby Baccalieri, the affable gangster in The Sopranos television series, though he didn't find the comparison amusing thinking it painted all Italians with the mafia brush. His aging features the result of experience and more than three decades on the job. These days he weighed somewhere between two hundred and two hundred ten pounds; but exactly where between those two markers depended on if it were before or after Thanksgiving and Christmas. The fat still girdered by muscle, though. His face, however, was a perfect home to his vituperative deep baritone. At least he didn't have the red, striated nose and equally crimson face that evinced a fondness for strong potations. When you mostly have only two glasses of red wine with dinner that isn't given to happening.

The First Grade Detective truly looked the part of a thug, though no one would believe he was. Unless you messed with his family — blood or blue. He'd been known to administer beat downs no one wanted to be on the receiving end of. He never removed the fourteen-carat gold Saint Christopher medallion that hung around his neck that his beloved Ella had given him one Christmas when they were both young. Black, heavy-framed eyeglasses completed his look. Jesus, Mary and Saint Joseph; bifocals. His vision was going to hell faster than his waistline, but at least they weren't trifocals…yet. If he needed to buy a moment's time before responding to a question he'd pull a yellowing white handkerchief from his right rear trousers pocket and give the lenses a once over before answering.

Detective Third Grade Jay Park was a young Korean-American. Like most typical Asian kids, he had wanted to be number one in his class so as not to cast shame on his family. Only difference was, he had been number one in his class at every grade. Then off the chart as a uniformed patrolman. Aced the detective's exam and here he was. Young and still hard and hungry. Looked like he ran a 10k every day and lifted weights for an hour and a half after the run. But the sad part, for most mere mortals, anyway, is it was most likely the byproduct of good genetics. Way more than fit, he had a physique similar to that of the late actor and martial artist Bruce Lee. Jay came to America because his parents brought him. He didn't have any say-so about the migration. As so many immigrants do, they had thought New York the capital of Earth. If he hadn't believed it then, only because he was a mere child, he believed it now and was proud to be a New Yorker. Equally proud that his familial demonym was Korean.

They put down their literal roots in what was now becoming known as New York City's Koreatown or, more popular with its inhabitants, K-Town, a gentrified neon-bright area of West 32nd street between Fifth Avenue and Broadway at Sixth. Not nearly as famous or notorious as its Asian brethren, Chinatown. But the miasma of aromas — of kimchi, bibimbap, and Bulgogi cooking — continued to pull people to the southwest side of Manhattan.

Rossi, the third one named Salvatoré, his family calling him Trey until he was sixteen when he informed them he was too big and too old to be a Trey; besides, he thought his given name, a strong sainted Catholic name meaning savior, was a legacy, fourth generation to be on the job. NYPD blue in his red-blooded DNA. His grandparents were pious. His parents pretended to be. Because it was expected of them. He just thought they were overly strict. Took it out on him. Sent him to Catholic schools but additionally made him go to Catechism class on Sunday. Got special permission from the Monsignor for the overkill. Just to make sure he knew they were in charge, and could.

He never made the outrageous claim to be Pope, but for the most part, he was a croyant and believed he was a good guy. Always had been. A not-particularly steadfast member of the Knights of Columbus, but then, that wasn't a requirement for being a good guy or even a good Catholic.

Even the one who came before the subsequent generations, his great great grandfather, had been one of the Carabinieri, Italia's finest force of *la polizia* dealing with organized crime back in the Old Country. With his heritage being the determining factor, it was all Rossi had ever wanted to do. But he was no elegiac, mourning for the law enforcement days of yore, holding tight onto dreams of catching William Poole, better known to historians as Bill the Butcher.

First Grade Detective Rossi relished being a present-day cop in New York City. The capital of Earth. He thought it was somewhat more than a little honorable profession.

Park was still trying to find his way. He'd loved being in uniform;

felt a kinship, a camaraderie, with his brothers and sisters in blue that started at the academy. Back when they were all wet behind the ears. When he was still literally too young even to shave.

At the academy nobody saw black or white or yellow, only NYPD blue. He already felt that was missing in the detective ranks where it seemed every man or woman was for himself or herself. Who had the most arrests? Who got the biggest bust?

In the patrol car he confided in his older partner. "I don't know, Mr. Sal. But I'm not sure I'm cut out for this."

It wasn't that unusual for young ones to have doubts. "Sure you are, kid. You're smarter than the average bear. With my looks and your brain we'll make a good team," he said with a droll wink. "You just keep an eye on me and do what I do, and you'll be fine. And we're partners. Don't call me mister. It's just Sal."

"Okay...Sal. Wait, smarter than the average bear? What the hell is that? Where the hell did that come from? Just how old are you anyway?"

Salvatoré shook his head disbelievingly. He thought sure the kid would know about Yogi Bear, at least from the reruns on the Cartoon Network when he still wore messy diapers. Sal remembered watching the animated shows from first runs on Saturday mornings on a black and white TV. His family had been the last one in their building to get a color set. But kids today weren't like his generation. They took their studies seriously. Especially in the Asian culture, every one of them had to be number one in their class. It wouldn't do to bring shame on their family name.

"Okay, listen. Listen. This is something my old man told me. Same thing his father told him. I'm a fourth generation New York cop. So you can take it to the bank. A man has got to figure out who he is, what he's not, and what he's got. What you got is smarts and family. Those things will take you wherever you want to go."

"Your father was a smart man. You learned well."

"Well you hear me and learn it from me."

"Yes, sir," he said, only somewhat a little less than sincerely.

They were the last to arrive. The two detectives from the elite Special Investigations Division of the Detective Bureau, in what was their usual fashion, would take charge. Although the feebs were first on the scene, they'd be butting heads with them for control. In a multi-agency case it was a competition. Nobody wanted to lose to the Feebs, and they in turn didn't want to lose to other departments that they looked down on or thought were beneath them.

There were three of those FBI assholes. Two males, one female; each somewhere north of forty, but not yet fifty. Veterans, probably over twenty years in for each. The men wearing blue suits, white shirts, blue or red ties. The woman, the feminine version of those minus the tie. The FBI always thought they were in control when multi-agency was used to describe the scope of the investigation. That pompous description was the key phrase. The SID was highly secretive, much like the United States Army's Delta Force, in that the NYPD denied its very existence. Before getting out of the unmarked car, each detective checked their weapons. Rossi did it because it was a habit over thirty years in the making. Park did it because Rossi told him to do everything he did. That was only one of the things there was to like about the kid; unlike so many of the newbies who thought they knew it all, Park listened with his mouth closed.

Rossi grinned watching his young charge following his lead. The kid was going to be okay. Among many other action items, he'd have to find his own informants — stools, snitches — and learn to work them, but Rossi could help to get him started with that. They weren't that hard to find, and some were better than others.

The best work with the FBI, NYPD, the staties, or all of them. Some work both sides, the cops and the mob — the Italians, not the Russians. The Russians were stone-cold killers, and if they even suspected you were working with the cops and might betray them, you weren't long for this earth. It didn't matter even if you were law enforcement.

All informants are venal, venal as hell. But you didn't want one who was too venal. You didn't want one that would work with just anybody. You needed to find the right one. He had to have a baby-face, a fresh-faced innocence about him. You didn't want one with battle scars. He wouldn't make a good impression in court. He needed to dress decent. Not like a fuckin' street junkie, even though that's what most of them were. Find him. Work him. Buy him clothes if you had to. But be careful because according to the letter of the law even that was illegal. Still, all the top arresting detectives did it. Treat him right and you'd have a good one. One that would stay with you as long as he thinks you care. Some of them made a pretty good living as informants. They even had homes and families they had to take care of. They'd work hard to keep that.

Park needed to find one that looked like himself. One who looked like he loved his mama. Innocent looking even if he wasn't.

Rossi and Park did the usual things detectives do at a crime scene. They'd been taught the basics of crime scene investigation at Criminal Investigation School, but they'd learned most of it by doing. In the case of Park, he would learn it. It was to be a long day. Canvas shop owners in the surrounding area, check their security camera footage. Search for any physical evidence. Today, there was a lot of blood. Probably only the vic's, but they'd still have to get the lab to check it out. And a lot of footprints; cheap sneaker treads and crocs, most of them probably restaurant workers taking trash to the dumpster. Maybe a few dress shoe soles. Nothing they could hang their hats on. Been there since the last rain. Nothing but people taking a shortcut. No more, no less. Even though it was probably an effort in futility, question everyone on the sidewalks. See if they saw anyone carrying a long bloody blade.

Flashing their shields, "Excuse me. Did you see anything?" they inquired of all passersby. Of course the answer was no. Everyone was on their way to work. None had been in the neighborhood in the wee hours. But until the medical examiner gave them an estimated time of death, they had to follow that line of questioning.

They had to explore every possible option because the Unholy Ghost seemed to choose his victims capriciously, and so it was hard to predict or determine a pattern. In fact, all of the real work was done at the precinct. Searching records for anything. Similar crimes. All arrests across the area. Hospital records. Anything might be useful.

* * *

Grayson got up around seven. Late for him, but he wasn't well-rested. He was tired, muscles ached. Especially those in his hands. Not like he'd been in a fight, but sort of like he'd been grappling with someone. He recalled crazy dreams. More like nightmares, actually. Of a struggle. Yeah, that had to be it. Another nightmare where he seemed to be viewing a murder like a witness to the crime. He probably shouldn't have had that last Old-Fashioned before turning in. Maybe that was why he was tired and achy.

But at least the images in the dreams were giving him more fuel for his new book. He'd forego going out for coffee and brew his own. He needed to work on his new book and couldn't waste time walking to and fro. If he felt like he could waste that time later, after he'd stopped hurting, he'd go down to the massage parlor in the next block. Get one of them to work on his aches. He'd done that one time before and wow, that little Chinese lady worked him over but good. But he felt better after she stopped.

The expensive widescreen TV in the green antique Chinese armoire was on for background noise. Grayson couldn't write in a vacuum. He actually had to have all of his senses involved when he wrote. Hearing, maybe the most important.

A national special news report caught his ear and interest. It seemed that the Unholy Ghost had struck again overnight. But what was most interesting was that the killing the news reporter described seemed almost identical to the one in his nightmare. But that was impossible. It had to be due to his being exhausted; literarily his brain playing tricks on him.

Before Grayson got too focused on his writing, and even though it was early autumn and only beginning to turn chilly, he laid a fire in his study's wood-burning fireplace. He loved the smell of the woodsmoke in the neighborhood when all the neighbors had fires going, and he enjoyed doing his part to contribute to that pleasant fragrance.

* * *

It had been a long day for Detectives Rossi and Park, interviewing everyone who, unconcerned about getting involved, didn't wave them off; searching the alley and the sidewalk for trace evidence; attempting to develop a timeline of events. With almost full rigor evident, the ME returned a TOD of approximately eleven thirty pm, give or take a little bit, the night before. That at least gave them something to work with.

After the FBI's icy attitude and the stressful day's work Salvatoré offered to buy his young charge a pint or three at Byrne's Irish Pub to decompress. Jay appeared surprised at his partner's offer and quickly jumped to accept before it could be rescinded. They got in the special edition silver Crown Victoria Police Interceptor, commonly known as a CVPI, with its powerful V8. Even though they had been discontinued and it was getting a little long in the tooth, Rossi preferred it to the smaller, less powerful Ford Taurus that was finally taking its place. It was as comfortable as a familiar handshake and just as firm. It smelled of his classic Old Spice. If he were to be honest, though, he thought one of its tires was looking worn and would soon become traction-challenged if it wasn't already. Wouldn't do to get in a chase with some asshole and have the tires give out. He'd have to let the motor pool know.

Rossi behind the wheel, the unrelenting depression in the old, cracked vinyl bench seat conforming to his ass, Park riding shotgun, they both buckled up. Departmental policy, wherever they were going. Furthermore, it was also departmental policy not to have a beer and get behind the wheel of a squad car. But he wouldn't have more than two, his home wasn't that far from the pub, and besides…what they didn't know…

He rolled hard to the curb on 53rd Street between Park Avenue and Lexington. Pulled into a no-parking space, jammed the unmarked car into park, and tossed the NYPD laminated placard haphazardly onto the dash. Anyone would take the large Ford for either a cop's car or a well-worn rental. The placard removed any doubt. Rossi continued, "Byrne is a retired cop. From what I hear he used most of his retirement check for the down payment and borrowed the rest against the revenue, for the equity and startup expenses, on a long-term note. That's one good thing about cops. They might not have a lot of cash, but they usually have good credit; they're a good risk.

Park whistled in conservative disbelief and said, "Sounds like he should have just gone on a gambling junket to Southeast Asia. The casinos over there would have loved him." Park, like most Asians, eschewed borrowing or using credit, preferring to pay cash to make his way, but did love their gambling. The casinos in Southeast Asia as magnificent as any in Las Vegas or AC, a testament to the huge amounts of cash spent there.

"Fortunately for me, even though the Irish cops that hang out here are pretty clannish, going back to the Old Country, micks don't seem to mind the occasional wop cop joining them. That's good for you because it means they're diverse and will accept you graciously. I agree with their informal motto — get drunk to celebrate when you close a big case or get drunk to console yourself if you lose one.

Either way, it's a good day. Anyways, it's the precinct's main and most popular watering hole. A lot of our brothers extend their tours at the end of the day by coming to Byrne's…an unpaid extension, of course."

In addition to being brothers in blue, the other commonality the wop and mick cops held was an ardent love for the liquid courage.

They locked the unmarked's doors, stepping from the warmth into the suddenly dropping temperature. Park took hurried short steps to keep up with the taller Rossi's longer strides. A bell over the door announced their arrival as they entered the prototypical New York Irish pub, except for this one being run by a cop, for cops. They were greeted with grunts of greeting from featureless faces in dark booths, and others crowded shoulder-to-shoulder at the bar. The habitués would've recognized Rossi as a cop even if they hadn't known him. The weary mien that comes from too many hard years on the job. His service weapon causing his cheap suit to bulge. The wary experienced eyes checking out everything and everyone. The done-in look after a long day, but still ready for business if need be. Rossi would have known the Irish cops even without the red hair turning to yellowish-gray. Without the freckled faces. Or the drinking problems.

The broad chests and thick bodies handed down from the previous generations of farmhands were immutable giveaways.

Jay glanced around, bright-eyed and open-mouthed. Sal said what was manifest to anyone who was a regular. "Safest bar in the city. Any scumbag tries to roust this place won't live long enough to regret it. Outnumbered by the quantity of guns and larger calibers. And...better shooters."

Jay nodded, soaking up the sights and sounds like a youngster listening to a wise and worldly uncle generously sharing his knowledge. Indeed, everybody in the pub was carrying two things — a deadly weapon and a willingness or, somewhat more than likely, a desire, to use it.

Byrne's was dark, almost too dark to see. But one knew they were in the right place from the pungent, damp pong of old age and hoary history. Built in the early 1800s, it smelled like it. Mortar hardened by decades wormed its way down the fusty walls from where it had been troweled in the crevices between stones more than two-hundred years before. The only modern conveniences: one TV over the bar for watching only the team from the Bronx — don't even think about watching anything else; sconces on walls, and tabletops and bar lamps with small, red-shaded bulbs designed to look like flickering candles; and one huge cooler to keep Guinness and Murphy's icy cold.

A roaring blaze in a fireplace constructed from stones even larger than the ones forming the walls warmed the small space. Booths on two walls and small tables crowded the decades-old, wide-plank wood floor that creaked under ponderous steps. Creatures of habit anyways, the bar was comforting to cops. Not all, but most, preferred it over their own homes, and the company of their brothers in blue more than that of their wives. Rossi wasn't one of those, however. Not to say they didn't have their problems — they did — but he still loved his wife, and fortunately, most of the time, even liked her.

The place had no frills. No Thursday Night Team Trivia or Tuesday Tacos or Live Wednesday Music! The only form of deterrent to drinking was a dartboard on the wall, for those so inclined, with a Guinness logo on the wooden-doored hinged case. Music groaned from an ancient jukebox. On this night, Dropkick Murphys, a Celtic punk band from Quincy, Mass, was making a lot of noise. Sounded like their huge hit *Rebels with a Cause*. That noise and the companionship of their brothers was all most needed.

Saying he'd had enough of that shit from those no-talent assholes from Beantown, as he described them, like he'd truly had all he could stand, a huge young cop stomped hurriedly over to the previous-century music box and dropped in some coins. Satisfied with himself, he announced, "That'll be enough of that shit," before the pleasant opening riffs of *Days Like This* by all Celts' favorite native lyricist, Van Morrison. It was obvious that from a tender age his parents had raised him well on the soft stylings of the famous artist.

Byrne's didn't get a lot of action. It was an orgy for the senses, however, with the dim lighting, the organic tangs, and the sounds of warm conversation. The only time it ever changed would be in about two months when, Christmas approaching, Byrne's wife made him (otherwise he wouldn't have done it) place a gaily lit tree in a corner with gleefully wrapped and bow-festooned empty boxes surrounding it. That was the subtle signal that meant the clientele would change from cops only to include those who had no place else to be for the happiest, and most forlorn, of all holidays. Over ten million people in the naked city and nobody called it home. At Christmas, the city could be the coldest, loneliest place on earth for those on their own. Most places, the temperature inside as cold as the melancholy and dramatic December outside.

It made Rossi grateful he wasn't one of those wretched creatures with no place else to go. But Byrne was already late getting the Halloween decorations up. He didn't much care though. He wasn't a big fan of the pseudo holiday except for getting to eat the leftover candy he didn't give out to the kids. Thoughts of Christmas hadn't even entered his mind yet.

With Rossi leading the way, he and Park bellied up to the scarred but opulent mahogany bar crowded shoulder to shoulder but not three deep like patrons at the more popular chain fern bars in Midtown, and ordered pints for himself and his partner, since going out had been his idea and he'd enticed the kid by promising to buy. Typical of most Italians, Rossi usually drank red wine — while eating pasta with red gravy, or as some Italians called it, Sunday sauce — but if he found himself in a quaint Irish bar, it might be the only time he found it made sense to pound back a pint or few.

Byrne, a doughy sort, of the flaccid frank face and red hair turning to fatigued gray, handed him two cold mugs, condensation forming on the sides, and said formally, "Salvatoré, you old sod. How are you my friend? And who's this? A newbie?" Byrne was one of the few who didn't use the diminutive of the big Italian's name.

"Angus, meet Detective Third Grade Jay Park. Just got his gold shield. One of, if not *the* first Korean American detective on the NYPD. I'm trying to train him up right. You know the drill. Never talk about the job to anyone who's not on the job. Never do anything off the job you wouldn't do on the job. Never give up your integrity. Respect all living things. Never trust a hooker — or a newspaperman unless it's Jimmy Breslin —"

Rossi turned to Park and explained. "Serial killer Son Of Sam's primary connection to the police and the public through his letters, but Breslin died two years ago."

Rossi turned back to Byrne. "— or Steve Dunleavy, but he died last year. Every cop knew those two could be trusted, but since they're both colder than dirt that isn't a problem we have to worry about now, do we? Jay, say 'how do you do' to Angus. He's the publican of this fine establishment. It's not much to look at, but it's a damn fine pub. You wouldn't find any better in the Old Country, so they tell me. I haven't been there myself; and you know his last name. You saw it on the big sign out front."

"Nice to meet you, my boy," Angus said in a stentorian voice, strong enough to be heard above the din.

"You, too, sir," he replied meekly.

"I like this kid. He respects his elders. That will take you a long way, young man. Excuse me…Detective. Being respectful." One couldn't pay Park a higher compliment. To be sure, saying someone was respectful was one of the nicest things you could say about someone in the Asian culture.

"Thank you, sir." Never forgetting the culture of his homeland, Jay dipped a short courteous bow.

"See, he done it again. And it's good for you, Salvatoré, 'cause he won't give you any guff."

"He was raised right," Rossi agreed, as he turned to Jay and lifted his mug. "Cheers."

"Cheers, partner," Jay said. With English being his second language and not fully understanding some of it's more colorful, and lowborn, expressions, as Byrne left to visit with other customers, he asked, "What's this guff I won't give you?"

"Don't worry about it. He's so old he makes old-school sound like it's a youngster."

Jay shook his head and shrugged in resigned acquiescence.

They each looked longingly at the golden brew. Rossi said, "In honor of our Irish surroundings, *slainté*," and raised his mug to Park's. After respectfully having a healthy pull before setting it heavily on the scarred bar top, he aired, "Ahhh. The only thing better than one's first pint of the night is the second pint of the night."

Park took a healthy slug in agreement. "And why is that, partner?" he asked in unfettered curiosity.

"I think — and believe me, I have a lot of experience testing out this theory — it's because the first one gets your taste buds ready for beer, so that the second one tastes even better. But it doesn't continue with additional ones after that. The half-life dissipates with each subsequent pint." Rossi regarded beer in much the same fashion he considered holy water — that is, religiously; only one drank it instead of daubing it on the forehead. Don't even get him started on red wine. Jesus turned water into wine for God's sake. It doesn't get more spiritual than that. Recalling catechism classes, grapes for the purpose of winemaking were the most oft-mentioned fruit in the Bible.

"I bow to your experience," said Park with a half-ass salute to his older, more worldly partner, then continued. "In my country, you would be a much-respected elder."

"'Much-respected elder'?" Rossi said, feigning astonishment. "I like that much-respected part. But what's with that elder? And just when you and I were getting along so well." He'd said it with a huge smile on his face so the youngster would know he was throwing shade.

Jay shrugged and, unsure of his meaning, decided not to go there.

They pulled boiled eggs and generously sized crispy dill pickles from separate two-gallon jars sitting on the bar.

"If you're hungry, we can order something. The shepherd's pie here is to die for. And the bangers and mash is even better. Traditional Irish grub, you know," Rossi said, encouraging him so that, hopefully, Park wouldn't mind having something because Rossi didn't want to eat alone.

"I'm good with this," Park said, examining the pickle from all angles like he was trying to convince himself to eat it. "I'm not really a big eater."

In fact, Park stayed lean by eating little. But his good Asian genes didn't hurt. Rossi looked disappointed, although he knew it was better for his waistline.

A couple of rounds later Rossi said, "I think you're getting the hang of this, Jay." Even though it wasn't part of the deal, Rossi let the kid pay for a round; thought it would make him feel like a real adult. Then it was time to call it a night. They would need to be up early to get hot on the trail of the Unholy Ghost.

When they exited onto the sidewalk the rest of the block was dark with businesses closed for the night. A gentle rain had washed the streets. Neon-lit beer signs in the pub windows, the only ones still shining brightly trying to lure in the lonely, bathed the wet sidewalk in bright shiny colors.

Rossi turned on the heat in the car, then cracked his window to let in some cool fresh air before dropping Park off at the nearest subway entrance so he could catch a train down to what had been a once-huge Little Italy but was now being swallowed up by the increasing number of Asians of various ethnicities. Now known as New York City's Chinatown, it was way larger than the former all-Italian district it was rapidly eating up. After letting him out, Rossi turned east toward the FDR before heading home, south to the building that was no more than common by New York City standards. Constructed during the time of *I Love Lucy's* original run, it had been all they could afford in the city on a detective's salary.

Far from a tenement, but closer to that than one of the luxury high-rises on Park Avenue. The building didn't have a doorman for first line security, but all the other tenants were happy that an NYPD Detective was their neighbor. They judged rightly that they were safer with a well-trained armed protector than with an aged overweight unarmed doorman.

The hardest thing for Rossi to accept were the changes in the old neighborhood. A mom-and-pop pizza place that had the biggest slices on the east side replaced by an OTB place. Dry cleaners in the next block, the hair salon, the small family-owned drug store, all now national chains. The Halal restaurant that never seemed crowded, but due to the city's huge Muslim population it managed to survive and, in better times, actually prospered. All were hardworking folks with dreams. Truly, they were not dreamless.

The only thing that bothered him, confused him, was not knowing when the city changed from black and white to color. He knew no one would get the joke but him, but he'd always thought from watching all the old black and white films with Doris Day, Rock Hudson, and Cary Grant set in New York that at one time the city must have been nothing but monochromatic shades of black, gray, and white, before becoming colorized. Must have happened sometime in the '40s and '50s, after those films but before he was born. The city didn't change fast. Not like the ephemeral nineteenth century. Then, a man would be steering a horse and carriage one day, a motorcar the next. One day living in the country, the next on a broad city boulevard.

Ah well, nothing lasts forever. Even him.

He would never forget the places he took his kids, the small neighborhood park, the arcade, and more. In his worst nightmares he woke up coming home to find his building boarded up, or worse, knocked down. That's when he woke up in an icy sweat. Because that building tethered him to New York. No, tether was too weak of a description. It anchored him to the city.

That was New York's most evocative quality. It was always changing, but it stayed the same. If one needed it to. Rossi thought that he was indomitable, like the city, or wanted to think he was indomitable like the city and that he stayed the same, too.

The city wouldn't forget those places, either. The city that never sleeps likewise never forgets. To do so would be a travesty. Ah, the stories it could tell. One would think them fiction, but one would be mistaken. Non-fiction. True all.

The fragrant aroma from the spices of Indian food — mostly, cardamom, clove, and cassis bark — settled low on the dark hallways of the first floor like a heavy sweet-smelling blanket. A mountain of empty tan cardboard boxes was stacked next to one door in preparation for a move. The apartment soon to be untenanted and bereft of the life and energy of a family. Using the skills of a seasoned detective he detected that whoever lived there was a good customer of the purveyor of alcoholic beverages across the busy avenue since all of the boxes were printed with matching Amstel Light logos. He chuckled softly. Proved to himself he still had it. Could detect the crap out of crap.

Even though their unit was only on the eighth floor, the tiny and interminably slow elevator, common for buildings of that era, made it seem higher than that. After forever, the caged doors painfully took their time to open and he stepped out. A burned-out ceiling bulb made the hall darker than it should be. Rossi walked to his right. With his aging eyes, he had to search for the correct key before unlocking the third steel, high-security door that he came to, one that he'd installed himself. From years of practice he made his way sure-footedly into the dim two-bedroom apartment they'd chosen to keep after the kids were grown only because it was easier than packing up lock, stock, and barrel, and moving to a smaller one. Two bedrooms, and modest. Certainly not showy, but likewise, not pity-inducing for an NYPD senior detective. Being rent-controlled didn't hurt. They'd lived there for so long, casting their own shadows, their own ghosts, that the ones from previous decades didn't even bother them. They wouldn't dare. Even if they did, he'd have to live with them. He could never be unmoored from those thirteen hundred square feet plus small terrace. The terrace was kind of stingy, but it was on the south side of the building, and the nighttime view of the Empire State Building and its exterior lights changing color with the holiday and the Chrysler Building and its shiny silver spire made from the hubcaps of early twentieth century sedans, was the stuff of travel magazines. If Rossi squinted real hard, south of Manhattan Island, out in the bay, he could almost, almost mind you, make out the tarnished green glow of the Statue of Liberty against the maudlin nighttime sky.

He was convinced that the funeral home hearse would have to call for his woeful remains at this address. That conviction somehow gave him more than as much comfort as New York City's most famous sites.

Even though it was dark in the house, he could sense the love, its heartbeat and energy. Especially the love. Or maybe it was the garlic, but to Italianos garlic was love. He could still remember when he was a new cop and he and Ella opened the door for the first time. He carried her over the threshold like in a fairytale. Good thing she was small and he had been young. It wasn't a home then. Not yet. Not like it is now. A living, breathing organism with a heartbeat, smells and memories. Those of husband, wife, kids, and grands.

Oh, the grands. He had no idea it was possible to love those tiny toddling Italians so much. He could remember when his eldest grandson —thrilled his son had named him Sal — was four and asked his Nonna if she would make him some milk. Of course, he meant pour him some milk, but he didn't say that and she said, "No, I'm not a cow." The expression on his face was priceless. Sal the elder still laughed about that one and loved throwing shade at Sal the younger about it. Now that the younger was ten going on twenty and beginning to notice the fairer sex, he had even begun to ask Sal the elder for advice about girls. That made him happier than he thought possible, even though he wasn't sure what he thought about a ten-year-old being interested in girls. If he had to guess, he'd guess he was more like his grandpop than he knew.

The apartment looked well-lived in but was clean. Nothing out of place. Furniture wasn't of a name brand designer but wasn't cheap. Sturdy, good quality for a reasonable price. The smartest kind of purchases a policeman would make. Or a policeman's wife. Not that there was much difference in the two.

Sofas and chairs upholstered in flowery fabric before being slipcovered in clear plastic, in the way of New Yorkers, to protect them from stains, of which there had been many with three children and four grandchildren. Mostly red gravy and red wine. Ella's mother and Nonna, stern women both, had made a habit of the practice and so she did. Better to be safe than sorry, even if damp skin on a hot summer day made a sound like a king-sized whoopee cushion.

Family pictures and what would be called tchotchkes if they were Jewish, suffocated the surface of every table in every room. But since the Rossi's weren't, they called them knickknacks or bric-a-brac. That's the way it's done in nuclear Italian families. Some, cheaply-framed photos of family members in dated dress, gone, but forever remembered. Others, children in baseball uniforms or cheerleader uniforms, most in black and white or faded Polaroids. Age and fashion made the subjects appear gauzy and schmaltzy. Additionally, newer pics of grandkids, likewise in uniforms at the same age as their parents. The quality finer, though, and not marred by the passing of time. Then, in a place of great honor, a rendering of Saint Francis of Assisi, and on the wall above it, a crucifix with the Christ's bloody hands and feet apparent.

Although fustily kept, in the manner of the elderly, the house appeared pleased with itself. Keeping a family.

The intoxicating aroma of love and warm garlic and red gravy from where Ella had been cooking all day, filled the space. All from scratch, and love. She would have died before using canned sauces. Her mother and her nonna, the sainted *materfamilia*, would quite literally roll over in their graves in Holy Cross Catholic Cemetery of Brooklyn if she had dared it and would come back to haunt her.

People only think little old Italian women are mean. They can't hold a candle to little old Italian women spirits. Try to imagine an anguished tribulation led by pissed off female Italian ghosts.

No whole grain pasta for her favorite dishes either, even if it were healthier. Semolina pasta had been good enough for Mama and Nonna so it was good enough for her. Indeed, most Italians were predisposed to being panivorous. Besides, whole grain didn't taste the same and they could eat healthy with other dishes, and besides, everyone knew moderation was key in all things, even moderation itself. Rossi's wife's personal mantra when it came to cooking was the same as those strong Italian women that came before her: If all else fails, add more garlic.

Besides the notion, she thought it especially salubrious.

But Sal, taking her idea about garlic to the extreme and just to be on the safe side, lifted the lid from the still simmering pot and dropped in some additional cloves he'd found from where she'd left them on the chopping board. His mantra was, if a little garlic is good, then more has to be better.

Hearing the lid rattle, Ella sang out lyrically but softly from the darkened bedroom. "Are you messing up my gravy with more garlic?" It was an age-old argument among Italians, even among those of the same family, whether the necessary red foodstuff was called gravy or sauce. Whichever, it had to be ready for Sunday; so that usually meant simmering all day Saturday. Then they could agree on calling it Sunday Sauce. But only on Sunday; then they'd go back to the age old gravy-sauce argument for the rest of the week.

In a stage whisper he said. "Don't you worry your pretty little head about it. You know you never use enough."

"Did you even taste it first to see?"

"Didn't need to," he said, still talking softly to try and not wake up the entire floor.

He'd have to make sure he made it home in time for dinner the next day. As much for Ella as himself, to show her that what she did for him was appreciated.

Rossi didn't turn on the bedroom light and even showered in the dark in a vain but nevertheless thoughtful attempt to keep from disturbing her further. He brushed and flossed in the same, consoling himself with the fact that even in his mid-fifties he took no prescription meds. Only a supersize aspirin a day, because his doctor, an almost lifelong friend — they'd met on the playground in primary school — said it was a good idea. What his friend, the doc, had told him was if aspirin were invented today it would require a prescription. Rossi thought if he could avoid any foot chases with young hooligans his heart would probably work for another thirty or so years.

Away from the aromatic pull of the kitchen's heavenly aromas, he detected the floral scents of Ella's bath soap and the moisturizer she used to keep her skin soft and supple for him — as she never forgot to remind him. Trying not to disturb her, he climbed in on his side of the bed, closest to the bathroom for those nocturnal trips that were becoming more numerous with increasing age.

"Hmm, I'm glad you're home" she said, sleepily.

"Thanks. I'm glad to be home."

"How's the kid?"

"I'll tell you tomorrow."

"Mmkay. Good night."

"Good night, luv." Rossi leaned over and gave her a loving peck on the cheek. Then rolled over to listen to the nighttime sounds of the city that never sleeps. The car horns and sirens that even if it took awhile, everyone eventually became accustomed to. Truth: probably couldn't sleep without. And that was when even transplants became New Yorkers.

Pray before sleep. Bless his wife, kids, and grands. Forgive him his sins. Especially the ones committed on the job. Most of them in his younger, more morally ambiguous days. Before he became more evolved with age; like any necessary beatdowns he may have given to get information or save lives.

He hoped he'd never sold his soul in order to be the best policeman he could be. Or if he had, that it hadn't been seen or never found out.

It wasn't that Rossi was particularly pious, but with maturity came a sense of urgency. *Memento Mori*. Although he was only a child when it was changed, he missed the days when the liturgy was in Latin. Not that he understood a word of Latin, he didn't. But he thought the mass more meaningful in the archaic language of those bygone days. He did like it, however, that Vatican II had turned the altar around. Besides, the most important part, to him anyway, the homily, had always been in English.

* * *

Grayson woke, not to the sound of his smartphone's gentle alarm, but to its annoying-as-hell klaxon-like ringtone, instead. It was still dark. *Who the fuck would be calling me at this ungodly hour?*

"Hello?"

"You ready for the *Today* interview?"

"Now?"

"No, not now," his agent laughed, as if he were saying 'you dumb son of a bitch.' "Tomorrow."

Joseph acted like his father. Grayson almost thought of him that way. If an ethnic European Caucasian could have a Jewish father from the Old Country.

Still trying to will his brain to function like a normal human being, he said, "Well, thanks for the advance notice."

"Sure. What are friends for?"

"I'm sure I don't know," he sighed. "So, if it's not until tomorrow, what the hell are you calling me so early for anyway? Couldn't it have waited until nine?" His logic unimpeachable even without a perfectly functioning brain at the inhumane hour and before hot coffee.

"I couldn't sleep and I figure if I'm going to be awake everybody ought to be awake. Besides, you know what they say about New York: the city that never sleeps."

Properly forewarned about the *Today Show* interview scheduled for the following morning, Grayson clicked off and, after crawling somewhat less than unenthusiastically from the large warm bed where he slept alone, started the coffee brewing. Getting up earlier than usual at least meant he could start writing before his usual time.

Inspired by the Unholy Ghost continuing to run amok, it didn't take him even half the morning to write a chilling scene about his killer meeting an attractive young woman in a dance club and after luring her outside, dispatching her with unmerciful alacrity.

Grayson was pleased with himself for taking a sad, solemn tale and making it his own.

Chapter Five

"Shoot"

Unfortunately and fortunately, hot on the trail of a killer in the twenty-first century meant poring over a computer and searching databases for similar crimes trying to make connections between victims and any other arbitrary detail one could think of. That's why it was possible Rossi and Park might make a good team.

Rossi was old school, all about beating the pavement, wearing out shoe leather. Park was from the generation that grew up with computers. Unlike older folks, he'd never lived a day in his life without them. It was almost time for lunch but from the intensity of his gaze, it appeared that Detective Park was willing to keep at it all day.

"Let's get out of here," said Rossi. "I need to clear my brain. Food will help. If we keep at it too long we won't be able to think and won't recognize a clue if it hits us over the head."

Rossi wanted to go to a diner known to east side locals for its pastrami sandwiches, the comfortably fatty meat sliced thin and piled high on rye, with Swiss cheese, Cole slaw, and mustard.

"Hey, kid. You like pastrami?"

As they walked out together, Park said, "I don't know. It isn't real big in Korea. But I'm willing to give it the old college try."

"That's the spirit. But this place has other sandwiches if you like. No rice, though," he said with a shit-eating grin.

"My parents still eat rice three meals a day, but I don't," said Park thinking Rossi was serious before he saw the wan smile on his face. "Oh, I get it. You were trying to be funny. That was a good one."

They exited the precinct into the late morning air, the sidewalk clogged with people as usual on a Tuesday. Rossi eyed his reflection in a building's tall window, sucked in his a little less than ample stomach, and pulled his suit jacket close against the heartless bitter wind, no mere susurrus sweeping off the untroubled gray Hudson. His rubber-soled black Ecco Oxfords, scuffed with age, were still good for chasing runners. Besides, even though they were old they'd cost more than his suit. He thought it important to invest in high quality shoes when you were on your feet as much as he was.

The morning was cheerfully sunny, but unseasonably cold. Except for the style of dress and the loud music — men would have been wearing dress hats and peaked lapel double-breasted suits and the women, dresses — the sidewalks of New York appeared little different in 2020 than they did in 1920. Hip-hop was coming from an open car window. Rossi, not that he was an expert, even though he did grow up in the Bronx, the birthplace of rap, thought it sounded old-school, maybe Grandmaster Flash and the Furious Five. Wouldn't have heard that in 1920. Rossi was a young man when the group first appeared on the rap scene, so along with the buildings, sidewalks, and culture, even he seemed old to himself. Not 1920s old maybe, but old, nonetheless.

Everyone focused on themselves, their jobs, their world. New Yorkers are often thought of as cold. Truth is, they're not any colder than people anywhere else. They're just more focused than most.

It had been estimated that on a typical Tuesday with the normal population of the city combined with commuters, plus visitors — business travelers, vacationers, and others — the total number of people swelled to over double its actual size, with twenty million people in the ten square miles of Manhattan alone.

It was a five-minute walk to Lilac's Diner, though these days locals just called it Craig's. An African American, Craig was the second-generation owner. His parents opened it after World War II, and operated it until retirement and Miami called, as it does for many retiring New Yorkers looking for warmer climes. They were delighted that Craig wanted to take over the operation of the little restaurant he'd grown up in. There was little difference between back in the day and the present. At first Craig had thought about changing the name from his mom's, Lilac, to his own. But then he decided to leave well enough alone. Same with the menu. New York City comfort food. Meat loaf, mashed potatoes, hot bread, and the like, when his mom ruled the kitchen with a spoon as large as a scepter. It was warm inside and the place was crowded with the usual lunchtime crowd.

"Detective Rossi, good to see you." Craig knew all the regulars if not by name at least by face.

"Thanks, Craig. You, too."

"Your usual?" Craig not only knew all the regulars, but he also knew their usual orders.

"Why change now?"

"I like predictability."

"I'll have what he's having," said Park.

They got their food just as a young couple was getting up from a coveted small table.

Rossi said, "Anything you need to know in the neighborhood, Craig can tell you. Keeps his ear to the ground. He's kind of like the mayor of these few blocks, so just ask him."

"I've got a question for you," he continued.

"Shoot."

"Do you know karate, or judo?"

"Because I'm Asian?"

"Well, yeah," he said somewhat more than a little embarrassed, "you know, Bruce Lee and Jackie Chan and all that shit."

"Let me tell you a little about the martial arts."

"I'm all ears."

"Karate is from Okinawa. Judo is from Japan, and kung fu is from China. If you'll allow me to be even more esoteric, then you have escrima, or kali, Filipino stick-fighting, properly called either, due to the multitude of dialects of Tagalog, the main language of the Philippines. Even though they're all part of Asia, the cultures are very dissimilar. You with me so far?" He didn't wait for Rossi to answer. "I'm Korean. Tae kwon do was invented in Korea. So was Tang Soo Do. They are similar to karate in that they consist of kicks, blocks, and punches. Likewise, they have katas, but they're different, too. All children start classes in elementary school. It is required curriculum for physical education for youngsters. Not all stay with it, obviously. But I did. I'm a second-degree black belt in Tang Soo Do."

"Hey, that's great. So that means you've got my back if anybody tries to get wise."

"Yeah, you can count on me, partner. Don't you worry about it. And you're right, this pastrami is pretty good," he said, ripping a paper towel colored with violet flowers on the edges from a roll on the table and wiping his mouth aggressively.

"Told ya," Rossi said. "And remember, the fiber in the cole slaw'll keep things moving. So it's good for you." After lingering a short while over their sandwiches, Rossi said, "We should probably oughta get back to the department and at least look like we're trying to catch the Ghost or the lieutenant's gonna have our asses."

"Let's do it." Park, like most Asians, was already showing an affinity for hard work.

* * *

Back at it and an hour into their case research, Park yelled, "I think I've got something."

"Whatchu got?"

"It looks like there have been murders in every section of the city except the Upper West Side."

"And?"

"You know most killers don't want to shit in their own sandbox."

"Good catch, detective. It may not be anything, but then again, it might."

It was the first time Rossi hadn't called him 'kid'. He'd earned the small prize. "I think he's smart and brazen, but not brazen enough to kill in his own backyard. Maybe he's afraid he might be seen and recognized by someone who knows him."

"So, what are we supposed to make of that? It's not like we can knock on every door on the Upper West Side."

"That, partner, is the bitch of it, isn't it?"

Chapter Six

"If it works, don't fix it"

Since Grayson was awake, he started coffee, woke up his iPad he used for writing, entered the password to unlock it, and brought up MS Word. He'd just begun using a password. It would be bad enough if he lost his iPad and his work-in-progress. But as soon as he got a new one he could restore the manuscript from the cloud, but if someone found it in the meantime and figured out what they had — an unpublished manuscript by a best-selling author, no telling what they'd do with it. the thought of that scared him. The aroma of rich Starbucks dark roast filling the room alerted him to when it was ready. He didn't want to write a word until he'd had at least a quick injection of caffeine. He knew it was psychological, that there was no logical reason for it, but it had become habit and he thought that his writing was better after the first taste. The murder scenes he wrote lately seemed to be getting more intense, ghastlier, and more realistic. So, like they always say: if it works, don't fix it. Inspired by music, Grayson pulled up the music on his iPad and started *Psycho Killer* by Talking Heads. Feeling it in his soul, he put it on repeat play and let it continue to play the entire time he wrote. Sometimes, he wished he weren't so normal, then maybe writing about serial killers would come easier. Grayson needed to get as much writing done as possible since the *Today* interview would take up too much writing time the next day.

* * *

The next morning, Detective Rossi entered the huge squad room. Park was already hard at work on the computer. All the desks held ancient beige desktop computers, each denied flight by heavy monitors of the same color and age, even though most of the detectives used iPads in the field.

"Trying to make me look bad?" he asked of his charge, passing him by.

"You know I'd never do that," he replied in a look of feigned Asian innocence. He was already learning to give as well as he took.

"It's okay. Look out for yourself. You need to look as good as you can right now." His young partner grinned knowingly.

Chapter Seven

"What's going on?"

Today sent a car for Grayson to deliver him to their studio at Rockefeller Center. He guessed that Joseph must have talked them into that. A nice gesture and a welcome convenience.

He only thought his agent's call at seven the previous morning had been early. The car collected him at five a.m. which meant he had risen at four. It wasn't a matter of just craving coffee but requiring it if he wanted to be functional and communicative for a national TV interview. He hadn't seen four a.m. since his undergrad days, and then only if he was still up from the previous night's events.

He was delivered to the green room before one of the show's makeup artists, a cute young Latina barely out of college and looking younger than that, came for him, to do her magic. He'd done enough of these things to know that this was his least favorite part. Seating him in what resembled a Sixties-era barber chair, she tucked a tissue paper in the open collar of the shirt he wore under his wool sport jacket. The young woman began her job to make him presentable for the cameras.

Five more minutes and the producer called for him. After the commercial break they would introduce him. Lester Holt was set to do the interview. Grayson was glad for that. Everybody in the business knew him as a nice guy and a softball interviewer.

Seated again in the green room to wait, after a couple of minutes he was called, but it felt like they had to wake him up. His eyes weren't closed and he wasn't dreaming but he felt like he was unconscious. When he stood, however, he was alert and felt more alive than he could remember.

A young intern — *Where do they find all these cute girls?* — led him to the studio where Lester, seated at a desk getting his own makeup touched up, gave Grayson a smile and a timid wave when he noticed him entering. Lester probably wasn't a fan. Grayson was sure the famous host had googled him to find out what he looked like. After they returned from the next commercial, Grayson was introduced as the best-selling author of serial killer novels.

It was going the way of the typical interview until Lester asked him if he had been using the Unholy Ghost for inspiration. Grayson gave him a somewhat more than ambiguous answer.

"I get inspiration from killers, yes." He didn't specifically admit to stealing from the nation's current most-famous killer, but admitted to following news reports about various killers for fresh ideas.

Soon after that question, for the better part of a minute, Grayson, for lack of a better description, blacked out. He was conscious and his eyes were open but he couldn't respond to anything Lester said. Torpid, mentally and physically. The show's producer went to an unscheduled commercial break and an always-present medic came to the table. By that time Grayson was regaining lucidity.

Coming to with the medic taking his blood pressure, Grayson asked "What's going on?"

Off the air, but with cameras on, Lester asked, "What happened? What's wrong?"

Grayson focused on Holt. "What are you talking about?"

"We lost you there for a minute."

"What do you mean?"

"You couldn't answer my questions, it was like you were awake, but unconscious. You don't remember that? It was right after I asked if you were inspired by the Unholy Ghost."

"Come on. You've got to be kidding. That sucks on live television."

"We went to a commercial. It'll be okay."

"That's good to know, at least." Grayson was relieved. He wouldn't want anyone to think he was drunk or on drugs. His reputation as a professional fabulist was at stake and book sales might be hurt if people suspected anything was amiss.

For the return trip home it was a different stretch limousine complete with a bar containing the makings for a morning mimosa. Grayson didn't indulge. He didn't like the bubbles, and besides, he had work to do. The black stretch Lincoln, the unmistakable smell of Lysol and air freshener heavy in the car, delivered him home. Out of habit, as soon as he sat down at his desk, Grayson checked Amazon Author Central to see how his books were ranking with readers.

His only wish was that the interview would help to make *Rapacious* debut high on *The New York Times* Bestseller List when it was released in time for the long holiday book-buying season.

The weeks before a new book hit the shelves is an interesting time. Busy with preparations, checking in with editors, making changes, and battling nerves. All authors had doubts. Would people like it? Would anyone buy it? How would it be received by the public, by other authors?

Would it measure up?

Grayson finally took a deep breath and tried to relax. Blanton's small batch would surely help. But it was too early. He thought lesser brands of bourbon were just too pedestrian. He worked through the day, then went to bed earlier than normal because he had to make appearances at three Manhattan bookstores the next day. Each in a different section of the city.

Chapter Eight

"Flying solo, my good man."

The streets of New York City after midnight on Halloween are a visceral experience like most have never had and never will.

Gordon awoke and decided to go out to play. He dressed as a pirate with a fake mustache and a black eyepatch and mingled among all the witches, ghosts, sexy nurses, cowboys, presidents, and hobgoblins of various sorts. Other pirates would have worn a plastic cutlass on their belt; Gordon's, however, was shiny stainless steel. No mere prop it. Purchased with cash in one of the all-night shops in Manhattan that contain a trove of unnecessary items no one could possibly want or need but that they somehow managed to sell anyway. Mostly to the tourist trade. Gordon considered it a necessity. One good feature of the costume was that it was also a disguise and he could ditch it later, if needed, no one the wiser.

What Gordon had discovered about himself was that the cacoethes that drove him to kill were strong. Since he had blissfully come to terms with those desires, remorse was allowed no part or place in what he did.

He walked south on Seventh Avenue in the Fifties, enjoying the spectacle. Men and women alike all out for a party, in some cases wearing the skimpiest costumes the law would allow…or not. He felt that with the right motivation, or enticement, that this might be the easiest in terms of effort and most productive in terms of numbers of his redoubtable killing career. One could always hope.

In front of the site of the infamous Jack Dempsey's restaurant, now a drugstore, a couple, male and female, Batman and Wonder Woman, caught his eye.

"Dude! You and your girl look like real cold people. Youse want to go to a happening Halloween party?" Gordon gave his best party-boy smile. "I'm headed that way. My friend Nicholas, er, Nic Cage,—he told me to call him Nic—is already there. Festivities are just getting started. Yeah, and he's as wild as you've heard, I assure you." He lowered his voice conspiratorially. "No telling who else is going to show up, but all kinds of A-listers will be there." Gordon was selling hard, barely pausing to take a breath he was so excited about an opportunity for two kills. But, from the expression on the guy's face at least, the hard sell looked like it was working. Gordon spread his arms wide and laughed. "As always a few minor celebutantes. Always a few at these sorts of things. But, hey, at least there won't be any Club Kids, right? The Limelight is closed and they haven't been around in years. Even if they are still alive. Though who knows; they overdid some serious drugs, you know. It could be worse. Could be those asshole wannabe players that went to Danceteria, right?" You could tell the way he poo-pooed those hangers-on how he really felt about them. He could tell the guy didn't want to be embarrassed in front of his girl. "Whaddayasay? It's gonna be in all the papers tomorrow morning. Come on. Live a little."

"Where is it?"

Gordon waved a hand for them to follow him and said over his shoulder. "Hell, not even a block west of here." He put a little energy in his step in time with some internal beat that only he could hear, and said, "Less than the length of a…football field. Shorter than a Tom Brady pass." Then he turned and began walking backward. "Who knows, Tom might even be there. He and Giselle keep a home here in the city, you know."

That seemed to sell it. "Come on, honey. Let's go."

She looked somewhat less enthusiastic about it than her boyfriend, but nevertheless acquiesced. "I guess so," she said. They smiled and began to follow Gordon, timidly imitating his dancing movements

Gordon detected an Eastern European accent. Maybe Russian. In any case, he knew he had them. "I'm Gordon, by the way."

"I'm Nelson. She's Elena," the guy said, nodding at the girl.

"Nice to meet you, Nelson. You, too, Elena."

"You, too," said Nelson.

Elena was quieter than Nelson…or wasn't as comfortable with their new acquaintance. Her women's intuition at work. They should have heeded it. The east-west streets were deserted compared to the major avenues. Dark, with many places of opportunity. Nearly all the brownstones on the West Side had steps up a half story to the main floor and steps down a half story to the lower level hidden by the steps above. Gordon kept up his faked party-boy patter as his eyes scanned for his next killing field. He picked out a particularly dark section.

"Down here," he said, bouncing energetically the six steps to the lower-level entry of a darkened townhouse.

Elena stopped and said, "It doesn't look like they're having a party."

Gordon just waved them down. "Oh, the party is on. But it's up on the next level. This is just the easiest way in." Gordon was getting better at making this shit up. Nelson took Elena's hand and laughed, joining him in the dark entry vestibule. Gordon turned and, obscured by the steps above, he said, "You should have trusted your instinct, Elena."

He pulled the shiny blade from its dark scabbard.

A sweeping horizontal slice took Nelson's head off. A second in the opposite direction followed, taking Elena's. Clean and quick. Soft thuds as the surprised heads hit the rough concrete surface. Blood drenched the tile-covered concrete. Gordon paused to enjoy the scene, then wiped the blade on Elena's Wonder Woman blue shorts with white stars and replaced it in the scabbard. He quietly slunk up to the sidewalk. The nearest passersby, which weren't, didn't even pay attention. With luck on his side, nobody would find the gruesome scene until the first light of morning. He casually left the scene.

He smiled. The night's physical exertion raised his appetite. He made his way to Seventh Avenue and a couple blocks north to the theatre district, to Martini's Restaurant, a dark, ultra modern glass and steel place for beautiful young people. Gordon entered, passed the coat check; the maître d' greeted him in front of the high-ceilinged dining room with Corinthian columns framing the entry. "How many, sir?"

Still riding high from his successful evening he all but danced in and answered happily, "Flying solo, my good man."

"Very good, sir. Follow me."

"Could I possibly be seated at the bar?"

"Indeed."

Because it was Halloween, in sharp contrast to the dark intimate space, the top-shelf liquors were backlit with bright orange lights. Much like the Empire State Building which changed colors with the holiday. Kelly green for St. Patrick's Day, red, white, and blue for Independence Day, and red and green for the extended Christmas season.

There were others seated at the shiny black marble-topped bar. Gordon thought some of them might be entertaining. With two kills freshly notched on his belt, even though it was late, one never knew what the night might bring. He chose a seat next to an exquisite brunette dressed as a witch, pointy black hat completing the outfit.

A blonde middle-aged but still-attractive female bartender asked him what he desired.

"I've had a busy day and I'm famished. I'd like a dozen escargot and a bottle of your best white burgundy if you please."

"Our escargot dish holds six. A dozen would be two orders."

"Let's do it, then."

"Sounds good. My best white burgundy is a Louis Latour Meursault 2016. Will that do?"

"Perfectly," Gordon said with a satisfied grin.

Soft standards by Neil Diamond, and the chairman of the board, Frank Sinatra, and Tony Bennett — New York- or New Jersey-grown all — filled the dark space *sotto voce*. Those mellow tunes setting everyone up for a surprise: *Somebody Put Something In My Drink*, one of the biggest and loudest hits by the city's own Ramones.

The witch leaned toward him and said, "You have magnificent taste. White burgundy and escargot. Two of France's greatest treasures. Of course, there's Paris in the spring, too. So that makes three." She smiled at Gordon. "Are you from there?"

She looked like a graduate of Convent of the Sacred Heart all-girls Catholic School on 91st St. and Fifth Ave. Then, of course, college at Columbia right here in the city. Ivy League through and through. And it showed. She probably called the university by its original name, King's College. Most likely legacy parents and grandparents before her. She'd know which fork and spoon to use and when. Surely she lived in an outrageously expensive Soho warehouse loft. Purchased using family money because her father, like any father, would want her to be safe. He though, had the wherewithal to ensure it. Ironic, now, since she was anything but.

"Thank you, but no, I'm just fond of its esculent national treasures."

"It just occurred to me. You look familiar. Are you famous?"

"Hardly," he chuckled as if flattered. "I'm a salesman from Iowa. In town for a few days. Don't you recognize the Midwest accent? But I do love the big city and, since I'm not at home, I decided to dress up and join the Halloween party."

I think I'm doing a good job of selling that story because I'm not ready to "be famous" quite yet.

"Really? Oh-oh-oh! I just remembered. You look like that famous author. What's his name? Oh, yeah! Cole. Grayson Cole. You could be his twin. I saw him on TV just the other day talking about his newest book."

Grayson Cole? That must be why I have credit cards with that name. But that still doesn't explain everything. I need to deny any kind of connection there.

"If he's that famous then he must be rich. I wish I were him, but…"

he shrugged slowly, "I'm a working stiff."

She extended an elegant, long, black, witches-begloved hand and said, "I'm Jocelyn, by the way."

"Gordon."

"And your name is even similar to his. Grayson. Gordon. Both begin with G."

Gordon attempted to laugh and appear confident — anything but diffident — although at this particular moment confident was the last word he would use to describe himself. He shrugged again saying, "I agree. Pretty big coincidence. But…sorry. That's all it is." He wanted to return the focus to her. "So, what do you do?"

"The cosmetics counter at Macy's."

"That explains it," he said.

"Explains what? What do you mean?"

"From my experience the prettiest women in the city work at cosmetics counters in the department stores."

"Aren't you sweet? I always feel like I don't measure up."

"Well, you need to get that silly thought out of your head."

"Thank you, Gordon. I'll try."

The blonde bartender was back and unbouchoned the bottle of expensive wine, offering Gordon a healthy pour of the white burgundy in a large globe Chardonnay glass and placed it before him. He was delighted that the restaurant knew Chardonnay glasses should be large. Many didn't. He asked her to pour another glass for his new acquaintance. Jocelyn heard him and quickly pushed aside the dirty martini she was drinking. A classy drink yes, but the white burgundy would be much better with the garlicky escargot in the event he decided to offer her one. It wasn't long before the seasoned professional barmaid returned with two servings of escargot. The warm aroma of fresh garlic and butter caressed his senses.

"How lovely," said Jocelyn, as she breathed in the scent.

"Would you like one? Maybe two. But no more," he said, thinking he was displaying an attractive sense of humor. It almost felt like he was on an actual date, that he was somebody normal, someone with a conscience.

Have I ever had a conscience? If I had, I lost it somewhere along the way. Even worse, do I have a soul? But doesn't everyone have a soul? Or is it in the realm of possibility I could have been born without a soul?

That was the only conclusion he could come to; that he hadn't been born. That he'd just occurred.

Her pretty demure personality brought him back to the task at hand. "Oh, I shouldn't," she said.

"Please. I insist," he replied.

"All right, then. But only because you asked twice. And insisted." She flashed dimples deep enough to hide the two-carat diamonds she wore on her sexy lobes.

Each small white dish came with its own diminutive fork for withdrawing the succulent, fat, buttered snails from their shells. Gordon slid one over in front of her and said, "I was only kidding when I said no more than two. You can have as many as you like."

"I just want a small taste," she said lifting the delicate fork gracefully.

"I'm curious. Why is such a pretty woman as yourself all alone on Halloween?"

Jocelyn wiped her mouth fetchingly with a black cloth napkin before explaining. "I actually had a date. First meeting, to tell the truth. From a dating website. You know how those things are," she said, not expecting a reply. "At Tavern On The Green. Well, anyway, there was no chemistry at all. Not like with you and me," she said, pouring on the charm. "So I didn't give him my last name and a few minutes later I told him I was going to the restroom and I ducked out the patio entrance. I hated to do it. I've never done anything like that before...but now..." She smiled at Gordon. "...I'm really glad I did. And I hope you are, too."

He tipped his glass her way with a grateful smile. She had no idea how glad he was.

"Where are you staying?" she said with more than what one might call a passing interest.

Will it always be this easy? He smiled slowly.

"Marriott Marquis. Times Square."

"Right in the middle of the Crossroads of The World. Great place. Have you been to The View yet?" She was referring to the well-known hotel's famed revolving restaurant and bar on the 52nd floor that slowly and completely rotated once every hour providing a three-hundred-sixty-degree view of the New York skyline.

"I was just getting ready to go for a nightcap. It's only two blocks. You wouldn't want to join me, would you?"

"I'd love to. Besides, tomorrow's my day off."

She thinks she's hit the jackpot. She only thinks she'd love to. How deliciously bittersweet for her. Too bad she won't have time to revel in the emotion. "I'll settle our tabs and we can be on our way."

"That sounds delightful."

Exiting onto Martini's corner patio, the temperature had dropped since he'd entered and a nebulous dense fog draped and becalmed the city. The spire on the top of the Empire State Building rendered vaguely by the penumbra of white, but because it was not as tall, the flat top and the letters spelling out MetLife on its namesake building a few blocks away, made it a visible sentry, looming unobscured by the haze obscuring the taller, more famous one.

When it was the Pan Am building, the huge flat roof accommodated large double-prop helicopters that landed on it to ferry city dwellers to Kennedy International Airport, then named Idlewild, to sleek Pan Am jets waiting to whisk them to destinations around the world. Which, as frightening as it sounds, wasn't nearly as dicey as forty years before that when dirigibles were expected to fight high winds in order to anchor to the uppermost point of the mast high atop the Empire State Building before releasing a swinging gangway for disembarking passengers to make way to what was then the world's tallest building's open-air 82nd floor observation deck.

Now, after midnight, and the sidewalks were still crowded with scarily- and cheerfully-costumed revelers, depending on one's bent. There were sure to be some brutal hangovers come morning's unwelcome but nonetheless inevitable dawning. Gordon shivered in his pirate's costume but still managed to wrap a gentlemanly arm around Jocelyn, dressed less than comfortably for the cold in her little more than skimpy witch's garb.

The warmth of her feminine body is causing me to tingle...but what is this feeling? It feels nice, but not like a need to kill. Could I be satisfied with the feel of a woman without having that need to kill? What the hell is that shitty smell?

He looked ahead in the distance and saw two mounted policemen at the curb. The officers didn't even glance their way when they passed. They'd apparently been there for some time as there were two steaming piles of manure in the street behind the large equines. His nose wrinkled in disgust at the source of the stench.

Two blocks later, the neon lights of Times Square, bright lights of song, and scenes moved on large screens on the walls of tall buildings protecting the square like those shielding the habitués of a fort. Though the area looked like a different universe now, Times Square was no longer like it was in the Seventies with the unending sex shops and peep shows, theaters, and stores from a different era. Appearing like bright sunny daylight, the Square beckoned them onward to the warmth of the Marriott Marquis' open air first floor where people take one of the six capsule-shaped glass elevators to the eighth-floor lobby. It, the lobby, the center of the hotel's actual and Times Square's metaphorical universe.

But first, to tread sidewalks littered with leaflets accepted from hawkers of men's clubs, clothing stores, and diners, to be immediately discarded, and avoid the hawkers and the pickpockets with the same vigilance.

The intersection still bearing the name given it when *The New York Times* began construction of its new headquarters building in 1904, before then being known as Longacre Square.

Arriving at the main floor, even though it was near one a.m., for all the activity, it might as well have been one p.m. The jewelry store, the I Love New York store, and women's shoe stores, all open for business and chockablock with shoppers. Gordon and Jocelyn congregated with the group in front of the elevator that would speed them nonstop from the 8th floor open atrium lobby to the 52nd floor and The View.

The first ones to enter moved typically to opposite corners, until others entering filled the entirety. As usual, no one uttered a sound. Tomb-like quiet. Like in a public restroom, especially the men's. Gordon stood with his back to the glass wall; Jocelyn placed herself strategically in front of him, her ample derrière pressed against him. The warm fragrance of her perfume, Victor&Rolf Flowerbomb, on her neck overwhelmed his senses, dulling them.

What is that fragrance? How do I recognize it? Where am I? Why am I here? I know what I do. I know who I am. I'm Gordon...fuckin' what?

He couldn't remember his last name...or if he even had one. All he knew was that he was a killer. The scariest motherfucker of the night and he had to kill. To harrow the city. That thought focused his brain and helped him remember the night like a movie. Film fragments. Black and white flashes of city scenes. Was the night an illusion? A delusion? A montage of stills. Killings, cocktails, and snails. A flashing, clicking, black and white film without audio. If there had been sound it would have been eerie late-night music too unreal to be real.

In his distorted unreality, wasn't everyone like him? Everyone needed an answer to that most basic but deepest of existentialist quagmires: Who am I? But for Gordon to know what he was was enough. Unsure if he was alive, if he'd ever been alive, it was ironic that when he was killing was the only time he felt alive. At least at those times, he knew what he was. That was unequivocal. No dissonance in that.

Midway to the top, they passed a high-ceilinged fitness club filled with treadmills, steppers, and weight machines that looked like ancient torture devices. Men and women alike, perspiring profusely, getting a workout in the wee hours. It was truly the city that never sleeps.

Another quick half of the building's height and the elevator slowed, then braked to an abrupt stop. Gordon and Jocelyn were the last two off. Into the dark carpeted lobby. The center of the restaurant and bar, stationary, anchored to the tall building, dining and bar areas rotating around the center.

After having to wait in line for a short while, they were greeted. Gordon asked for two seats in the bar area, but as near to the glass wall as possible. They were seated at a small table for two, arranged in the arc of the window that at that moment faced north to the vast dark of the lightless Central Park and the bright lights of historic Harlem not far beyond and further still to the electric neon of the Bronx.

Gordon liked the dark. He was comfortable with it in the same way the good people of New York were growing afraid of it. Another reason he would need to strike in the light of day. So they'd be afraid no matter the time. Afraid of day or night, light and dark.

He wanted — No, needed! — another kill on the night though technically it was after midnight and thus the next day, but why quibble over technicalities? At the same time he wouldn't consider it to be momentous or something to morbidly celebrate. Nothing more than another chapter in the sordid tale of the Unholy Ghost. His reputation growing longer by the day. He had to keep fueling the fire as he somehow understood the half-life of a serial killer's fame only lasted until the next arrived on the scene seeking a higher body count as if it were a competition.

A server approached, introduced himself as Sean, and asked, "What would you like this evening? Although I guess it's morning." Then with the reality of time dawning on him, covered a yawn.

Jocelyn said, "Chardonnay? A glass of Plumpjack? I might as well stick with chard."

She and the server looked toward Gordon. "Very good choice. And what will the gentleman be having?"

"I'll have the same," Gordon said with a delighted smile. Sean gave a little bow and walked away.

"I remember Sean from the last time I came here," said Jocelyn. "He's a real nice guy."

"Seems like it."

"And I recalled they had Plumpjack. Not many places do."

"I'm glad you did. An excellent choice."

"Thank you. Of course, I'm sure he doesn't remember me. Not dressed like a witch, anyway."

"Doubtful." *With any luck, Sean won't be able to remember me when I'm not a pirate.* After much small talk and finishing their wine, Gordon suggested, "Since I haven't been there, why don't we go upstairs a level and check out the restaurant?"

"I have. It's lovely. Let's."

In the dark lobby of the lounge, there was a long line waiting on the elevator. "Let's take the stairs," Gordon said.

"Are you sure?"

"Of course. I'm sure the employees use it to go between the two levels when they're in a hurry." Though Gordon hoped it would be empty.

"Alright, then."

They opened the steel fire door. Gordon softly eased the heavy metal portal to. As they moved forward, their footsteps echoed on the empty concrete expanse.

"Come on," Gordon said, taking a laughing Jocelyn by the hand and hastening up the broad stairway. Halfway to the next floor was a landing before the switchback to the next level. Under the pretense of needing to catch his breath, Gordon doubled over, gasping. Jocelyn moved closer to comfort him with a gentle hand on his sturdy seemingly trustworthy back. When he raised up a shiny steel blade was in his hand. The demoniac look in his eyes told Jocelyn all she needed to know before a blood-curdling scream could leave her mouth. He sidestepped the blood spray; her head fell from her already lifeless body and tumbled, rolling fourteen steps to come to rest on the floor where they began their trek, leaving a moping path of blood and gore, the witch's hat a step above it.

He started down the stairs in a rush but was unable to resist a last look at the macabre sight when her dark, dead eyes pleadingly caressed him to stop. He bent over the formerly attached necessary body part and, from her delicate ear, ripped one of the large diamond studs for his newest souvenir. He placed it in his mouth for safekeeping. It tasted of her perfume and bloody saltiness. The taste would've fueled his urge, nay, need to kill had it not just been sated.

Continuing his rapid descent, he tore off the black eyepatch, the black kerchief that covered his head, and the large, clasped, gold hoop earrings that completed his costume, rendering himself virtually unrecognizable from his most recent visage. On the next landing — he thought he remembered the floor number, forty-two, painted over the exit door — panting from his ten-story run, he threw the accessories aggressively into a mid-height black plastic trashcan, along with the now bloody sword and its scabbard, before stepping calmly out of the stairway onto the next floor's red and gold carpeted hallway. Noticing a security camera, even thought it was pointed another direction, he ducked his head and covered a fake sneeze. Appearing as any other guest who couldn't sleep.

He'd hated to trash the ravenous cutlass since it was a fine blade, but it would be somewhat more than a little conspicuous now that he wasn't dressed as a pirate. Oh well, if he wanted to, he could always get another one at any of the twenty-four-hour shops, abundant in Manhattan with troves of unusual objects, usually frequented by tourists for souvenirs. He made his way around half the floor to the bank of elevators that would take him down, just short of the gates of hell, but no less precipitous.

Inside the polished descending bullet, he studied his reflected image in the glass wall bearing a day's worth of fingerprints.

I need a haircut. But where to get one? I can't remember ever having had a haircut. What does that say about me? If a man has never had a haircut, is he really a man? If I've never had one, my hair should be past my waist, yet here it is only beginning to look a wee bit messy.

He ran fingers through his hair.

I want to get that tattoo I've been thinking about ever since…ever…since…when? At least a week. I can't remember anything before then except for…blood. But it feels like I've wanted one for ages. So, haircut first. Then, a tattoo…maybe a knife dripping blood?

But when he did get the tattoo, there would be no on else to care. He was alone. Depending on where it was put on his body, would anyone ever know? Who indeed?

Reaching ground level, and worried about his unkempt hair, he nonetheless pushed it aside — the worry that is, not his hair — long enough to deal with the current predicament. Since it was cold and pushing the hell out of three a.m., he let the all-night, burgundy-uniformed doorman summon with the whistle that seemed to never leave his lips one of the yellow taxis queued up twenty-fours a day, year round. He palmed the man a five-spot for his trouble.

Not too generous, but not cheap. Unremarkable, like myself.

Looking like nothing more than a boringly respectable businessman who got hungry and was going out to find something to eat. His usual routine of faking a cough into his hand and ducking to cover his face. He'd done it so much it was routine. He didn't even have to consider it. He'd have the cabbie drop him off a block from his building...just in case.

Chapter Nine

"Son of a bitch"

Detective Rossi was having an everything bagel with lox and a schmear. He added capers and fragrant arcs of red onion. His opinion was that the Jewish people had gotten it right with their choice of toppings, and right here in the city that birthed the prototypically New York creation. He always bought them at Carnegie Deli and brought them home by the bagful. Occasionally, when he couldn't resist the temptation, he'd buy one of their world-famous cheesecakes. Probably was somewhat more than a big reason for his stomach beginning to camber over his belt.

He was finishing the breakfast delight, hoping it might help to improve his attitude about their lack of success with the Unholy Ghost, or at least his early-morning torpor, when his phone buzzed, vibrating in his inside jacket pocket.

"Yeah, Lou."

"The Unholy Ghost."

"Fuck. When? Where?"

"Won't know when until you and the medical examiner get there. Where is a stairwell somewhere between the resto and bar levels at the top of the Marriott Marquis. Get over there forthwith. I'll call the kid and tell him to meet you there." The lieutenant was displaying his somewhat more than serious earnest side, in other words, he was acting like he usually did.

"10-4." Rossi could play his game, too.

"And, hey."

"Yeah?"

"Find a clue this time." The lieutenant clicked off quickly knowing his order wouldn't be well-received by his most experienced detective.

First Grade Detective Rossi knew the lieutenant was serious about him rushing because he used the term forthwith. Cop-speak for get your ass in gear; his commanding officer never used it unless he was deadly serious. Indeed, he possessed the rare talent of being able to convey nuance even over the phone.

Rossi returned to the bedroom long enough to kiss Ella goodbye — and tell her to have a nice day and that he hoped to be home in time for dinner — and brush his teeth. He'd floss on the drive to the Marquis.

From his east-side apartment it was almost due west as the crow flies to the luxurious hotel in Times Square. Of course the crow didn't have to deal with Midtown traffic. The further west one got, the worse it got, as drivers queued up to enter the Holland and Lincoln tunnels making their way to Jersey. He figured he'd still beat Park there, easy.

Rossi'd been to the Marriott Marquis before for a wedding reception, so he knew he'd have time to grab a cuppa at the Starbucks in the hotel's lower lobby. He pulled to a hard stop next to a fire hydrant, called johnny pumps by New Yorkers, on West 45th Street on the south side of the hotel, and threw the NYPD laminated placard in the dash.

After the lieutenant's call, Park practically ran to the 9th Street Station, breathlessly calling Sal on the way to get an update, before he'd catch the PATH Train, standing along with the other straphangers — professionals, hard hats, and service workers — for the four-minute, barely more than two-mile high-speed trip to the Times Square 42nd Street Station, the busiest in New York. He didn't mind riding the trains at night because they weren't very crowded. People were more afraid to ride them at night because of the criminal element, making them less than crammed full. But during the day, especially morning, it was another story entirely. Everybody on the trains competed for seats. It was like a race when the cars' doors opened. Everyone eyed the competition, until the race was on.

Park always let an elderly person or the pregnant have the last seat, but then someone else, not as kindly as he, might get to it before the one he intended to have it, and if they did he would shame them for it; and if they tried to make a thing out of it, he'd flip open the leather case holding his shield. He loved watching them stutter and stammer and attempt to explain how things were; but now it was his station and time for him to dodge cars crossing the street and people on the sidewalk on the way to the Marquis.

A nor-easter, not a tempest but nevertheless a juggernaut, had come in overnight. The smell of the aeolian chill rain roiling through the gusty west-to-east canyon off the torpid but ever noble Hudson River. Unusual for October in New York, the sullen leaden sky's tenuous grip portended an early frost and snow squall arriving on a nor'easter before Christmas. Promising less than clement weather. One could never know, however, if it would sneak in duplicitously like a thief in the night or if it would arrive on a tempest for everyone to see and, worse, feel. Indeed, the city itself, buildings, sidewalks, streets, possessed of a despondent gray cast. The unmindful stain of the clouds matched most of the substantial brooding gray buildings — they of a similar color to Manhattan's underground bedrock.

A 737 Boeing jet, the blue, red, and yellow of Southwest Airlines, flying north, began a low banking turn, to make its final approach over the shallow waters of Long Island sound, unexpected and unsettling for travelers, and on into LaGuardia, named for Fiorello LaGuardia, the mayor of New York when the airport was built in 1953.

Most likely not a coincidence. The zigguratic walls of certain structures hewn as they were from the granite underpinning below, part of the undercrofts as deep as the buildings are high; most of them not what one would call attractive, but historic, inspiration-evoking, and awe-inspiring nonetheless.

With legs pumping and his hard leather-soled shoes slipping, Park hopped over the river of street wash that had formed at the curb — at least the rats would get a much-needed bath — carrying trash along with it, and onto the wet sidewalk; dashing past people and ducking under umbrellas, passed a wet, dirty homeless man pushing his shopping cart possessed of all his wet worldly belongings.

At the moment Park wished he were one of those New Yorkers who carried an umbrella every day because they didn't trust the TV weather person. Just in case. Of course, it would be too late at this point. He slipped past the dozen umbrellaless standing in respite under the awning and gazing skyward wishfully for a break in the storm. He ducked into the Starbucks next to the hotel's first floor entrance and bought a grandé cup of green tea. He removed the plastic lid to better enjoy the aroma as the hot white steam rose from the surface. Even though he was hungry he resisted the urge to order a cheese danish. He hadn't had his usual side of rice with his bacon and eggs earlier. A mistake he didn't often make in the morning. He'd been raised with Far East habits where eating rice three meals a day was common. He didn't do that, but thought it was important to have extra carbs for breakfast at least, before work.

The rueful scene of the homeless man outside the large window made him pause, and after thinking about it, he bought a second cup, this time the larger venti, and took it outside. Maybe it would warm the man's spirit, even if it couldn't do anything for his soul. Park always looked for opportunities to improve his karma in the world. And chasing the Unholy Ghost, he'd need all the good karma he could get.

After having some tea and feeling altruistic about helping the homeless gentleman, Park had a smile on his face, but upon arriving upstairs and opening the heavy steel door to the stairwell landing and seeing a uniformed officer keeping watch along with his senior partner on one knee leaning over a bloody headless corpse, his smile was replaced with a determined resoluteness. The man he already looked at as his mentor squatted next to a venti cup of Starbucks dark roast, black, Rossi believed apt for his tough-guy image, that sat on the cool concrete floor next to him.

Except for the head being fifteen feet down the stairway and a bloody trail leading to it, the inert body was in considered repose.

Seeing his partner enter, without even looking Sal reached into the outer flap pocket of his sport coat and pulled out a pair of latex gloves, some canvas booties, and what most people would call a surgical mask, all matching the ones he wore. Handing them to Park, Sal said, "Here, kid. Put these on. Shan't run the risk of contaminating the scene."

The slow steel door clanged shut behind them. They wouldn't need to touch the body in a vain attempt to find a pulse since, minus its head, it would be obvious to anyone with half a brain that the victim was deceased. Park nodded, even though Sal didn't see it as enthralled as he was in examining the bloody stump of the victim's neck. Park sat on the concrete, cool through his worsted wool trousers, and wrestled with putting on the protective items. Booties first, over inexpensive black lace ups. Rubber gloves next. Mask last since breathing would be uncomfortable with his nose and mouth covered for very long.

Since it was Detective Park's first experience with a hideously gory body, he felt somewhat more than a little hot acidic bile rising in his throat and swallowed to tamp it back down, happy now he had not purchased a danish earlier. He nonetheless tried to convince himself and his partner it wasn't a big deal and joined him in leaning over the wretched body and in an exaggerated display of machismo he really didn't feel. Shaking his all-of-a-sudden heavy head, he said, "Son of a bitch!"

"Couldn't put it better myself, but aren't you a little young to be using language like that?" The incredulous but nevertheless amused cast of Jay's dark eyes showed he couldn't believe Sal had said that.

"Believe me, kid. You got to look for the humor in these dark things or you'll end up eating your gun. The damage a nine mm parabellum does going through the soft palate and into your brain at faster than the speed of sound isn't pretty. Besides, your suicide would reflect badly on me. So, we got to do everything we can to make sure that that don't happen."

Park couldn't believe he'd made another weak attempt at humor.

"Moreover, your mother wants you to come home. And my hand to God I'm going to do my best to make sure that happens. I'm sure I don't want a little old Korean woman pissed at me anymore than I do a little old Italian woman." Park nodded in agreement with that correct though ethnically offensive comparison.

Sal pulled a plastic bottle of Tums from his trousers pocket and chewed three. A huge gulp of the caffeine delivery system washed down the leftover crumbs of the masticated antacid. His heartburn had been acting up since he awoke and the gruesome scene wasn't helping it any. "You want one?" he asked, holding out the bottle to Park.

His junior partner ignored him. Pretending not to hear and attempting to man up. Rossi put the bottle back in his pocket.

Park began to turn green and looked like he was about to heave. "Hey, kid," Rossi said not inconsiderately. "Why don't you go find some water? I can handle this."

"I'll be fine, besides don't we need to interview employees?" Park managed to finally say.

"The restaurant won't open for a few more hours, so anyone that would have been on duty when it happened won't be here at least until it opens for lunch. For now here comes the fun part. We need to examine the head," he said, gesturing without looking, toward the trail of blood and neck offal, down the stairs to the next landing where it had come to a rest.

Park placed his hands on both knees to raise up from an otherwise unassisted squat, and stood with a groan that belied his youth. It was more about knowing what lie ahead and that it was somewhat more than likely that it would be much worse than the scene he'd just viewed. But he had no idea how much worse it would be. Like the remains in a particularly bloody slasher movie; only the film wouldn't be as bad as this.

It wasn't only the young detective for whom it was bad; it was the worst thing Rossi had seen in his thirty-plus years on the job and they both regretted ever setting eyes on the grievous appendage. Rossi questioned his career path and wondered why he hadn't decided to become a chef in an Italian restaurant, instead. Park wished he were back at university half a world away.

"Look," Park said, getting his head back in the game. "Both ears are pierced but there's only one diamond. From the looks of the lobe it must have been ripped from her ear."

"Good catch, kid. You've been paying attention," Rossi said somewhat lightheartedly and egotistically, even though he knew it didn't feel right. "Our guy's known for taking souvenirs. Guess we're lucky he only took the earring."

Both he and Rossi nodded their heads in agreement, glad the ears were still intact. A young African-American officer in a sharp dark blue NYPD uniform haltingly opened the door to the stairwell. Rossi was glad to see he was at least clean-shaven. He was old school and in the minority with those of the opinion who didn't support the easing of departmental regs requiring officers to be clean shaven. Truth be told, his dislike went deeper than that; he wasn't sure he trusted those who had beards.

"Excuse me. Detectives? We found something."

"Yeah, whatchu got?" Detective Rossi said impatiently, showing he was already exhausted and running out of patience with the perp but taking it out on the young man.

"A sword."

"A sword?

"Actually, sir, I think it can technically be described as a cutlass." The uni seemed scared to death of the senior detective.

"A cutlass, huh? I take it you're not talking about a Sixties-era, two-door coupé made by Oldsmobile."

"Uhhh…no, sir…I'm not."

"Well, how about we go take a look-see, then."

"We can probably get there faster by taking the stairs."

"Let's do it then," Park said.

Rossi turned to the uni. "You must be pretty smart, knowing what a cutlass is."

"Not really. I just read a lot."

"That's good. What do you read?"

"Fiction, mostly."

"Doesn't seem like you'd learn much reading fiction. Just sayin'."

"Are you kiddin'? I peregrinate the world learning every step of the way by reading good fiction. Good thing I can too, on a cop's salary".

"Peregri-what? You need to use language a dago cop understands." Detective Rossi wasn't highly educated, but even though he tended to play it down, he was possessed of a vocabulary grandiloquent. But the young officer had used a word with which Rossi wasn't familiar.

Rossi liked when people underestimated him. Even though he was wise in the ways of the street, he was smart, his vocabulary practiced and the argot of professors and the like. It was his burden. His wisdom wasn't of just any streets; it was those of the worst parts of the deteriorating Gotham City. Which had been ultimately a good thing since being alone gave him the proverbial heebie-jeebies, anyway. To him the northern reaches of Central Park were the back of beyond, or its even more remote cousin, the hinterlands. To Manhattanites, parks were revered as the geographical and metaphorical heart of New York, nay, the world.

"It means journey on foot. To journey on foot."

"Thanks. The day's not a waste, then. Learned something new and the day's not even half over." Without a doubt, he enjoyed increasing his vocabulary and felt like it was a good day when he could.

The entrance to the forty-second floor was impeded by the ubiquitous yellow crime scene tape. Peeling off just enough, they ducked through and entered.

Peering over the hinged top of the dirty black plastic waste can, Rossi said, "Let's see what we got." Sure enough, a bloody steel sword with gold-colored hilt, some of the blade still shiny, was crammed point down into a corner of the can. Rossi withdrew it slowly, as if it were a treasure of the highest order. He stood it in the concrete corner, point down, and peered into the can. If only with a magnifying glass would he have looked Holmesian. "What have we here?"

Still wearing the latex gloves preventing transfer of friction ridges and/or DNA, he reached shoulder-deep into the receptacle and withdrew a black pirate's eyepatch, a red bandanna head covering, the scabbard that sheathed the sword, and a furry black caterpillar. Nope, the caterpillar lookalike was a fake mustache. Handing the odds and ends now thought to be important evidence to the officer, Rossi commanded, "Bag this and get it to the house."

"Will do, Detective."

"Speaking of the house, let's head that way our own selves," Rossi said to his partner. "We need some help with this shit."

"What you mean?" asked Park.

"Street help."

Park shrugged, unable to do anything more than trust his partner's judgement.

Rossi's phone rang. He glanced at the display. "Yeah, Lou, what's up?"

"We got another one. Actually, two more. One scene."

"Fuck."

"Yeah, looks like our asshole was busy last night."

"Where?"

"Not far from where you are, but I've already got you guy's backups on the way. You and Park circle up."

"You got it, Lou."

The precinct was buzzing when they arrived. There was always a lot of activity after a murder. Or three. Especially when it was the work of the Unholy Ghost. The lieutenant caught them up on the other two murders and they updated him about their catch. His heart finally slowing down after the morning's intensity and two cups of coffee on top of that, Rossi looked at Park and said, "Let's go to Craig's for lunch. I need his help."

"How can the owner of a diner help you?"

"He knows Bookworm."

Park imagined ominous strains of dramatic music. "Who, or what, is Bookworm?"

"An informant. His number changes, but Craig always knows how to reach him."

"Is he good?"

"Craig?"

"Bookworm."

"He's the best. He has the heartbeat of the city."

"Cool. Let's do it, then."

"Cool your jets, detective. No offense to my favorite football team."

Properly chastised, and with tail appropriately tucked, Park returned to his desk and waited for Rossi to call him over again.

Chapter Ten

"Zip, zero, zilch"

They entered the diner to aromas of oregano, fresh garlic, the nuanced bouquet of extra-virgin olive oil, and more difficult to discern but just as pleasing to the senses, other lesser-known spices popular with all chefs.

"Welcome back, detectives. Same as last time?" Craig said enthusiastically in reply to the bell jingling over the door, and kept chopping onion for potato salad.

"Sounds good," Rossi said. "How about you, Jay?"

"Definitely."

A minute later Craig delivered two open-faced pastrami sandwiches with thin-sliced beef brisket piled high on huge slices of rye bread with brown mustard and Cole slaw. "On me, today, for our men in blue." The sandwiches looked even larger than usual.

"Thanks, Craig. Have a seat?" Rossi said.

"Just for a minute."

Feeling like he didn't have the time to waste, Rossi got straight to the point. "You seen Bookworm lately?"

"He usually comes in a couple of times a week. At least when he's flush."

"Will you ask him to call me next time?" Rossi said, extracting a business card from his leather shield case. "He should have my number but you never know with Bookworm."

"True, but yeah…no problem. I'm sure he'll be in for breakfast before the week's over. He always says it's the most important meal of the day."

Rossi laughed. "That sounds like something Book would say."

"Sure does. I should get back to work, now," he said, glancing at his watch and then at the rapidly growing crowd of lunchtime regulars."

"Thanks, Craig. See you soon."

Curiosity piqued, Park said, "What's the story with this Bookworm?"

"His name is John Campbell. Tall, good-looking brother. Real smart. Supposedly went to Princeton on an academic scholarship. Book wasn't really that street-smart. He grew up middle-class Bronx. But he wanted to make positively sure no one think him an arriviste.

"Book could've played football and looks like he still could. The Jets or the Giants could probably use him. Sons-a-bitches. He was an all-city wide receiver at prep school, grew tall and strong, but in some ways he didn't grow up. He's still that kid in many ways, but he worked on his grades. Double major in philosophy and finance. No autodidact, Book. Did it all with verve.

"Anyways, story is he used to read all his textbooks the first week of the semester and never open them again. And get all A's. He still likes to read, classics mostly — Dumas, Melville, Fitzgerald, Bronte. The best gift you can give Book is a good book, no pun intended. And believe you me, you want him on your team if you're playing trivia. I'm quite sure he could recite the Boy Scouts' oath from memory. He probably was an Eagle himself. God, Mom, apple pie, and all that crap."

Rossi took a bite, barely chewed, almost swallowing it whole. "Book knows the names of the lions flanking the entrance to the main New York Public Library on Fifth Avenue. I lived in the city all my life and didn't know that until he told me."

Ripping off another chunk of sandwich, Rossi had Park on a string, waiting for more of the story. This time he chewed slowly and dragged out the suspense.

"Patience and Fortitude. That's their names and now you know, Jay. Mayor Fiorello LaGuardia, called Fio by some, he of the airport, which I like better than JFK, by the way, gave them those names in the early thirties because he said that's what New Yorkers would need to survive the depression."

"Patience and Fortitude." Park nodded and said nothing more as he tried to remember all this information.

Rossi continued. "Anyways, I digress. Book's schoolmates started calling him Bookworm. I just call him Book. Him and me, we're on a first name basis only, you know. Of course, he likes to think himself as D'Artagnan, you understand." Park stared blankly. "From the Alexander Dumas book? *The Three Musketeers?*"

Park nodded like he knew and Rossi continued. "He's never been what one would call diffident or reserved. His energy is kinetic and swallows up everything around him like a huge black hole sucking up matter.

"But like I said Book made nothing but A's. Dean's List all four years. Graduated on time with honors. Was on his way to becoming the prototypical Princeton man until he came back to the city after graduation to chill for awhile before getting serious about his career and his smarts while staying cooler than the other side of the pillow." Rossi grinned, liking his analogy.

"Look, Park. The worst thing I can say about Book is he's something of a rascal. Fell in with the wrong people, them who work the streets, and now he runs them. Used his smarts to take them over. 'Course probably wasn't that hard to take over a group of semiliterate street thugs. But he could've gotten hired to teach philosophy right there at Princeton or maybe gotten a job at Merrill Lynch, Pierce, Fenner, Smith, Wes and Bean. I still call them by their original name. Old-school habit."

Park laughed. "I did not know that."

"Oh, yeah. It's still their legal name, by the way. But Book liked the street too much, so he decided to become an informant. Can you blame him? Who would want to go down either one of those other career rabbit-holes? He's servile to no one and no one's servile to him. He considers himself a modern day paladino."

"A what? Pala...deee...nooo?"

"Sorry, old habit. Forgot you don't speak Italiano. A paladin is a gentleman supporter of causes and a defender of the victimized underdog. Book probably makes low six-figures a year keeping the Law informed. Tax free. No nine-to-five and doesn't have to wear a suit and necktie. What would you do?" Rossi said, holding his hands palms out to the side in an as-if gesture.

Park had never heard Rossi talk that long before; he was impressed. "Wow. That's quite a story."

"It is, isn't it? What I like best about Book, though, is that he isn't given to rodomontade; he doesn't take himself too seriously."

"Do you have to use words like that?"

"Like what?"

"Whatever that word was."

"Oh that. Rodomontade. Given to boasting, bragging." Indeed it was their mutual love of words over which Bookworm and Rossi first bonded.

"Why don't you say that, then?"

"I'm trying to help you. You know, with English."

"Don't do me any favors."

Rossi shrugged noncommittally. He was pretty sure that that was a promise he'd be unable to keep if indeed he made it. "Well, I needed that," he said, judiciously applying to his mouth a plain white paper towel ripped from a roll on the table. "But we should oughta get back. You've already figured out how Lou gets when he can't lay eyes on me."

A full stomach made it hard to concentrate on anything but a wished-for nap, but they had work to do and an asshole to catch.

* * *

Rossi exited his building into the early morning's chill, passing graveyard-shifters going home. He could tell which ones they were by their tired clothes and the need of a fresh shave. He was a detective, after all. An Entenmann's truck, full of delicious, sweet pastries and thus giving people a reason to drink coffee and face the day, was making an early morning delivery. It backed up to the curb in front of the bodega across the street beeping an annoying too-early-morning warning for pedestrians and vehicles to stay out of its way. Except for the beeping, the silence was fierce. Yet it wasn't. The city is never silent, not in the way one would consider silence, anyway.

Gotham silence meant one could hear one's thoughts. Not easy to do unless surrounded only by somewhat less than meaningful noise. So silence meant all a person heard were somewhat less than important sounds, allowing them to hear, really hear their thoughts. Which, hopefully, were important and not heart rending. To them at least, anyway.

The city bursting to life in the morning woke Rossi better than any amount of hot coffee, and nourished and abetted the New Yorker in his soul. Caffeine's most important duty is to help one make it 'til happy hour. A good thing it does, too, because New York doesn't allow for easing into anything. It throws shit right and left, and one better plan on some of it sticking because it's going to, like it or not. The city does not come with an owner's manual, or instructions…something real New Yorkers would scoff at. One has to be clever enough to figure it out on one's own and on the fly. And if one can, then like former Mayor Ed Koch said, "You're a real New Yorker, no matter where you're from."

Instead of a screaming hive of angry bees like a typical morning for the NYPD, on this morning the precinct was but a dull drone when, a little before nine, Rossi entered to the sound of phones ringing, angry loud men swearing, and the tension of knowing a heavy blade could fall at any minute. All of the lights on his multi-button desk set landline were flashing when he sat down. He picked up the sheet outlining the cases that had come in the night before and been assigned to him. Didn't appear to be anything that would be more important than working on the Unholy Ghost case. It wasn't long before his cell phone rang.

"Sal, you Fuckin' dago," the disembodied voice said good-naturedly. "How are you, my friend? You still fat?" Rossi could hear his smile.

"Book! You do know this is really an undercover disguise, don't you? I'm actually a lean athletic brother. As a matter of fact, I look a lot like you, complete with the fro. For real. We could be brothers." He winked at his young partner listening disbelievingly to one side of the conversation. While he did, Rossi hit the save button on his smartphone to capture Bookworm's newest digits.

Caught off guard, Bookworm couldn't even think of a smartass response to that, so he got right to business. "Craig said you need my help. Let me guess. The Unholy Ghost."

"You got it."

"Tell me, *¿qué pasa?* Whatchu got?"

"Zip, zero, zilch."

"The big Triple Z. That sucks."

"Tell me about it."

"Well, I got to tell you, Sal. You sent up the smoke signal at precisely the right time. I'm just about down to my last piaster." Bookworm didn't try to be risible, that was just Book being Book, unfailingly farcical.

"That's what you always say, man, but you always seem to have a few more lira in your pocket. And what do I always tell you about mixing metaphors? Smoke signals and piasters? Shit."

"Me? Listen to you. *Lira?*"

"At least I'm Italiano."

"Yeah, sure you are. You're as much Italian as I am. When was the last time you were back in the Old Country, or even on Ellis Island? Besides, your name's not even Tony. You know, To-NY. To New York."

"Yeah, like I haven't heard that stale old joke before. Anyway, when can we meet?"

"Tomorrow? Noon at Craig's? I'd like to go there because we can help a brother out at the same time."

"Sounds good."

"You're buying."

"Don't I always? Or at least the city of New York does."

"Just making sure so there's no hurt feelings."

"Noon?"

"Be there or be square."

For someone who thought you could find his picture beside the word *cold* in the dictionary, Bookworm sure could be a nerd.

Chapter Eleven

"Smart ass? Me?"

Rossi and Park arrived at Craig's place at ten before the appointed hour to be sure and get a table and to watch Book enter. At exactly twelve noon, he walked in like he owned the place, dressed like Carlton on *The Fresh Prince of Bel Air*, complete with a classic wool sport coat, starched khaki-colored chinos — most likely J. Crew or Polo — and an autumn-colored plaid dress shirt topped with an actual hand-tied bow tie, it looked like Brooks Brothers. The outfit made Rossi wonder if Bookworm could do The Carlton Dance, but it wouldn't have mattered how he was dressed. Bookworm had an all-encompassing presence and charm that transcended dress, or stature, or status. A presence that came from within. All the great ones had it. Reagan, Jesus, Elvis…even Hitler, but only when in front of a crowd. Bookworm was birthed with it, but don't be mistaken, he'd also spent time developing it, honing it, and using it. He didn't so much charm people as overwhelm them…to get what he wanted. Information mostly.

He was followed by a young man who, in contrast to Bookworm's earnest preppie appearance, had more the look of a thug. Wife beater tucked in low-hung dungarees.

Bookworm hesitated, glanced around the room. Upon seeing Rossi, a huge grin flushed his handsome face. That grin revealed that he thought this was more than a business meeting, indeed lunch with an old friend. He pushed away from his accompanist in a rush.

While he made his way through a maze of tables Rossi rose and extended a meaty hand in a somewhat more than small friendly gesture. Bookworm saw it, brushed it aside with something less than no interest at all, to embrace Rossi in an enthusiastic bear hug. True Bookworm, through and through. With him, nothing was an act. What you saw was what you got. Warmth.

"Sal, good to see you, my friend."

"Thanks, Book. You too," he said, extricating himself from the suffocatingly affectionate bear hug. "Meet my partner, Jay Park."

"Nice to meet you, Detective."

"You, too," said Jay reservedly, not quite knowing what to think about the amiable young man.

"And this is my new protégée, Reefer." Bookworm liked using

words like protégée. Reefer barely acknowledged the introduction with an over-the-top cool, almost imperceptible, nod of his head, a gamy set to his eyes, and mumbled something indecipherable. Stolid to his core. The opposite of the verve of Bookworm's personality. Reefer had taken his nickname from the title of the 1936 film *Reefer Madness*, his pops had told him about.

"Bookworm and Reefer," said Rossi, appraisingly but not unkindly. Getting it.

"I know. Right? Who would think it? It just be's that way," said Bookworm with his ever-present charming grin. Even though he spoke perfect King's English, he had to throw in some street occasionally just to remind Reefer and anybody that might be listening, that he hadn't forgotten where he came from...even if he hadn't come from there.

Reefer's light skin showed off a wary face full of incomprehensible tats, making him resemble an African-American Post Malone. Or hip hop artist-turned-fellow police informant Tekashi69 who, perhaps, Reefer aspired to considering his new career path. It was probably the first time he'd ever had a social interaction with The Man and he wasn't sure how he felt about it. Even though he was young, he was discerning enough to be pretty sure that the feeling was mutual.

Strictly on appearances, Rossi wasn't sure about Reefer. The thoughtful detective hoped his friend wasn't making a serious error in judgement with his selection of a trainee. He probably took Reefer under his wing as an acolyte because he reminded him of himself, the way he might have turned out, had he not gone to college, gotten educated. An elegiacal moment which, if left to fester, alas or happily, take your pick, he never would. It would have been a waste of his natural and practiced talent because Bookworm was right where he should be, doing what he should be doing. But Reefer certainly didn't display the overt sense of friendly charm that his mentor did, though. With regard to being charming, Bookworm was nonpareil.

Rossi grasped Bookworm's elbow, directing him to the table, and like a welcoming Italian host, said, "Sit, sit."

Bookworm sat back, fingers interlaced behind his head, confidently stretching out his long legs, and examined a spot on the wall with his intense gaze. "So, how are things with the Five-0? Tell me whatchu got," he said.

Reefer had positioned himself so he could have a sweeping view of the room and keep an eye on the door. It seemed that Reefer held a dual position with Bookworm that included bodyguard as well.

"Like I told you on the phone, basically we got zilch."

"I remember. The Triple Z."

"Eloquent," Rossi said, unable to contain himself, with a conflicted chuckle.

"What's happening around the precinct because of that?"

"You know what they say, shit rolls downhill."

"Tell me about it," Bookworm said, shaking his head empathetically, even though, having never held a hierarchical professional position, he really couldn't relate.

Park and Reefer listened silently to the odd pair chatting like two old commiserating friends, who hadn't seen each other in awhile.

"Well, usually we never hear anything from anyone above our chief, but apparently the commissioner, and don't think it stops at One PP, because even Hizzoner, the mayor, is pissed off about this."

"Well, you know that other thing they say, don't you?"

"What's that?"

'Better to be pissed off than pissed on."

"You aren't joking," agreed Rossi, glancing at a menu, followed by, "We probably should oughta order."

Bookworm ordered a huge juicy cheeseburger, bleeding, with a mountain of onion rings on the side. He wouldn't gain an ounce. Rossi ordered a burger-well-done, sans cheese, with fries. Eschewing cheese allowed him to convince himself that he was eating healthy. Park ordered a cut of tuna, blackened, with a side of steamed broccoli.

Reefer ordered an all-meat omelet, breakfast potatoes, a ribeye steak, and onion rings finished off with a pair of New York's famous Black and White cookies and an Irish coffee. It appeared that he couldn't make up his mind between breakfast and lunch, so he decided on both. Or he just knew he could stick it to the police by taking advantage of a free meal. Since he didn't pay taxes, he wasn't vicariously paying for his own meal. It was good for him that most New York diners served breakfast all day. He'd pick up a large bag of Doritos at the first bodega they passed, unless he encountered a White Castle first, in which case, like their commercials suggest, he'd have to take home a sackful of the juicy, small, square delights — the first sliders — drenched in delicious bits of cooked, rehydrated onion, and fat. Of course he'd probably eat the entire sackful before he got home. Apparently he'd been smoking some of his namesake that morning.

The food arrived surprisingly quick considering they had to wait for Reefer's huge order. Bookworm took a huge bite from the juicy, fat burger dripping melted cheese, and said, "You know, Rossi, you should invite me for dinner sometime. Since y'all are Italian, I bet your wife's a good cook. As the great Clint Eastwood said in the classic movie, *Coogan's Bluff*, filmed right there in my neighborhood in the Bronx, 'I'm always ready for spaghetti.'" He grinned sheepishly at the rhyme-intended but weak joke. He knew it was weak. Indeed, Italian food is the great equalizer.

Rossi smiled and said, "And as the greatest comedian of all, Jerry Seinfeld, said in the TV show filmed near my neighborhood in Manhattan, 'Maybe I will, Lois. Maybe I will.'" He knew the Upper West Side where they filmed the eponymously named TV show wasn't really that close to his Midtown 'hood, but why let facts screw up a good joke.

"Touché", said Bookworm, realizing his ante had been raised cleverly before he spoke warmly and calmly. "So, if I can infer from what you're saying, Hizzoner and the Commish, being estimable gentlemen of great self-worth, have a keen sense of profundity, but the problem is that they aren't street cops, so they think you should simply be able to fire up the computers and go pick him up, whoever the computer tells you the son of a bitch is."

Rossi nodded sardonically. "That's it in a nutshell, Book, but you left out the part about them thinking I'm a Luddite, and that's why I'm going to hell. And I need your help if I'm going to keep that from happening."

"So what I hear you saying is you want this guy pretty damn bad. No problem. We can start this afternoon."

"That's good, because as the greatest Yankee of all, Yogi Berra, once said, 'It's getting late early.' If I don't get this guy soon I'll be working security chasing teenage truants and shoplifters at the Manhattan Mall. Look. I think this son of a bitch is the worst piece of shit since that asshole, Ted Bundy, and I want to bust this guy so bad I'll make sure he gets a bottom bunk at Rikers Island, then drive him to Sing Sing and throw his sorry ass in one of their shitty little cells and clang the fuckin' door shut my own damn self. Or if they ever reinstitute the death penalty in this state and want to fry his ass, I'll be happy to throw Old Sparky's switch and seriously kill the fuck out of him. If we don't find out who he is before that, then they can bury the loathsome piece of shit in a pine box wearing a twenty-dollar polyester suit in Hart Island's potter's field for all I care. And the cheap-ass plastic suit probably wouldn't even burn if they cremated him."

It was obvious to anyone that Detective Rossi was seriously pissed about the Unholy Ghost.

"Only one problem with whatchu said."

"Yeah, what's that, Book?"

"Derek Jeter is the greatest Bronx Bomber of all."

Genuinely sorrowed by what he'd heard, Rossi shook his head lamentably. "That's the problem with today's younger generation. Youse don't know what greatness is. I feel sorry for alla youse." Without giving Bookworm time to consider that which he'd said, Rossi continued, "So, same rate? Two-fifty a day plus expenses."

"Sorry, I got to remunerate my man, Reefer, here. And he don't come cheap, no matter whatchu heard. Four-hundred, plus." Truth be told, Bookworm was probably pocketing twenty-five per cent of the extra one-fifty. It wasn't like it was coming out of Rossi's pocket, and if Book could gig the NYPD a little it's not like it would hurt his friend.

Reefer wasn't paying any heed to the money discussion even though it affected him directly. He was busy insouciantly checking out a hot young Latina sitting at a table in the front window looking out on the busy New York City sidewalk, making sure he was staying cold to all eyes while he did it. Her, wisely ignoring the worrisome-looking young man whether by lack of notice, or choice, was unknown.

"Man, you drive a hard bargain, but I'm sure we have it in the Crime Stoppers fund. I hear it's chock full of piasters."

"Smart ass."

"Smart ass? Me?" Rossi said feigning incredulity.

"I'm just sayin'. But you're getting a break 'cause he's not as good as me...yet. Else it'd be five-hundred big ones. You're getting the blue light special. Get it?"

Reefer clunked his large ceramic mug down too hard, coughed and apologized, "Sorry. Some of that Irish whiskey went down the wrong way."

"'We're cops?' Blue light? Yeah, I get it. Blue light special. That was pretty good. But I got a question, Book."

"Shoot. Not literally, though 'cause I know you're carryin','" Bookworm said, thinking he was being very clever.

Rossi ignored that comment. "How do you do it?"

"Do what?"

"What you do."

"The key to doing what I do is knowing a lot without knowing too much. Knowing a lot will get you respect. Knowing too much will get you dead. Internecine."

Bookworm enjoyed displaying his Princeton education and vocabulary, it without the expected Brooklyn or Bronx accent. He probably didn't have many opportunities to do so with his usual coterie, his street gang. Of course, as good as Rossi's vocabulary was, he would have to look up the fancy word in Merriam-Webster.

Bookworm liked what his education did for him. On occasion affecting a British accent, even, to go along with his extensive vocabulary, mostly because he likes how people, African Americans mostly, look at him when they hear a brother speaking with a limey accent. His skin color made him invisible, not in the traditional sense. It wasn't that he was unseen, but more overlooked, underestimated. Being a denizen of the streets, he wasn't expected to be or look to be anything but what he appeared, and that was others' mistake. Street smarts combined with book smarts made him someone not to overlook nor be taken for granted. One did so at their peril.

"Now me. Not a question, but a comment. Y'all need a cooler nick — like NY's Boldest. You know, those dudes in the Department of Corrections. They have the coolest name. The Boldest. Y'all and the fire department, y'all suck. No offense. New York's Finest and New York's Bravest. What's up with that? Boldest is bad. To. The. Bone. Just sayin'."

"Well, next time I see the Commish, I'll give him your recommendation," Rossi said with a smartass grin since he'd never laid eyes on the big man himself except on the evening news or on stage at large department-wide events. "But I'm not sure he can do anything, though. New York's Boldest is already taken."

Bookworm and Reefer stood. "Thanks for lunch. Don't call me. I'll call you. You call me, it won't do anything but slow us down. Oh, and let me know if you need any investment advice. You know, help with your portfolio."

Rossi ignored him with a grin and having anticipated an upfront down payment, two days being the norm, he counted out four Benjamins, and handed them over. Unlike the pre-lunch hug, the appetizer as it were, this time Bookworm fist-bumped Rossi and that set off a matching round between them all, even though Park seemed hesitant.

As they walked away, Park, true to his Buddhist nature, said, "I know I just met him, but I have a good feeling. I think he's going to help us get the Ghost. I think it's in our karma."

Rossi gazed floorward, and examined his shoes to buy a moment, then shook his head warily. "Might work for you, but I'm Catholic. Karma isn't an option for me. Of course, you're what? Buddhist, I'm guessing. Same God, though. Maybe He'll hear both our prayers. Or one of ours, if the other's isn't right. However, I do think this will become my crucible, unless we catch him...and fast."

"What's *crew-sha-ball*?" Park asked.

"That's *crew-sa-bull*. A test by fire."

"Test by fire. Cool."

Chapter Twelve

"Bring bagels"

Bookworm took Reefer to his office where they started working the phones. That's always where an investigation starts. Cover more territory faster, that way. Reach out to usual contacts to find out if anybody knew anything. Bookworm had rented the studio apartment next to his two-bedroom in Co-op City to conduct business. Now it was rent controlled. Next to nothing. Only way he could afford the extra space. He stood on the small terrace, with its mirthful bright view of the intersection where the Harlem River connects with the solemn gray East River which, with all of his esoteric knowledge, Bookworm knew wasn't a river at all, but a brackish tidal estuary, and Long Island Sound beyond. His latest generation iPhone was pressed hard against his ear to suffocate the loud sound of icy ocean winds at thirty stories above the city.

When he was young, growing up in the center of the Bronx, in a tenement much like many in the borough, he could only smell the fishy odor of the sea and not actually see the salt water that produced it.

That was the main reason why he so enjoyed the splendid view, and was proud of his legal, if somewhat more than a little less than respectable, way of earning a living. His profession wasn't something he talked about openly at cocktail parties or used as a pickup line at bars. Indeed, declaring he was a garbage collector would probably have earned him no less respect.

Made up of thirty-five brown high-rise buildings, with its tenant population of forty-five thousand, were it not one marginalized complex in the Bronx, Co-Op City would be the fifth largest city in the entire state. It built on the site of the former Freedomland, which, when opened in 1960 before Bookworm was even thought of much less born, was one of the largest theme park/family entertainment venues in the world, opening a year before the most famous of theme parks, Six Flags Over Texas. Now the Bronx neighborhood was a street jungle known for gang violence, cocaine, and crack. The largest cooperative housing development in the world, Co-op City was due east across the Bronx from the George Washington Bridge, which locals had cleverly given the upper and lower roadways the names George and Martha. George, of course, on top. If you didn't catch that old joke as soon as you were informed of it, the teller knew you were an import.

After a few hours time spent blowing up their contacts' phones, they looked at each other astonished, as both came up with the same results. The consensus was that the Unholy Ghost was a ghost, a phantom. Not in the lurid ghastly manner of film and fiction, but he managed to disappear himself, going completely off the grid, solid gone, after kills. Never to be seen or known again, at least until the next slaying. Those reports were not in any way nebulous, coming as they did from always-reliable go-to sources.

This, of course, was unacceptable. Everyone knows ghosts aren't real. Especially Bookworm — he, too smart and too afraid of the disembodied to accept the concept, the very idea, of ghosts.

It was getting late. Almost time for happy hour at one or several of the fashionable, but similarly nondescript in every way Upper East Side watering holes he frequented. After a Friday night of distorted realism aided by warm cognac and the heady fragrance of entrancing perfume, they would start anew the following morning. Who knew? Bookworm might even start believing in ghosts. Anyways, he knew his reality was unreal. Fictional, even. Wasn't everyone's?

Shit was getting deep.

The last thing Bookworm wanted to do was give Rossi the bad news that, as far as he and Reefer could find out, the Unholy Ghost was a real ghost. He knew the detective would want more than that sad conclusion in exchange for the city's dollars. Since he didn't want to think about giving Rossi what he was sure would be unwelcome news, he told Reefer to have a nice night and to be back by nine the next morning. Decided to give him a break and not start too early, since it would be Saturday.

"Bring bagels. And don't forget the receipt," he admonished Reefer, peeling off a twenty from a roll of cash as big as his fist. Bookworm suspected that, because of Reefer's unrelenting snack habit, he'd know where to find the best bagels in the Bronx.

Chapter Thirteen

"Are you famous?"

Exhausted from making the rounds of book promotion, Grayson thought he could use a power nap. It was three o'clock and if he did take a nap, he wasn't sure he would wake up before bedtime.

* * *

Gordon stirred. *Damn, I need to get a move on if I'm going to make happy hour and have a chance of meeting any hot opportunities.*

* * *

Bookworm didn't need much to get ready for the evening. He was still in his natty outfit, so he simply retied his bow tie, touched up the corners of his mouth with an electric razor, and dabbed on a little more Jimmy Choo Man cologne. When the stubbles began to come out of hibernation in the late afternoon was the only time he wished his caramel-colored hue was the color of dark chocolate so those little black hairs didn't stand out so much.

Stepping through mahogany-stained double wooden doors with etched glass panes displayed like art in each, he entered the shadowy, intimate, warm tavern that catered to a mix of the gentry, hoi polloi, and artistes, hitchhikers all passing guidebook-less through the galaxy that is the East Side. It had bright neon Budweiser and Miller Lite signs in the otherwise dark large windows along with a pair of local New York microbrew signs. One from the Bronx and one from Brooklyn. The pub didn't even have it's own name in the window or over the door. The name didn't matter. All that mattered was that it had alcohol, and the neon beer signs conveyed that message perfectly.

A typical pub on a Friday night in the city, it was filled to capacity with a laid back but nonetheless energetic crowd of somewhat a little less than genial native New Yorkers. Enjoying the pleasantly cool night before the city goes dormant until it wakes up again for the holiday season. On first glance, most observers would think they're human. But unlike among the tourists of Times Square bars, not a dad hat or fanny pack in the place. It was good being in the process of remembering that it was Friday. They remembered what it was like from the previous one.

The pub was not unlike the original Friday's that opened in the mid '60s, and but a few steps away on First Avenue, that the owner built just to make it easier for him to pick up girls, it was credited with creating the singles bar scene and setting the pace for the rest of the world to follow.

A tourist would never have found this place. Too far from Midtown and Times Square. They of bright lights and neon. The Upper East Side not as bright, more reserved. Darker, except for resolute red taillights of cars, fickle stoplights blinking green and red and a few small neon signs of various blithesome colors advertising that their emporium was open. It almost felt like a real neighborhood. A microcosm of the warren that was the Upper East Side, it a part of the warren that was New York City.

If a tourist had found it, they wouldn't have fit in anyway. Most of the crowd were regulars from the Upper East Side nabe. Music was loud, but not annoyingly so. The crowd sonorous, but not obstreperous. Indigenous New York or New Jersey music, but not Billy Joel or Neil Diamond because their music would have been too unhip for this crowd. More like all the bangers from the Talking Heads, Wu-Tang Clan, and Vampire Weekend. The even more truculent sounds of Beastie Boys or The Sugarhill Gang for the phatest of the crowd who wanted old school hip hop. Unless the crowd wanted old school pop, then it might be the laidback sounds of Brooklyn's hometown stars, Simon & Garfunkel; of course one mustn't forget any aging punks in the crowd, so the New York Dolls were always popular; or if the person in charge was feeling particularly magnanimous, perhaps the memorable blue-eyed soul of New Jersey's claim to fame, Frankie Valli and the Four Seasons. Not an opuscule among them.

Everyone was dressed like the people in the murals on the walls of the Monkey Bar in Midtown's Hotel Elysée. Fancy was the only word one could use to describe them. Unless one used swanky, but that term was kind of archaic. And there was nothing archaic about this crowd. The beautiful, well-dressed, sophisticates of New York. The fresh hot aroma of New York's favorite comfort food — meatloaf topped with cooked ketchup, and mash potatoes — warmly welcomed Bookworm into the homey dimly lit space. He moved further into the room, accompanied by the delicious smells of lasagna, nachos, and hamburgers from the closely-spaced tables.

Bookworm bellied up to the long, shiny, ebony bar that ran down the left wall of the shotgun space. The back side of the deep bar lined with draft beer dispensers — local micro brews and nationals, small fridges for chilling bottles of wine, and shelves of spirits, well, call, and top shelf. Typical of all bars everywhere, backed by an ornately decorated mirror etched in gold.

There was just enough room with an empty stool next to a guy and girl who sat chatting *sotto voce*. In contrast to the loud hubbub filling the rest of the restaurant. Looked like they were on a first date or maybe just met and were attracted to each other. The female looked interested; the man more interested, or rather, intent, than she. But isn't that always the way it is? A rhetorical question because everyone knows it to be so.

Recognizing a regular, and like any good bartender, recalling his preferred libation, and pleased with himself for doing so, the veteran of the New York City bar wars — a middle-aged man of Middle Eastern descent relentlessly affable since a dour one couldn't succeed in his chosen profession — placed before Bookworm a decanter of cognac and, like a Mexican restaurant habitually placing chips and salsa before every patron, added a basket of zwieback with warm butter, on the house.

The Caucasian male sitting at the bar was attractive in an unremarkable way. If one were perceptive, it would be obvious that he cultivated that look. Medium brown hair, not long, not too short. Plain khaki trousers, Columbia blue sport coat, white button-down shirt, no tie. Nothing he wore looked overtly expensive, but neither did it look cheap. Probably came from J. Crew or Polo. Bookworm guessed his underwear probably matched his socks. He appeared to be that put together. Literally topping off his outfit with a traditional blue Yankees cap. Soft-spoken, not calling attention to himself. Not a face one would recall the next day, but Book thought he looked familiar.

The woman, light-colored African American, or biracial, half-African American, half-Caucasian, very attractive. She appeared to be in her early thirties; him a few years older. Dressed classily in business-casual attire, extravagantly expensive Louboutin cheetah print ankle boots. Bookworm recognized the red lacquered sole. Set her, or somebody, back no less than a grand. She wore little make-up, but only because her near-perfect light latté skin didn't require it. Lovely long fingers caressed the stem of the tall glass of bubbly she held, probably a rich, toothsome prosecco. They would have been stylishly pretty even without the deep pink polish on all her fingers except for her right ring finger. It enhanced by a brilliant yellow. She wore three rings on one hand and four on the other. Not expensive, not cheap. The kind you might buy at Macy's mid-priced jewelry counter.

Bookworm examined his own manicure while he sat quietly and decided he could use a fresh one. He'd have to take care of that Monday. Wouldn't dare to go to a nail salon on a Saturday. Too crowded with housewives getting them done for Saturday night dates with hubs.

After a moment of close conversation the couple acknowledged his appearance next to them.

Bookworm responded warmly, asking of the man, "You look like someone I've seen. Are you famous?"

"Hardly, but it's okay. I get that all the time."

"I thought so, too," said the attractive young woman.

"See?" said the man, inclining his head in her direction. "Like I said…happens all the time." Then he said, "Excuse me, please. I need to go to the restroom."

A moment later he returned, wiping his face with a handkerchief, looking as if he were trying to wipe away the blushing, and embarrassing, yet troubling stain.

"Is something the matter?"

"This is New York, right. Weird has a permanent address here. But that was a first."

"What?"

"I'm standing at the urinal, right, and feel a finger poke me in the middle of my back and a man's deep voice said, 'I'm gonna kick your ass.' I pivoted, looked straight behind me at eye level and saw nothing. I turned back around and went back to tending to my business. A moment later the same thing happened and this time, I looked around and down, and a dwarf, no more than three feet tall, with a big ass grin on his face was about to die laughing. He might have come up to my waist. He'd obviously pulled the stunt before. I couldn't help but join him in his amusement. But I guess I shouldn't be surprised by anything. Like I said…this is New York."

It was fortunate for the dwarf that he'd made the dude laugh because what he had no way of knowing was that he'd just had a face-to-face encounter with, and not only that, but had also threatened the Unholy Ghost. Probably not too many people would be able to say the same and live long enough to talk about the experience.

"That is hilarious," she said. "Listen. I'm going to need to leave so

I better go to the restroom too." She lifted her purse from where it hung on an old-world brass hook underneath the bar top and started toward the rear of the pub.

Bookworm said, "I think I'll be on my way too. It was nice to meet you," he said to the man.

But, in a sudden act of caprice, the woman's new companion was leaving. Bookworm thought, the young man must not have thought he was getting anywhere with the attractive young woman.

When the woman returned she asked, "Where did Gordon go?"

"It was odd. He left without saying a word."

"That is odd. I liked him. But I should probably be on my way, too." It was still early but happy hour was ending and if she couldn't find a guy to buy drinks for her she might as well go home and drink, where wine from her own bar was cheaper.

"John," Bookworm said. Although she didn't seem interested, not even offering a perfect hand. Bookworm guessed she was only into white men.

Chapter Fourteen

"How'd you find me?"

The city was chilly and the air smelled clean, by New York standards. Even so, the chill was a sad, sick cold, not bringing with it the promise of anything. Gordon didn't go far. He tossed the Yankees cap in the first waste basket he came to, then stepped into a nearby previous-world telephone booth not many paces down the sidewalk, where he could keep a surreptitious weather eye on the drinking establishment's entry. Undoubtedly, considering the ubiquity of smartphones, not many of the crestfallen relics of communication from the first half of the twentieth century remained. The lights in the bar gave off a warm soft glow in the nascent dark. It was an ironic turn of events that, decades before, someone from the nascent communications colossus along with someone from the City Works Department decided exactly where the booths should be placed according to the public's need.

There were only one hundred thousand of the once ubiquitous commodity left in the entire country; and most of those were in New York City, even though there were far fewer of them than there had been once upon a time. Now they served the same purpose of providing a different public need. The need for a substitute restroom, a furtive place to relieve the call of nature. The dark, broken, white, glass disc with an image of a traditional blue bell topping it was a throwback to a different time.

After getting interrupted by the dwarf in the restroom, Gordon decided to unzip and take a piss in the confines of the filthy booth. It couldn't hurt it; the strong smell of ammonia from years of being abused as a toilet gripped the previous century necessity, now a nonessential, and wouldn't soon relinquish it. Undeniably, the sickly smell scoffed at the fresh breeze bringing with it a soul-quenching autumn rain. As to be expected, the once-shiny silver floor was damp, and sticky, yellow-stained, and grimy and littered with detritus, sandwich wrappers, crumpled coffee cups, most with familiar green logos, from years of abuse and neglect.

Besides, he was of the belief that when you lived in one of the planet's most crowded cities, and you had the chance to answer the call of nature you had better take advantage of it for you never knew when you'd get another opportunity. He pointed his stream at an angled downward slope against the blue-painted wall of the bottom half to keep it from splashing on his shoes. Hot steam rose in the chilly booth from the bodily function. Hands on his hips, he stretched his back while he pissed.

After finishing, Gordon saw the young woman, Hannah, exit the popular bar, pass the gathered smokers, against the crowd of people entering like a herd of wild gemsbok. He turned to face the busy street — a white plume of hot steam rose from a nearby manhole cover — the broken phone with the cord dangling from where he stuck it between his shoulder and his cheek, nothing more than an actor's prop to aid in shielding his face.

Hannah passed without noticing him, doubtless the only thing on her mind to get out of the suddenly crisp weather and the keening wind; and after giving her a moment to get ahead so she wouldn't accidentally spot him, but not enough time to lose him, Gordon gave her follow. And like the four horsemen of the apocalypse, hell followed with him.

To him it looked like she was whistling past the graveyard. But since she had no way of knowing what was coming, it only appeared so. They passed a pizza shop with a walk-up window counter open to the sidewalk. It next door to a shop with cheap men's *genuine* hand-painted silk neckties, five dollars each or four for twenty dollars; budget-priced knock-off smartphones and cheap sunglasses in the establishment next. The better shops kept their doors locked; customers had to be buzzed in. This was a nice neighborhood, but even nice New York neighborhoods had shitty businesses with even worse clientele. Although not all, most of these would close at a normal end-of-time workday, however, unlike Midtown and Times Square shops which might stay open for business until midnight or even later to be sure and capture their fair share of tourists' coveted dollars.

The autumn sun had set, and with that setting the temperature had dropped since he'd entered the bar. He raised the collar of his wool sport coat and pulled it close. Besides making him warmer it helped to disguise his face; and with it, he hunched his shoulders against the cold. Then exhaled a harsh warm breath on his fingers. Cold fingers made you cold all over. He knew he'd heard that somewhere, but he couldn't recall where. Then he pulled a black knit watch cap from a coat pocket and tugged it down hard on his head to give him a different look, in the event she looked around or anyone else noticed him following her.

One positive that comes with the arrival of autumn is that the cooler temperatures and chilly rain help to kill the tired hot smell that's part and parcel of the city's summer heat. Without giving away the location precisely to curious ears unknown in a bar — not for nothing city-hardened New Yorkers are cautious, if not careful — a fourteen story mid-century structure with an attractively mansarded roof where Hannah had alluded to living, was no more than three blocks away. And because north-south blocks were short in Manhattan, it was no more than a tenth of a mile, a little less than two football fields in length. A fast runner could gain the distance easily in less than half a minute.

Gordon had improved his tailing skills over the past year and this was a simple one. One of his easiest. All it took was to walk a hair faster than Hannah, to time his arrival and catch the door to her building before it closed behind her, without her noticing him. Then repeat the act at the elevator door, getting in before it left with her. And make up a good story on the fly as to what he was doing there. Lately he'd been getting even better at making up good stories than he was at tailing people. He didn't know why, it just seemed that he had an innate ability for storytelling, but equally inexplicable was from whence the gift came.

Phase one of his inchoate plan went without need for deviation or ad-libbing. Nor adjustment in the commando-like tactics.

The locking glass door was six inches from closing when he grabbed the long silver handle, already cold to the touch from autumn temperatures; it allowed him easy and silent entry. With no doorman with which to pass muster, fate smiled on him again. Since Hannah was absorbed in foraging through her purse — probably looking for her favorite hairbrush, to attend to the effects of the rapidly-increasing cold wind — instead of paying heed to her surroundings. As he approached, the elevator's tarnished brass doors opened, letting her in.

Scurrying, but arriving almost too late, Gordon offered a hand in sacrifice to gods ancient and antediluvian, they of the closing door. Lo and behold, the gods accepted his sacrifice and the doors parted. Hannah was still pressing the open button when he stepped in. Her surprise at seeing who it was was betrayed by a wan smile, which did not reach her eyes. Combined quizzical and curious.

Indeed, nascent uncomprehending wrinkles creased her forehead.

"Hi again," he said with all of the charm and innocence of a guileless youngster holding a puppy.

"Why, hello? How'd you find me?"

"I didn't. You passed me on the sidewalk and I decided it couldn't hurt to see if you'd like to have another cocktail."

"Well, I guess it wouldn't hurt," she said guardedly, yet curiously just the same.

"Then, why don't I see you to your door. For safety's sake."

"I'll be fine. I live here."

"Now, now, I insist."

She was still somewhat more than a little reticent, but was slowly lowering her guard. He was cute, so "Alright, but only because you insist."

Hannah pressed the button reading twelve. It lit up cooperatively and the well-used compartment began to move, as if drawn upward like a marionette on a tether, slowly but determinedly toward its programmed goal. The small cage smelled of old age. Might have been the begrimed and corroded mechanics of the aged lift...might've been from elderly residents in the same condition. Gordon didn't want to consider the funicular people carrier's mechanical condition. Especially it's cable. He was, simply put, quite the worrier and if he thought about its appearance and condition, and of what was most assuredly a tether worn by age, that it might come crashing down with them. And he needed to stay focused.

No small talk in which to be engaged, anyway; they stood in silence uncomfortable, staring into opposite corners of the automated box. Which he thought best. If he looked at her too long or too hard, she might suspect what was coming and start screaming or try to otherwise alert her neighbors. If he looked her in the eyes or they started to talk, he might dissuade himself from his mission. Nothing but the sound of silence deafening, and the elevator's mechanism, muffled by the closed doors.

A short time later, the elevator jerked to a bumpy stop. Once the doors opened, Hannah let them exit and led the way down the unremarkable dimly lit hall to the left. As was the lobby and the elevator. Unremarkable and dim. The elevator too old for the door to chime upon opening. Or maybe it once did, but declined to continue as it aged. That's not unusual. A small dog barked from behind the first door they passed. Maybe a toy poodle or a chihuahua.

"Don't mind him. That's just Buck. He barks at everything. His parents are country music fans. Named him for Buck Owens."

Gordon looked at her questioningly.

"I know. Right? Country music fans in New York? What's up with that? They had to explain to me who Buck Owens even was. Apparently he used to be a pretty big deal."

The third, cold gray steel door on the left was number 1213. Thirteen would be her unlucky number this evening.

Chapter Fifteen

"Oh, you don't like honesty?"

Hannah had waited until their arrival to dig her key from her handbag. She inserted it into the door's lock and as she began to ease it open, Gordon shoved it with both hands and slammed into her back with a hard shoulder, knocking her to the unsympathetic parquet wood floor that dated the building's construction. It was more tumult than which he was accustomed to using. He didn't have to do it, but shock and awe were sometimes warranted. Took most of the crying and fight out of them. He was of the impression that this one could be a fighter. All in all, made it easier for everyone concerned.

She screamed, loud and shrieking.

The thought crossed Gordon's mind that he wished she weren't so recalcitrant and hoped the walls weren't so thin. Couldn't have that. He clocked her hard in the mouth, the force from the heavy-handed cuff stopping her. Additionally, he straddled her, bringing his full weight onto her middle and throttling her with one strong hand on the throat. It hadn't taken him many times doing this to figure out people stop resisting if they can't breathe. Using his free hand he pulled plastic gloves out of a pants pocket and after stretching them on with a firm pop, withdrew a roll of silver duct tape from a coat pocket and ripped off two long pieces. Covered her mouth securely with the tape, not being careful as he did so, pulling her hair and bruising her delicate face as he did it. He made sure he got her right hand controlled first because he pictured her in his mind's eye at the bar holding her long-stemmed flute with her right and if she struck him he wanted it to be with her weaker, maladroit left hand. He then violently taped her wrists and ankles together.

With Hannah under control, Gordon took a moment to look around at his surroundings. The apartment showed its age, but was fairly well kept considering the dweller was gainfully employed and had a full social life. Probably had a housekeeper come in. It wasn't like she was living out an actual *Looking for Mr. Goodbar* scenario from the '70s movie, but she had an enviable social life. In some ways proud of it, in others, somewhat more than a little ashamed. She might brag proudly to an acquaintance but keep secrets from her mother.

Before she left for the evening, Hannah had turned on a table lamp that gave off a warm buttery glow so she wouldn't come home to a dark apartment. It wasn't bright, probably lit by a weak twenty-five-watt bulb trying to clarify the space in vain. It seemed Hannah liked mood lighting, maybe for entertaining her male guests. The wall opposite the sofa was bare to allow for the Murphy bed recessed within. The apartment was tired, but not weary.

The ancient mid-century refrigerator in a dingy corner of the kitchen emitted a kind of subconscious half-humming, half-buzzing noise due to its datedness. The sound probably provided comfort to Hannah when she was alone. Gordon wondered how many people before her had lived in the place she now called home. The stories the apartment could tell. If they were only worth telling. Or were the lives lived here too lifeless, too humdrum? If it were to tell this one, would it be too sickened by what happens on this night to tell of it? Would it remain irresolute?

Seeing the wide roll of tape in his hand took Gordon back to the last time he'd had to use it on a worker at the original Nathan's hotdog stand in the shadow of Deno's Wonder Wheel at Coney Island. It had been a typical beautiful New York spring day, about six months before. The azure sky and the fair ocean meeting on the horizon. Jets on final approach into Kennedy International passing overhead, its taxiways always congested with huge airliners. Gordon preferred the huge airport's previous name, Idlewild, better, before it was changed to honor the nation's thirty-fifth president after he was assassinated in Dallas.

How do I know these things?

He smelled the ocean breeze and the salty air from the midway. He could hear the screams of delight from riders on the Wonder Wheel while he dined on a pair of Nathan's delicious all-beef hotdogs; mustard, ketchup, chopped onions, and relish. Gordon considered that there are only two kinds of people in the world: those who eat ketchup on their hotdogs and those who are wrong. The same applies to baseball: those who show up at the game early enough to take in bp and those who might as well not even go to the game at all.

It wouldn't be long before the nightly fireworks display would begin lighting up the sky.

The man was closing up for the night. His yellow and red plastic nametag read Earl. He didn't look like an Earl. Around sixty. Probably retired, maybe got laid off from the only job he'd ever held due to the economic downturn. A hard worker with a solid corporate career.

Working at Nathan's now, because he didn't have enough savings for a proper retirement. Times are hard. He was the only one there and he disrespected Gordon. Told him to hurry up and leave because he was ready to close up and go home, so Gordon simply had to impress upon the man the error of his ways.

The man was a scrapper; had put up quite a fight for an older man. He finished the evening by killing him with a plastic, yellow, mustard bottle. Stabbed him in both eyes with the business end. Then gave it a squirt. Left the bottle stuck in the... right eye? Hard to recall exactly which, now. A macabre look if he did say so himself. One he was proud of. Then from his cold dead head, he took the man's yellow-and-red paper Nathan's cap, similar to a military side cap, that matched the colors of the man's *Earl* name-tag, and wore it away, whistling contentedly down the famous boardwalk, passing the first roller coaster built in the United States in 1884.

How the hell do I know these things?

He remembered a teenage couple strolling along holding hands and pointing at his Nathan's hat, laughing. Must have thought he was a loser, working at a place like that. A street preacher was shouting his one-size-fits-all sermon of hellfire and brimstone to most who tried their best to ignore him. New Yorkers learn real quick to just keep walking around people of that sort. The ersatz minister paused for a breath when a train passing along the nearby shore threatened to render his life-or-death message unheard.

Gordon enjoyed reliving the memory but was jerked back to the present when a bead of sweat fell from his foreordained multi-generational nose and landed on her taped wrists. The splash a time travel stop. He swiped it away with a plastic-gloved hand, then tucked the black and silver rosary he wore back in his shirt, a memento of his first kill which was responsible for his nickname, then caressed one full breast firmly. Just because there was no one to stop him. The vein on the side of his head, right below the skin, pulsed with tension.

Moreover, feeling less than remorseful, but nonetheless gentlemanly, he helped her onto a thread worn pine green corduroy sofa that had been a hand-me-down from a beloved aunt. The played-out fabric made not a sound when she sat down. In her terrified eyes, he discerned the age-old question all killers get: "Why?"

He shrugged in an attempt to make it appear even less meaningful than it was if that were possible. "It's what I am. It's what I do," he replied. "I kill people. I will kill again unless, or until, they stop me. You've probably heard of me. They call me the Unholy Ghost. Look, this isn't about you. You aren't special. It could have been anyone."

He didn't know if that would make her feel better or worse, but in the end he decided it really didn't matter either way. It was the truth and would be for some greater power to determine if his honesty or the look on her face was more pathos evoking. He didn't particularly like the nickname; he would have preferred something akin to the *Serial Swordsman*, something more dramatic, something with flair; but it would be difficult to suggest it without drawing attention to himself.

His voice sounded languid and liquid to Hannah. She felt like she was on a coalescing mixture of drugs. She had guessed that he was probably the Unholy Ghost, but far too late for the realization to do her any good.

What I do must be good, or else why would I be called to do it? A calling? Hmmm...

Though he didn't exactly think it an afflatus, nonetheless it was not anything as mundane or as easily dismissed as caprice. At least he deemed that to be an honest take. Otherwise, why else would he be a homicidal beast? That was a rhetorical question because certainly, there was no answer to it, not one he could discern anyway.

Or maybe his victims deserved it. This was no pathological fugue. It might more likely be described by a professional as a psychosis. Gordon wouldn't wake up the next morning and suddenly disremember the events of the night. He always recalled every intimate second of the blessed deeds. Those eidetic memories continued to warm his heart.

He might like to make peace with the enemy but when the enemy is yourself, or at the very least, a beastly part of you, then how can that be done? Even if one could, what does someone do when they are only half of a whole, especially if they didn't know of it?

That residual feeling is what kept him doing what he did. What he couldn't remember, or know, was what he did between the occurrences. That concerned him more than anything he might do. At other times he wasn't even sure it was he who killed them, that it was some greater...or lesser, force. That was when he really got scared; not knowing who committed the murders.

She whimpered at what he'd said.

"Oh, you don't like honesty? Let's try something else then. A different kind of honesty. You're too fucking hot!" he spat, scornfully.

"Do you like that better? Will that make you feel better when you breathe your last?"

Hannah wished she'd thought to keep a knife under a sofa cushion for defense. She knew some women in the city did. Maybe she'd have had a chance, then. Otherwise, the best she could do was wish him dead. That wouldn't be very helpful. She regretted that she hadn't changed the beneficiary of her life insurance to her three-year-old niece. And she really wished she could see her again. She knew her family would miss her when she's gone. Funny the things one thinks about when they know they're about to die.

He glanced around, espying a small portable wine fridge. It was haphazardly installed in a small bookshelf below a large window that opened onto a million-dollar view of the Queensborough Bridge, spanning from Manhattan to Queens, its spires brightly lit in the night, Roosevelt Island nestled darkly underneath. Past the bridge, the world-famous Pepsi Cola sign in Queens reflecting on the river.

A clothesline ran from her window, the old school kind you could hang your wash on and spool it out further to make room for more. Nearly every apartment had one, crisscrossing all the floors of the building, shining in the naked moonlight. All bare. That gave him a glorious idea. Probably his best ever. As a matter of fact, this killing might make him famous, instead of just infamous, his ultimate goal, his desideratum above all others since reading that the FBI says there are twenty-five to fifty active serial killers in America at any given time.

Of course, he could always target a few of them and decrease the numbers of his competition and at the same time be doing law enforcement a huge favor by discouraging copycat killers. At the same time, he wasn't impressed with those numbers because many serial killers used guns. Anybody could do that. Man-up and use a blade. Up close and familial. Cutting implements made the killer and prey one with the other. He believed it the greatest of all intimacies.

Gordon had a tendency to get somewhat more than a little distracted at times like these, right before he managed to refocus on the task at hand. In reality, the Upper East Side view was distracting. He didn't have anything like it on the West Side.

How can I afford a townhouse worth seven figures on the Upper West Side without any visible income? I don't ever remember making a mortgage payment. And what about that antique Chinese liquor cabinet with its magical never-ending supply of booze and the credit cards and cash in my pocket?

He couldn't remember ever going to a liquor store or a bank. He knew it possible that he was solvent, but didn't even want to consider how it was he came to be able to attend to his financial obligations.

There I go again. Getting distracted. Again. Goddammit. Concentrate.

"Please, don't try to scream. It'll only make it worse for you before it ends. Would you like a glass of chard?" he asked. "I certainly would. All this excitement has made me thirsty." A glass of wine would help to relax him. "Oh, silly me. I forgot. You can't have any with that tape covering your mouth. See, you shouldn't have screamed. Then we could be enjoying that nice glass of wine together that we talked about. We'd be having a lovely eventide by now."

He leaned down to her eye level. "I know what you think. You think I'm insane. But I'm not crazy...or anything. I'm just... just...like everyone else. But better looking."

He stood, straight and tall and continued his speech. "Compared to all the great killers in film, I'm positively pedestrian. It's not like I'm Hannibal Lecter feeding Ray Liotta's character little bites of his own brain sautéed in garlic and butter. Mayhap that's what I need," he said clapping his hands enthusiastically. "Hollywood screenwriters scripting my little transgressions into bleak but nonetheless thrilling dramaturgies."

What even he had to admit was interesting, was how he knew about that macabre scene in the famous film since he couldn't remember ever having visited a cinema or even watching TV. Indeed, how had he acquired so much esoteric knowledge of all sorts? He began going through her shelves.

"How will I be remembered for posterity? How have my killings measured up to those of the most famous, or infamous, on which history reminisced and measured such things? Because I know I can't go on like this forever. Killing is such a Sisyphean task, I couldn't possibly keep it up for years longer. Eventually I will be found out. I almost look forward to it. That's why I have to be concerned about my legacy. To make sure I collected all the style points that are my due."

Hannah shuddered at the thought of being fed pieces of her own brain and said a silent prayer thanking God for any small miracle He could spare. Even worse, what if she liked the way it tasted? She did like butter and garlic, after all. She kept her eyes on Gordon as he kept on.

"What I am adept at is planning; planning enjoyed with quirkiness, and situational opportunities, too. Flights of fancy if you will."

He felt like he'd hit the proverbial jackpot when he discovered a bottle of oaky and buttery Kistler, the seal unbroken. One of Napa's finest.

"By the by, where is your stemware?" he asked. "Oh right, there I go again. You can't talk all taped up like that. I typically don't like using tape, but one must be prepared since one never knows how these things will play out. Don't fret. I'll just look for it myself."

Gordon searched cabinets in dim light until he found a cabinetful of the coveted glasses, selecting a beautiful, large, crystal globe Chardonnay glass. He sat in a comfortable chair, took a draw. "This Kistler is really good. I wish you could've had some. You'd have enjoyed it." He tilted the glass in a gloved hand toward her in a morbid toast. He finished the glass in a final draw.

It felt like a scene in a noir crime novel. Truly, Gordon had an urge for the entire vesper to be performative. It must remain that way until the act was discovered. It would reflect badly on him if it weren't. She looks at the clock on the Keurig coffeemaker. Stares at it uncomprehending as it reads forty-five after eight. It's been fifteen minutes since she last looked. No. It hasn't stopped. It's changed into an hourglass. It's just moving ploddingly slow. One grain passing through the needle's eye of a channel at a time. Her eyes widen in internal thought!

I really would have liked a taste. Alas, I've enjoyed my last glass of Kistler Chardonnay, or any wine, for that matter. No! That can't be. Time has stopped. It's going to be quarter of nine for eternity. But then, maybe I'll live forever at 8:45. I'll wake up in the morning, nightmare over, but still the time will be 8:45.

Her life playing out in Sisyphean fashion. Never-ending. A cruel trick of fate to be played upon her. Her attention came back to Gordon.

"Just think," he said. "If your God is real and you've been faithful, you'll go straight to the Elysian Fields, which will certainly be a better place than here. If I were you, I'd thank me, thank me for being merciful. That's it!" he said snapping his fingers. "You should sing my praises. Hymns of praise are what I deserve."

The look Hannah gave him was easily recognized as eloquent skepticism mixed with a healthy portion of disbelief. His brain was a scary place, and it looked like she had seen into its deepest and most frightening recesses. He began to hum, a horrifyingly ethereal tune, keeping a sickly syncopated rhythm with the snapping of fingers, trying, but somewhat less than successfully, to locate the melody of *How Great Thou Art* from somewhere within the disturbed deepest parts of his tormented mind. If he tried hard enough, he could convince himself that, at best, he was on a mission from God. At worst, nothing more than a public display of frighteningly outré behavior.

If she could only get her hands on a carving knife she'd kill him before he could kill her. The fourteen-inch Wusthof heavy meat carving knife from the block set she'd bought herself when she'd moved in here. A self-bestowed housewarming gift. The collection had been expensive, but in her mind, worth it. Hard to believe it had been over four years already. She only used it for carving the traditional celebratory roast turkey for Thanksgiving. She used Martha Stewart's turkey recipe. Four holidays now. It was the only time of the year she hosted the rest of her family. A newish tradition.

She'd never get to again. Or go to the Macy's Parade before having the holiday meal. She so loved selecting a prime spot on Sixth Avenue to watch the parade and listening to the marching bands playing Christmas carols while eating warm chestnuts from the small white paper sack bought from one of the street vendors that hawked the delicious treasures on every corner during the holiday season. Putting the sack of hot nuggets in a jacket pocket and using it to warm her hands for the length of the parade. It was less than three weeks away, now. The official start of the Christmas season, which for anyone who'd ever been to the city during the glorious time of year knew it was New York's finest showing. Lamentably, she was sure she'd done that for the last time, too.

She loved Christmas and it upset her to no end that she would be unable to celebrate it again. Tears threatened, but she bravely held them back. She had to think clearly.

The huge knife was sitting on the counter inserted in the blonde wood block in which it came. If she could only get to it. Distract him somehow. Then, two-handed, taped together like they were, she'd stab him square in the chest. Bury it to its heavy wooden hilt. Or maybe in his throat. That would do the job.

But Hannah was kidding herself. She'd still have to get to the knife and distract him enough to get it and plunge it into his throat. Besides, she knew it wouldn't be easy to kill him but she would if she could only get to it. An hour ago she had liked Gordon. She'd been thinking about having sex with him. Not making love, just sex. She'd just met him and she was already planning on giving in to him. Now she was hoping for the opportunity to kill him. Funny how life could turn on a dime.

That wasn't like her. She'd slept with men the first time she met them or on the first date, only five or six times. Not that she kept count, but it was rare enough that, the times she had, made them easy to recall.

"You know what I'd like to know? You don't know yet, anyway. I mean you will anon, but as soon as you do, you won't be able to tell me because of a real but nonetheless utterly unfortunate consequence of this loving act. But I desire to know if one sees the bright light at the end of the tunnel when one dies. Once you find out you won't be able to tell me. So, in a way, I'm envious. You're lucky. You're getting ready to find out. You're getting ready to leave this vale of existence and understand it all. You don't have to wait a lifetime to know. I take it upon myself happily to do it for you."

On a philosophical roll, he continued, "Do you think most people believe they're going to live a long time? I don't mean hope. I mean believe it. Everybody hopes they're going to live a long time. And usually they're right. They live a long, monotonous, mind-numbingly shitty life. But you, you aren't going to be faced with that. You're going to have a lively, exciting end to yours. At what? Thirty-two, thirty-three years old. I have to say. You're lucky. Very fucking lucky."

Feeling relaxed and heartened, Gordon decided to finish the bottle of fine Kistler before finishing the business at hand and going on his way. It would only take two more refills of the large Chardonnay glasses. If he gave himself good pours, and since he thought of himself as both a considerate bartender and a good customer, he was sure he would accommodate himself. Besides, he had nowhere else he had to be.

Hannah's eyes began to well. Then came an explosion of raw emotion and her cheeks shined with the salty wetness. A transpicuous, dispirited circumstance that was highly manifest in light of the evening's sickening episode.

Gordon finished the next glass of fine Chardonnay leisurely while Hannah watched him, tears still rolling down her cheeks, dispirited, hoping he might show an indication of changing his mind. Not damn likely, she thought. What had started out as a perfectly lovely autumn evenfall at the tavern had turned into the most hagride, most likely the last, event of her life.

Gordon took a last draw from the glass, and decided he didn't need the last pour hiding around the bottle's punt. Placing both of his hands on his knees, he pushed off from the old sofa and said, "Like every good Broadway show, the final curtain has to fall for it to be ended."

He went to the kitchen to locate a tool with which to complete his show. Finding the blonde block of wood with the fine carving knives, he smiled to himself. The longest would be more than suitable for his plan. He returned to where she sat awaiting death, wiping the stainless steel blade on his sport jacket sleeve as he did.

The look of terror in her eyes terrified him, but only momentarily. Until he picked her up to place her gently on the floor on her back. Then, straddling her middle once again, with the knife held in his still-begloved right hand, he raised it high above his head and looked deep into her eyes. The blade felt pulsatingly alive in his clench. Even though she shook with fear, he could see in the returned gaping stare that she had never had that depth of a connection with anyone ever before. Indeed, few would experience it. Someone taking life from someone connected them for eternity, across the eons.

"Remember, pain doesn't hurt. It's only a reminder that you're alive." That was his pathetic attempt at comforting her — and being philosophical. Someone might give him an A for effort, but he most certainly would get an F for execution.

With eyes wide open he plunged it into the soft, white hollow of her throat, and felt it tear through her trachea, ribbed with rings of cartilage. He heard and felt the rush of warm air on his face from the unnatural hole in the main pathway for oxygen from the mouth to the lungs. With life-giving oxygen unable to get to her lungs, she would have died of suffocation even without the loss of blood and catastrophic injury. A fleeting thought crossed Gordon's mind that he wished he'd studied anatomy, but then, he didn't know what he'd studied, if he had any sort of post-secondary education. He knew he was fairly smart, but he had no idea if he was educated.

Gordon reached down with his left hand and started to close the lids over her estranged eyes, but changed his mind. He liked the look better with the cold, dead eyes open. Using the edge of the pointed knife, he rent her head from its natural place attached to the torso. It wasn't as easy as he thought it would be, sawing with a kitchen knife through cartilage, bone, ligaments, and skin making it harder than he even imagined. The lesson he learned was that one focused high-speed slice with a long blade did the job much easier than sawing steadily with an equally-honed short blade.

He made sure to direct the eruption of blood, gore, and detritus away from himself; didn't want to get any of that disgusting shit on his trousers, since the night was still young, and who knew? He might want to hit another watering hole before going home. He'd be sure to wave down a cab though, considering how cold he knew it would be getting by now.

For the next act, he picked up the severed head and, holding it carefully so as not to get any of the bloody shit on him, carried it to the bathroom where he unceremoniously placed it face-up in the immaculate toilet bowl. She had been a conscientious housekeeper or, at the very least, had one in her employ.

Then, returning to the body, he took off his belt. Fortunately, it wasn't very expensive, a faux alligator print stamped on leather. *Where had I bought it?* He looped the brown strip of sturdy leather around the body's waist and made sure it was anchored snugly below the underarms and, being careful not to step in the sticky yet slippery blood spreading patulously on the floor, carried the headless torso to the kitchen window to where the clothesline that could be fed out on a spool was anchored. He propped the decapitated body in the deep sink and raised the wood-framed window. Taking two heavy-duty carabiners used for hanging heavy wet garments he'd spotted in a small plastic basket by the window, he hooked them onto the belt and then spooled the cold hard line with the headless body attached, out in the dark, above the deserted alley bottom, twelve floors below.

Moonlight illuminated the desolate artistic form from above. A luminous non-phantasm forever embedded in his gray matter. In the dark scene under the pale moonlight it resembled a black and white Hitchcockian TV drama or a dark Orwellian novel. As he stood there viewing his artwork, he wondered how long it would take her family to forget her. He hoped they would forget her soon, for their own benefit. So they wouldn't mourn for too long. Gordon didn't have long to admire his artistry, however. Tearing himself away from his vision, he jerked himself back to reality. Glanced around the room to see if anything he needed to do came to mind. Decided he hadn't left fingerprints on anything of consequence after donning the surgical gloves. But after the three glasses of wine he decided he just had to take a piss before he left. He couldn't take long with the tarriance, but it wasn't like he was going to take a shower. He went to the one bathroom where he had carefully placed Hannah's head in the toilet.

He unzipped and for a moment thought about pissing in the sink. Pissing in the face of the head seemed a bit much, even for him; but then he figured what the hell difference did it make? If he weren't already proceeding straight to the gates of Hades, then this lone sadistic act wouldn't put him over the edge, and he began to relieve himself in a disgusting *coup de grâce.*

He murmured with a hint of sympathy, "Hannah, Hannah, Hannah. Alas, you shouldn't have been so demur. But demur and beguiling is an irresistible combination, at least for me it is. So where do you end up? In the toilet…and hanging from a clothesline."

But he considered his reflection in the wall mirror's shiny metallic surface rather than focusing on the indignity of the hot stream of urine splashing on the once attractive now mirthless face staring vacuously up at him from its ignominious resting place in the toilet bowl. At least the lack of jocundity wouldn't cause her to incur the wrinkles of old age of which Shakespeare wrote. That and dying so young. So he thought himself doing her a kindness: that of not having to face the indignities of old age.

Considering his own image in the mirror's reflective surface didn't displease him, and that caused him to believe he was entering a particularly epoch-making time of his life. He was singularly committed to making it happen. He believed everyone needed something to which they were committed. That's what made life worth living and not merely just existing.

The apartment made not a sound as he walked through it. Looking around one last time it occurred to him that someone would have to deterge the space of the orgy of blood and other bodily excretions before it could be rented, or even shown. Then wondered, not for the first time, how he came to acquire such an esoteric vocabulary. *Deterge.* He shook his head at himself with a lack of comprehending. It was like he was, or should be, a professional wordsmith of some sort.

Chapter Sixteen

That sure didn't take long...

Since he hadn't planned on killing her in her apartment or finishing with his physical necessity, he had to quickly make his way out of the building unnoticed and fall in with the late evening upper-crust throngs on the sidewalk. He encountered none of Hannah's neighbors while taking his leave furtively through the labyrinth of dark halls in her building.

The antiquated lift relinquished him to the lobby.

As Gordon exited onto the 2nd Avenue sidewalk, he ducked and smothered an ersatz sneeze, covering his face while doing so, in the event any of the security cameras were trained on the doorway. He turned south toward the Metropolitan Museum of Art in the shortest direction around the park, so he'd be walking in the general direction of his West Side condo.

Fell in among native New Yorkers, a typical Upper East Side evening, typical peoples, the paupers and prosperous side by side. Misery amid plenty. People who were defined by other people. New Yorkers were like that. They didn't even define themselves. Everyone defined others and allowed others to define them. If only everyone had defined themselves. That, at least, would have been honest even if not altogether accurate.

Nobody strolled. It appeared that everyone was on a mission, on no long and winding road they, somewhere they had to be that couldn't wait. Typical of New Yorkers. Residents of The Naked City. He wondered how many were like him. A frightening thought to someone who wasn't mad.

Halfway down the next block, the keening of ear-splitting sirens assaulted not just his hearing, but violated all of his senses, and he looked over his shoulder to see three NYPD marked Ford Tauruses with blue lights flashing, screech to a stop in front of Hannah's building.

That sure didn't take long.

Like the New Yorker he was, he shrugged, looked back down at the cracked sidewalk in front of his shoes, and kept walking. He concentrated his gaze on the dirty sidewalk in front of him, threading his way along. Felt the subway rumble under his feet. The anguished stories this cracked sober cement could tell. One step at a time. He thought about how in a different time, with different motivation, a different reality. Even he might have been a killer for hire for Murder, Incorporated, the infamous Mafia killing organization of hit men established in the 1930s that operated from a bank of phones in the back of the Midnight Rose candy store located under the Number 3 subway train EL in Brooklyn. Famous in tale and song. Most of whose members died in Sing Sing's electric chair, Old Sparky, back in the days when it was used liberally on anybody who deserved it, even if they were white. Back before the death penalty was abolished in New York State. For the last time, in '76.

Gordon certainly had the affinity for the organization's dirty business. Of course, he wasn't Italian or Jewish: an organizational requirement etched in stone, and, besides which, he was born too late to join the ranks of the Lord High Executioner, Albert Anastasia who, along with Bugsy Siegel and Abe "Kid Twist" Reles, co-founded Murder, Inc., before he was cut down by two masked gunmen while getting a shave in a barber's chair in the Park Central Hotel on Sixth Avenue. Gordon felt certain he could have bettered that organization's finest killer, Sammy "The Bull" Gravano's imminence of nineteen *admitted* kills and increased their estimated four hundred kills to one thousand… and proudly. Especially if he were using a firearm in place of a blade. But he felt sure he could still reach killer Sam Little's number of fifty confirmed murders — the most confirmed of any serial killer, and as many as sixty suspected.

Gordon looked no different from anybody else. Not in the least bit menacing. Fortunately for him, most New Yorkers stared head down at the path before them. If anybody had looked up, they might have seen him smiling. *They'll really be in for a surprise when they search the apartment.*

A busking musician stood on the next corner playing an inexpensive knockoff of a Martin acoustic and singing James Taylor's *You've Got A Friend*. Just a small part of the theatre of the street. He had a pleasant timbre to his voice, without attempting anything too acrobatic, and from the look of the small mound of folding money in his brown wicker basket, appeared to be having a successful night. Just one of the faceless millions in the cold harsh city with a dream of making it big.

I wonder what he does in his day job. Accountant? Subway train operator?

Gordon paused long enough to drop a five spot in his basket.

Chapter Seventeen

"Good Madre de Dios"

"You better come look at this."

The younger of the two uniformed officers, hardly old enough to shave and only beginning his third year as a policeman, stood staring, and called out to his partner in the kitchen. His partner, slightly older with a little more than five years of experience, entered the small bathroom and promptly vomited in the sink. Embarrassed, he took a moment to collect himself, and said, "Better call the sergeant. Looks like the work of the Unholy Ghost."

That foul-smelling shit in the sink won't help with collecting DNA evidence, he thought to himself. He would be embarrassed by it when the detectives showed up.

* * *

Detective Rossi had just climbed into the warm bed and snuggled up next to Ella, who he'd always said was his little toaster oven, when his cell phone, charging on his nightstand, sang out. The ringtone was the theme music to the Eighties TV cop show *Hill Street Blues*. Desk Sergeant lit up on the display in the dark room. The sergeant gave Rossi the victim's name and info.

"Shit," Rossi muttered and clicked off.

Ella sighed loudly. She knew from experience it most likely meant he would be leaving soon and if he were lucky would be home in time for breakfast. "What?"

"The Ghost again."

"Crap."

"Couldn't say it better myself. Unless I said shit again."

He hadn't even had time to get comfortable in the warm bed; moaning, he gently slipped out of the cocoon and shuffled softly toward the closet, where, after closing the door and flipping the light switch, he redressed, feeling sorry for himself. Then he thought about the victim and didn't feel sorry for himself any longer. Even though he hadn't had time to fall asleep, that didn't make it any easier going out in the dark cold city in the wee hours of the morning. The last thing he did was to strap on the holster containing the 9mm Heckler and Koch, commonly referred to as an H&K, his preferred weapon of choice. He wished he had a backpack to allow him to carry more of the gear he used as a policeman, but he was of the thought that no one who was out of school and had finished college should wear a backpack. That they were too old. Backpacks, like the breakfast cereal Trix, are for kids. Fine for his grandchildren but not so much for a grown-ass man and NYPD detective, besides.

He knew he should lighten the hell up, but being intense came with the job. At least it did for him. He didn't call Park. He'd let his young partner have the night off. Hopefully, he was on a date or at least having some sort of a life.

Rossi got to his unmarked car and drove with speed

* * *

Leaning against the hallway wall, Rossi bent over, slipping tan canvas booties on over his black Ecco lace-ups, then ducked over the lower slope of yellow tape and under the upper one the unis had already used to X over the open doorway to the victim's apartment. First thing he noticed: it didn't smell like his with the warm aroma of red gravy permeating all fabric surfaces.

If he thought about it he knew that all apartments didn't smell like red gravy, but it still caught him off guard momentarily because it didn't smell like...anything. He thought it joyless. It didn't smell like it should, like a family lived there. He knew he was being sappy, but he'd still have to remember to tell Ella about that. He was careful to avoid the massive amount of blood in the living room floor.

This was where he earned his pay. But knowing he was good at his job didn't make it any easier. He was glad to have other experienced eyes on the scene as well.

"So where is it?" he asked of no one in particular, referring to the body. The apartment was chilly from the kitchen window being open.

A forensic technician, a female wearing what looked like a surgeon's uniform from head-to-toe, answered. "In here," she said, walking from the rear of the small apartment, "and out there," pointing toward the window.

"What?" Rossi was genuinely confused. "I thought there was only one."

"Yeah. There is. It isn't pretty. Well, she used to be, but she isn't anymore. She'll have to have a closed casket."

Rossi went to the kitchen window, gazed into the space above the dirty alley floor. Saw the gory, headless body. He made the sign of the cross and said. "Good Madre de Dios."

"That's not the worst of it," said the forensic tech.

"Not the worst of it? What could be worse than that?"

"In here," she said.

Rossi looked doubtful.

"It's okay. We've finished our run-through inside, except for one thing. We'll take what we got back to the lab."

"What's the one thing?" asked Rossi.

The tech led Rossi to the bathroom, then stepped aside and, with a sweeping motion like Vanna White, gestured him in.

Rossi could smell the sickening sight before he got there and for the first time in over thirty years of viewing dead bodies, he lost his supper, spraying it all over the floor. The sight of the dispossessed head covered in piss in the otherwise meticulously clean toilet. He wiped his mouth, kept his eyes closed for a bit, then stood and stared at the ceiling. "Sorry for that. Never done that before." He stepped out of the bathroom to get his stomach under control.

Another uni asked, "What's wrong with people? Sick son of a bitch." He did not expect an answer, but Rossi felt compelled to provide one, or at least his thoughts.

"Nothing has changed. Things just like this…or worse, have always happened." He took a deep breath and looked at the uni. "Has anybody talked to the neighbors?"

"Yes, detective. It's in our report. Pro forma. Nobody heard or saw anything unusual."

"Nothing unusual except for a headless body hanging from a clothesline extending from the kitchen window twelve floors above a filthy alley."

"Yes, sir. Except for that. Apparently, she was known as kind of a party girl. Brought men home from time to time."

"Sounds like a normal, young, single woman in New York."

Rossi was embarrassed about vomiting, but he couldn't worry about that; he was too consumed with concern for the young woman's poor family. They didn't need to hear that the police thought their daughter might have brought this on herself. Nevertheless, they would need to be notified as soon as possible. Before he left, though, with his stomach reflexes now under control, Rossi took a couple of photos of the head.

"For the love of God, get it…er, her out of there," he told the tech.

"Yes, sir," she replied, none too queasy herself.

He went back to the window to get a few shots of the headless body in the scant moonlight. He knew cellphone photos couldn't be used legally, but he could use them for his investigation. Cell phone cameras made taking photos of crime scenes easier than when he joined the force decades ago during the time of Polaroids spitting out pictures that developed dimly right before one's eyes but only then if they dried properly. It was always hit or miss.

The ME and his crew would retrieve the body from where it was suspended over the alley. Rossi waited a few minutes to give them time, then snapped a closeup of the torso. Slipping out of the apartment, he texted all of the photos to Park and Bookworm. Might as well get Book involved right away, he thought.

"Hope I'm not waking you," Rossi texted Bookworm and Park, and attached the pics. Before he reached the elevator, his phone rang. Book.

"What's up?" he answered.

"Your vic. She looks familiar. I mean, can't be sure because of the damage to the face. But…"

"But how…where…what?"

"Well, I don't know her, but I think it's a woman I talked to last night."

"Explain, please."

"I went to an Upper East Side watering hole called…forget it. Doesn't matter. You wouldn't know it anyway. It's too cool for you. No offense. She was sitting at the bar talking to this white dude. I think her name is…was…Hannah. And…I believe his was Gordon."

"Good job, Book. Gordon and Hannah? Huh…you're right about Hannah. Hannah Whitehead. Maybe you're onto something." Rossi was getting excited.

"I don't think so. They didn't leave together. He left before her. So, he couldn't have followed her."

"Sure he could. We know our guy's smart. He could have left first, waited for her outside just to throw anybody off the scent who might've been paying attention. Like you. I'm getting a good feeling about this."

"I guess so," he reluctantly agreed.

"Just watch. I'm going to make a detective out of you yet."

"The city can't afford me," Bookworm said as a matter of fact.

"I know. I know. What'd this guy look like?"

"Not unusual. Late thirties, brown hair, clean-shaven. Casual clothes. Wore a Yankees ball cap. Looks like everybody…and nobody."

"If he's our man, first thing he'd do is ditch the hat. Sounds like…I don't want to say it…a ghost."

"I know, right? Maybe not so ethereal, though. Maybe just someone who's doing everything he can not to be noticed or remembered. Maybe both. It was like he was working too hard not to be noticed."

"Say, Book, you want to meet me at that bar tomorrow night? Actually, I guess it's tonight now. See if anybody remembers him or knows him? At this point you're the only eyeball witness we've ever had. This might be the big break we've been wanting."

"Sure, Sal. I'll meet you. I'll text you the name and address."

"Sounds good. I'll call Park after I get it, since I gave him last night off. Seven o'clock? So I can go to the Saturday vigil mass first?"

"Sure, Sal. You know, that's one of the things I dig about you. Even though you see the worst of what the city has to give, you don't let it get to you. You go on to mass and you live your life."

"Thanks, Book. Appreciate that, but I'm not as dauntless as I might appear. It's far more than ennui. My insides are in tumult. I get infuriatingly vexed by things like this. And believe me, the Unholy Ghost is seriously vexing."

Book took note of the words tumult and vexed. That was something he'd missed about regularly talking to Salvatoré: improving his vocab. "Well, you never lose your humanity, Sal. You remember what Dostoevsky said after he'd been in prison for awhile?"

"Not off the top of my head. Remind me."

"He said, 'The degree of civilization in a society can be judged by observing its prisoners'. Of course I have my own take on it. 'The degree of civilization in a society can be judged by observing its homeless, the disenfranchised — and how it treats them.' "

"Yes, I remember that and I agree. I also like yours better."

Chapter Eighteen

"Dude, we gots to do somethin' about this"

Bookworm started coffee brewing. Nothing like the aroma of freshly ground beans on a Saturday morning. Same as always, he was showered, shaved, dressed, and prepared for all the day might bring. Except for the purple rubber shower shoes he still wore; they would be the last change he'd make before carpe dieming.

ESPN was on the huge widescreen TV in the living room with talking heads making their predictions for the winners of the day's college football games. The living room was near fastidious; no one would think it the digs of a carefree young bachelor. But then, Bookworm was anything but typical. Checked his less-expensive-than-it-looked stainless steel Longines Legend with black face. Eight fifty-nine, it read. He grabbed a remote and muted the sound. He didn't need to hear them pontificating. What the so-called experts thought just bored the ever-loving shit out of him. He could call on his years of playing the game at the college level and do a better job than they. He might have played in the NFL if he hadn't gotten concussed one too many times. The neurologist had recommended he give up the game while he still had a brain.

The door buzzer sounded. Hearing a slight but familiar noise, he bounded across the room in two broad steps with the energy of a caged panther, and opened the door. "Reefer. Come in, come in. Right on time. I appreciate punctuality," he said, taking a quick glance at his watch again before flipping the wall switch to turn on the ceiling light. "How are you this fine morning?"

Reefer smelled the coffee as soon as he entered. Light on his feet, he walked confidently; a bit untidy, he looked like he always did, like he'd want to avoid himself if he came face-to-face with himself on the sidewalk. Especially if the encounter were in the Bronx. Face covered in ink, black dungarees with cuffs turned up two rolls and black hoodie covering his perfectly smooth shiny black head that was in sharp contrast to Bookworm's regal high altitude afro.

"Sup?" Reefer said, somewhat less than cheerfully, in other words, the way he always looked and sounded. Handed Bookworm a huge sack of large bagels, a little change from the twenty, and a receipt for the NYPD. Always a man of few words, and even less talkative than usual because he'd had a late night, he smelled of one of the new, hip young men's Old Spice fragrances and looked like he could use a shave, or maybe he was just trying out a new five o'clock shadow look.

"Dude, those are some bad kicks," said Bookworm, noticing Reefer's bright blue and white Air Jordan's.

"Cool, I got these at the Modell's on Seventh Avenue in Midtown. Howard Stern was looking at the same pair and I beat him to 'em. But we conversated. He was a good dude." He shivered slightly.

"Is it very cold out?" Bookworm asked. The room was pleasantly warm.

"Not bad." A man of very few words. "Not like it will be in late December, anyway."

Bookworm nodded in agreement to Reefer's observation and plopped the un-logoed white sack of bagels somewhat less than carefully on the uncluttered kitchen counter. "Help yourself to the java," he said. "Mugs're out."

They each poured themselves a large mugful, neither knowing it was much better than the swill they'd get at a hotel conference room meeting in Midtown because that wasn't among their life experiences. Bookworm walked to the fridge to retrieve a fifth of Irish whiskey. "How about a little extra kick for your caffeine? Help take the chill off," he asked, tilting it in Reefer's direction, before he poured a shot into his own green-and-white New York Jets mug.

"Now you're talking," said Reefer.

Bookworm proceeded to top off his associate's navy-blue-and-white pinstriped Yankees mug. The refrigerated Irish whiskey rendered the steaming coffee immediately drinkable. After a healthy swallow, Bookworm, surprising Reefer a little, said, "I don't know who invented coffee, but I could kiss him square on the mouth."

Reefer looked at him a little more than doubtfully, but said, "This is pretty good fuckin' coffee." Of course it might have just been the whiskey he liked since he wasn't a good judge of coffee given that he was more of a Red Bull or Mountain Dew man in the mornings.

"Especially this morning. I was up kind of late. Let me give you the latest," said Bookworm.

"Sup?" said Reefer again.

"On second thought, let's take our bagels and coffee out on the terrace. What I'm going to tell you won't be quite as bad over hot coffee and good food."

"Cold," agreed Reefer.

Bookworm wiped off the damp tabletop with a handful of paper towels. They set their mugs, bagels, butter, and preserves on the textured tempered glass top of the high bistro table for two, and sat in high-backed outdoor wicker chairs. The chairs were fairly new and hadn't gotten a lot of use as of yet so they weren't entirely comfortable. Bookworm, being a good host, politely slid butter and the small jar of cherry preserves closer to Reefer. At three hundred feet above the sullied and seamy Bronx streets, the breeze was chilly and stiff. The previous night's rain had moved out over the Atlantic and the skittish morning sunshine flashed and flickered off the salty whitecaps of Long Island sound not far away.

"Now, this is nicer," Book said. "A pleasant palaver between friends, over nourishing hot coffee and bagels before we talk business. Of course, who would want tepid coffee? That was rhetorical, by the way."

Reefer buttered his whole grain bagel and spooned on preserves without response. He was growing somewhat more than a little accustomed to Bookworm's magniloquence, and assumed a palaver was something good, especially a pleasant one, but he wasn't sure about rhetorical, so completely nonplussed, he held his tongue. Which he was good at doing anyways. Besides, it wasn't like Bookworm was trying to show him up. It was just Bookworm being Bookworm and besides, he had so many other good qualities. There was nothing spurious about the confident young man. One of the most genuine people anybody could know. Indeed, no one would ever be able to recall hearing him speak vituperatively.

The hot Irish coffee was delightful out on the chilly high terrace. Reefer had gotten the whole grain bagel because he liked its taste, not because it was high in fiber or healthy or anything like that. He was young. He didn't think about those things, yet.

"These are real good bagels," Bookworm said. "Where'd you get 'em?"

"The bodega on Third." It was right next door to a package store; made things convenient if one was so inclined.

"That's what I guessed. They're really good. There aren't many things better than a nice convo over coffee and bagels."

In the distance against the eastern horizon, though hard to make out against the bright early morning sun, further out on Long Island one could just make out the silhouette of the mysterious Tesla Tower, also known as the Wardenclyffe Tower, which Nikola Tesla built in 1902 for the early transmission of messages, telephony, and even facsimiles across the Atlantic to England and ships at sea.

Bookworm was a bit of an amateur historian and found it fascinating and beyond exciting that he could see the significant historic site from his apartment. Even if it were only about an inch high at arm's length and most people wouldn't know what it was. If he were giving an out-of-towner a historic tour of the city, he could show them the rundown Midtown New Yorker Hotel where the dying eccentric lived out his final years. His room still a shrine and museum, unavailable to rent, with a plaque by its door emblazoned The Nikola Tesla Room. The hotel itself, a dark stone with gilded accents, was known for being the subject of a famous painting by the renowned southwestern artist, Georgia O'Keeffe. Bookworm pointed the tower out to Reefer and explained its history to him.

"That's dope," Reefer said with as much subdued fervor as he was capable.

Bookworm wasn't sure Reefer could actually appreciate it or only pretended he did. Which was okay, as long as Bookworm was opening him up to a new experience. Eventually he'd probably understand how life-altering it was and what it had meant to the future of global communication. He picked up his smartphone from the table and touched the photo gallery icon, bringing up the images of the discrete suspended body over the alley and the head in the toilet.

Before handing it to Reefer, he said, "We got another victim. Detective Rossi sent me these about two o'clock this morning. What's even worse is I saw her at a bar last night. I might have been the last person on earth to speak to her before she was killed. Excepting for the killer, of course."

Reefer took the offered iPhone, last year's model. But it didn't take but a moment for him to set it harshly back on the glass-topped table as if it were contagious. His street-weary eyes gazed unfocused toward the eastern horizon, staring both deeply and vacantly into it rather than at it, then spoke, slowly, carefully, as if every syllable pained his everlasting soul. "Shit. That's disturbing…on so many levels. What kind of barbarian does it take to do this kind of evil?"

Reefer said it so quietly, head now bowed, that Bookworm could tell he was badly shaken. He was impressed that Reefer knew the word barbarian and how to use it. Reefer continued to be lost in his stare. It was like he had forgotten Bookworm was there.

"Evil has been around since before Iago betrayed Othello, Reef...and even long before that. In the form of jealousy or covetousness, both the most common impetuses to murder," Bookworm said sententiously. He was fairly sure Reefer didn't know who Iago, Othello, or their creator Shakespeare were, but it was too good of an analogy not to use.

Reefer looked up at Book, staring him in the eye. "We. Me. You. And your man, Rossi. We gots to bond, be solid, to get this scourge off the streets of our city."

Bookworm couldn't believe Reefer used the word *scourge,* and called New York *our city.* Obviously, he'd not only been listening to him, but hearing, too. "Couldn't say it better myself, Reef. Rossi's a real good guy...you know, for a cop, of course. There's a lot of unsavoriness in the world and Rossi cares. I mean, really cares."

Bookworm saw in Reefer's jet eyes a depth of humanity of which he didn't know the young man was capable. They betrayed a presence of seriousness that most had never been privy to from the tough young man of the street. If Bookworm didn't think it not possible, he would have thought he saw a tear. His admiration for the Bronx-hardened young man grew.

Then, Reefer, with all the cool of Bogart, produced a near empty pack of cigarettes from the pouch pocket of his hoodie and bounced the last stick from the cellophane-wrapped package. He continued softly. "Dude, we gots to do somethin' about this."

He crumpled the now empty pack, took a drag from the cig. Then changing his mind about wanting it, flicked it over the terrace wall, and continued, "I need to conversate with some of my crew I used to roll with. Somebody's gots to know somethin'." He wasn't typically that high-minded, but he'd obviously been deeply affected by the images he'd seen.

"Sounds like a plan. I'm going to meet Rossi about seven this evening at the bar where I saw her last night. I can't ask you to come with, but maybe you could reach out to some of your boys while I do that. Then we can catch up later. We've got to get a handle on this malefactor."

Bookworm grinned when he surprised himself by using the fancy word. His intent wasn't to be disrespectful of the newly deceased by trying to be amusing, and it certainly wasn't levity on his part. He truly couldn't help himself. Princeton would be pleased. He could be counted among their most scholarly verbalistic successes. Brandishing words for their meaning instead of merely speaking them.

But as classically erudite as was Bookworm, Reefer was just as genuinely street, and shrugged. "If by 'get that malefactor' you mean get that motherfucker, then...for real."

They went inside to the warm living room where the rest of the morning was spent setting aside the palavering. Instead, discussing possibilities, options, and Reefer's thoughts on what Bookworm had observed the previous night. The young man leaned toward agreeing with Detective Rossi that Bookworm may have had actual face-to-face contact with the Unholy Ghost. But not even sure he'd recognize him if indeed he had, and if he were to see him again, Bookworm hoped the employees of the Upper East Side Tavern would be able to help with the man's identification. Who knew? If God looked down on them favorably, they might even be able to produce a credit card receipt.

By early afternoon they were confident they had exhausted all possibilities and their brains were tired from performing cognitive calisthenics.

"So, we have our game plan, right?" said Bookworm.

"Coolio," Reefer nodded.

"Good, let's lean into this, then talk tomorrow, unless you run across anything I need to know. In that case, you know how to reach me." Bookworm extended a long arm across the table for a fist bump.

Reefer nodded and reciprocated. Took a last warming slug of Irish coffee before heading back out into the chilly November air, tottered a bit, a slight torpor making an appearance. Apparently Bookworm had gone somewhat heavy on the Irish whiskey, or at least Reefer's. Bookworm seemed fine. Or maybe he just had more experience with morning drinking. But Reefer had work to do. Run down his boys and find out if anybody knew anything or knew anybody who knew anything. He rediscovered his balance and moved toward the door with even less spirit than with which he entered, but more determination.

After Reefer left, Bookworm texted Rossi the name and address of the bar where they were to meet, along with the admonishment not to dress like a cop. Bookworm was afraid if Rossi were recognized for what he was, his, Bookworm's, own reputation might be irreparably harmed by associating with an unsavory element. Rossi probably wouldn't find that amusing.

Chapter Nineteen

"Listen to you using the kids' words"

At seven in early November, the sun has already given up on its daily quest and surrendered to full dark. The pleasantly cool temperatures of October replaced by the new month's near-bitter chill and more like late December when the howling wind blows through the high canyon walls of the tall buildings. Bookworm entered the tavern crowded with loud Saturday evening revelers, and spotted Detective Rossi sitting at the dim bar not far from where Hannah had sat the previous night. Salvatoré waved, and Book returned it somewhat more than sheepishly. He'd rather that anyone paying them heed believe them two strangers who casually struck up a convo at the bar, rather than think their meet was prearranged. Obviously, his friend Salvatoré wasn't as nuanced when it came to matters of fitting in and going unnoticed.

Salvatoré stood and hugged Book. So much for being inconspicuous. Truth was, Sal was looking forward to a convivial evening with Book since it wasn't often that he did something like this with anyone other than his brothers in blue.

At least he was dressed street, his coolest outfit, as Bookworm had suggested: jeans, button up striped shirt, dark blue Giants cap, and heavy brown leather jacket. Even so, he'd never be mistaken for Serpico. And Bookworm was sure his friend was armed.

"That's the same bartender that was working last night." Book nodded at the bone-thin, middle-aged man approaching while gently but firmly extracting himself from Salvatoré's embrace since the last thing he wanted to do was hurt his friend's feelings. Bookworm sat on the high seat next to Sal. They ordered cocktails: Book's usual snifter of Hennessy, and Sal a glass of Tullamore Dew Irish Whiskey on the rocks.

"Cheers." Sal tilted his highball toward Book. "I'm paying, by the way."

"Cheers. Whether you pay and expense it, or I pay and give you the receipt to be reimbursed, ultimately it's coming from the same place. The City is paying."

"I like the way you think, Book. You're right. Tonight is on the City. So, drink up." Salvatoré put the glass to his lips and threw it back, the rich liquid warming him from the inside out as it passed down his gullet. "I think what I'll do is talk to the barkeep first and depending on how that goes move outward to others."

"Good plan, but I'll do it. No offense, but you'd scare them. You look cool, but still look like a cop being cool. You know how bilious you can get."

"No offense taken…I think. You know, I used to be cool."

"I'm sure you were, Sal. It shows."

"Thanks. How's the food here, by the way? All I've had is a communion host and the last half goblet of red wine at the pontifical vigil mass. His Excellency, the Holy Archbishop, served it himself. You know, the body and blood of Christ. I always get at the end of the line for communion so I can polish off the last of the wine. Old Italian trick. Gives you a head start on Saturday night, and saves you money. I didn't even stay for bingo. If I had I could've at least had some coffee and donuts, and somebody, probably old Kelleher, would've brought a bottle of Irish whiskey to make the coffee more, er, shall we say, interesting. Unless his wife caught him, then there would have been hell to pay."

He hoped they could get some information that would help him catch the Unholy Ghost and then have a pleasant confabulation. It wouldn't hurt if he could combine some pleasantry with police work.

"Food's real good." Book said reaching over the bar top and getting Sal a formerly white battered and stained cardboard menu.

Sal looked it over and said, "Looks like it. American with French and Pan-Asian influences." The Italian food lover in his soul was rearing its head. "If the City's paying I might as well eat good."

A young man overheard next to them asked the barkeep for a dead turtle.

Salvatoré said to Book, "What in the hell is a dead turtle?"

"Shit if I know. Ask him. As long as the bartender knows, that's all that matters, though."

Sal asked. The young man looked at him as if he were an actual living, breathing dinosaur, but said, "Equal parts vodka and pickle juice, with a dash of hot sauce. It's awesome…and deadly."

Sal turned to Book and said, "He said it's…"

But Bookworm was already looking away and gesturing to get the bartender's attention with a crooked finger. The aroma of sauteed onions and the frying of fresh fish off the boats at South Street Seaport downtown hung heavy on the unmoving air in the previous century's space that, in former iterations, had been a bank, a bodega, and other innocuous places of business until it found itself as a provider of food and spirits.

The mixologist gave Bookworm a return finger wave and a look that said 'give me a minute', so Book walked down to where the worker had begun wiping down the wood-topped bar, leaned in close and whispered, "Hey, man, you remember me from last night?"

"What do you think, my friend? Any bartender worth his rupees never forgets a face."

"Cool, then you remember the couple I was talking to, right?"

"Yeah, you mean the woman murdered after she left here, right?"

"Yeah. Had you ever seen the dude before?"

"Never. You think he did her? You a cop?"

"No, dude. I just figure if I do something to help out Five-0, they might help me out down the road. You know what I'm talkin' about."

"Yes, my friend. I hear you," the bartender said, leaning closer, conspiratorially. He felt like he was being let in on a big secret.

"Anyway, you sure you don't know the dude?"

"Positive. Never seen the man before. Before you ask, not sure I'd recognize him if I saw him again. He was…ordinary. Funny, now that I think about it, he never looked directly at me. Kept his head sideways to me all night. Even when he paid his check. In hindsight, it was like he was trying to avoid my eyes."

"Did they come in together?"

"No, he was here first. Sat alone for one drink. In fact, if I can read customers — and I can after twenty years of pouring, listening, and observing — I think he was getting ready to leave after he finished that one drink. Then the chick…no disrespect of the recently deceased intended, my friend. The lady came in, sat down beside him and…well, you saw her. Would you leave if she came in alone and sat down next to you?"

"Yeah, no kidding. Okay, here's the biggie. He didn't give you a credit card by any chance did he?'

"Sorry. No. Cash. Three twenties for his and the lady's drinks."

"Well, shit. That's unusual, isn't it? Don't most people use credit cards, these days? But thanks anyway. Speaking of drinks, give me and my friend two more."

"Is he a cop?"

"Him? No. La Cosa Nostra. Italian, you know." Reefer was enjoying a joke at his friend's expense.

"You're kidding. Really? The Mafia?"

"I shit you not. But they don't like that name, so don't let him hear you use it."

"Sure thing. That's really cool."

"I'll tell him you thought he was a cop. He'll get a kick out of that."

"Well, whatever you do, don't tell him I called him Mafia. Don't want him to be angry with me."

"Don't worry about it. He's cool."

The bartender, thinking he was in a new role of undercover cop, overanxiously asked, "You want me to call everybody over so you can talk to them?"

Picking up on the notion that the man was digging this Bookworm said, "No, we need to do this somewhat on the q.t."

"Yeah. I gotcha." The bartender felt included in the undercover escapade. That was one of the reasons people were just naturally drawn to Bookworm.

Over the next thirty minutes Bookworm casually approached a pair of servers and a busboy and got no additional useful information. While he talked to some of the staff, Rossi finished a platter of nachos, heavy on the jalapeños, then decided they'd found out all they could and that they should enjoy themselves for the rest of the evening.

So more drinks were poured. Copious amounts of alcohol cemented their friendship and working relationship. It was good for them both. Pounding them back like Keith Richards having his last bottle of Rebel Yell of the night. Rossi's nerves had been on edge for months and it was getting worse; he needed this. And yet, he was still working.

The alcohol taking its maximum maudlin affect, Rossi said, "I miss the days of the Guardian Angels. Seeing at least half a dozen of them every time I rode the subway. They did a damn good job, too. Violent crime? Down! You know what, Book? I think you would have made a good Angel."

"You know, Sal, I've long thought I could've been one, and I certainly would have looked cool in one of those red berets."

"What was the founder's name? He should oughta run for mayor. I think he could win. I know I'd vote for him."

"Curtis Sliwa. He has a radio show."

"That's right. Curtis Sliwa. Mayor Sliwa. I like it. I'll have to listen out for his show. What Channel?"

"77 WABC."

"77 WABC. Alright." Rossi continued, "You know, Book, I think we're up against something more than just your typical garden variety evil."

"I hear you, Sal, but what are you thinking?"

"I'm not sure. Remember, I'm just sort of thinking out loud here, okay? Spitballin'. But an escaped mental patient, maybe? A military experiment gone wrong? Or, hell, I don't know, maybe even multiple personality disorder. He might have more people in his head than there are in this bar. Hell, one of them night even be Spider-Man."

Book laughed out loud. "You're shittin' me, right? Spidey? If it was anybody, I'd say it'd be Batman. He always was kind of crazy, anyway. Watching his parents get murdered. Wearing that scary black costume. Driving crazy vehicles. Rolling over and crushing shit."

"Whatever. Just the prospect of him getting off on a psych eval scares the ever-lovin' shit out of me. I'd hate for our guy to get shrunk by some third-rate defense team psychiatrist, be declared a bedlamite, and get off scot-free."

Rossi pounded the table with a fist. "I'd have to beat the son of a bitch dead, *Totis viribus*, with my own hands before I'd let that happen. Give every damn one of his fuckin' personalities an anointing while he pleads for *misericordia*." Rossi was on a roll using the Latin for which he didn't often have opportunity. "He'd rather flagellate himself than let me get ahold of him."

Indeed, nobody would want to be on the receiving end of Rossi's ire. A Golden Gloves and PAL boxer in his youth, he was still swift of hand and could pack a wallop. His nickname had been "Fists of Iron".

"I hear you, my friend," Book said, patting Sal ruefully on the back. Book knew he meant it. "So we need to find this son of a bitch, *forthwith*." This was no pettifoggery; they were working out some serious shit now.

"Hey dude, forthwith. That's a police term, you know."

"I know it is. What? You think I haven't been paying attention?"

"Course not. I'm just shadin' you."

"Listen to you. Using the kids' words."

"What can I say?" Salvatoré laughed. "Told you I was cool. Now, maybe you'll believe me."

"I know. I remember. And you were right."

"'Course you could just say we need to festinate."
Bookworm looked confused.
"Festinate: hurry. We need to hurry."

Chapter Twenty

This is perfect for the surprise

Grayson woke on the early side of normal for him which, on a Sunday, was elevenish. It was the only day he could sleep in without feeling guilty. He cooked a comforting hot breakfast with challah bread French toast, his favorite, with real maple syrup from Maine, turkey bacon, and copious amounts of coffee.

Starbucks dark roast was his preferred caffeinated vice. Whole beans he took pleasure in grinding himself, was good anytime. He guessed it could be called lunch according to the hour, or at the very least brunch. As the meal came together, it was an aroma for all the senses. He was dismayed to see he'd let himself run out of eggs or it would have been even better.

He needed to go to the Manhattan Mall, the huge four-floor building that had begun life as the original Gimbel's Department Store, famous for creating the Thanksgiving Day Parade before turning it over to Macy's upon it closing. Nothing special to look at from the street, but inside the mall incorporated many of the store's original architectural elements into its common areas, staircases, and escalators.

Grayson hadn't been clothes shopping in some time and needed jeans, a new leather belt, a couple of fall wool sweaters, and a pair of lace-up boots to fight the coming cold season. He never knew what else he might stumble upon that he couldn't live without. When he got back home, he needed to lay out his winter clothes and move his summer clothes to the rear of the closet.

Finished with breakfast, and after a shower and a shave, he called for a car. The mall's location between 33rd and 34th streets in Midtown was over forty blocks away and too far to walk, even though it would be a pleasant enough day for a salubrious stroll.

The driver's small Honda sedan had both Lyft and Uber decals on the dash, so the young Indian man must have been trying to retire early by driving for each service. After fifteen minutes on a pleasantly dead Sunday afternoon in the usually busy city, the hoped-to-be imminent retiree pulled to the curb at the mall's main entrance on West 33rd Street.

Grayson hopped out and went straight to the Starbuck's. A hot drink would help stave off the chill. After getting a venti cinnamon dolce latte to go and hitting the restroom. George Constanza, in a hilariously realistic episode on the Seinfeld show for people who'd experienced it, had it right. Finding a fit restroom in Midtown Manhattan was a damn near impossible task and you had to know where the good ones were. Or you could end up in an ultimately embarrassing situation.

Finished in the restroom, Grayson exited Starbucks happily sipping his appropriate-for-autumn sapid hot drink, and made his way down the list of stores he'd entered on his iPad, to be sure he didn't forget anything. Although a writer, he was not a professor though sometimes he felt like the proverbial absent-minded one. Aeropostale and Nordstrom Rack, looking for sweaters and shirts. Then JCPenney for traditional Wranglers.

To rise to the second floor, he hopped on an escalator in the main space of the mall. It original to the building going back to when the entire structure was the dated early twentieth century Gimbels, but now open and white and cheery on a sunny Sunday afternoon. The escalator ascended and, as it rose, Grayson lost awareness, feeling a dizziness like when he appeared on *The Today Show*.

* * *

Gordon arrived at the top of the escalator. He wasn't so much nervous as he was confused, and more confused than somewhat about what he was doing at a mall. How'd he get here? After stepping off the moving stairway onto the second floor, he glanced around trying to get his bearings. He felt sure he'd been there before but he couldn't remember when or why. Wandering aimlessly and seemingly without focus, he drew the attention of three young toughs who resembled a modern day but deadlier version of the Jets from *West Side Story*. The look of Trouble with a capital T. It was hard not to notice them. Probably the look they were going for. But he kept his head down, looking at the Ipad he was carrying, focusing on it. At least, the toughs thought so. All to draw them in and set them up because he sensed he was about to encounter his newest opportunity.

He might have kept his head up, although it wouldn't have mattered. Recalling who he was and his purpose, Gordon proceeded into the homewares department of JCPenney, the young miscreants following. Gordon purchased a set of steak knives.

Just past the entrance to the department store was a small lighted sign reading *RESTROOMS*, in red, above two gray metal doors with crash bars, an obviously seldom used hallway for stocking stores and emptying trash through their rear doors. Feigning the need to answer the call of nature, he walked in that direction and opened one of the doors, hoping his prey, mistakenly thinking, to their peril, that they were the predators, would follow. He ripped open the package of knives, extracted one, and slid it up the sleeve up his lightweight poplin jacket.

This will serve my purposes perfectly.

Glancing around at the dim service hallway with its pale gray vinyl floor and dirty and scarred darker gray walls, fifty feet ahead he saw that the corridor made a right-angle turn.

This will be perfect for the surprise.

This was planning by the seat of his pants. Still, they fell right into his trap because he heard the sound of the heavy double doors closing behind him.

Good, they followed. Just like I thought they would.

Gordon knew his plan was in motion and so, he all but loped happily down the deserted hallway. He dropped his leather case-enclosed iPad into the sack with the rest of the steak knives only to make it easier to carry. At the end of the hall he made a tight turn to the right and, after one large stride, attempted to impress himself into the wall. He inched the concealed knife down the sleeve of his jacket where his left hand waited with the used Starbucks napkin, captured the weapon dagger-style, the typically innocuous dining tool now extending savagely from the bottom of his clenched fist.

Listening for footsteps, he timed his savage attack for the precise moment the nearest thug turned the corner. He didn't have to wait long. Two abreast turned the corner together. The third, a larger punk, a step behind. As soon as Gordon sensed movement he struck. A torturous karate-style bottom fist with the serrated-edge streak knife extended from his muscular hand. The victim had no time to react except for his eyes registering utter shock and anguish, as Gordon buried the ugly bone-handled knife hilt-deep into the hollow of the young tough's throat. The eruption of blood covering the one next to him as Gordon tore the knife free and slashed a jagged smile from ear to ear, across that one's throat; the thin strap of flesh remaining of his neck unable to support the weight of his head, it falling and rolling across the floor, where Gordon kicked it disgustedly further down the hallway, as if repulsed by the sight of the wretched thing. The two bodies landed gruesomely in a twisted heap, both deader than shit before they hit the dirty floor.

The third predator, now turned prey, paralyzed by fear and shock, raised his hands, and slowly backed several steps away before turning to run back the way they had come.

Gordon surveyed the sanguinary carnage and bore the passing thought that he wished he had multifarious methods of killing. The indistinguishable techniques were beginning to fatigue him intellectually. But then he remembered there was something to be said for doing something well, to take pride in the performance, and that banished the first thought from his consciousness. Positively verklempt was he.

So much for basking in the glory of his deed. He needed to get the hell out of Dodge. Squatted to plunge the gory knife tang-deep into the chest of one of the bodies, vandalizing it further, then bounded up enthusiastically, energized as he was by the dual kill. He needed this one: a double murder of males to show the world what he was capable of. Knowing it could just have easily been three had the last one not turned tail, emboldened him, his confidence growing with every malevolent act. He didn't want people to think of him as a killer of only the weaker sex in the manner of the infamous Ted Bundy of whom he didn't have a high opinion, believing he showed little creativity in his killings. Nothing was more important to Gordon than his legacy, and the double homicide of two despicable thugs would help to ensure it.

No one even paid him any heed as he exited the seldom-used corridor. Since most people had a belief that killers looked somehow different — like crazed animals — his attractive everyman looks and conservative attire served their purpose once again. Indeed nothing about him would give anyone pause; in fact, his good looks would give anyone, male or female, comfort, place them at ease. Even understanding all of this, he dipped his head and covered an unnecessary sneeze against the all-seeing CCTV eye. Just in the event. Best to keep the habit.

Chapter Twenty-One

"Don't give me a ticket"

Grayson remembered eating breakfast that morning, but had no recall of anything since then. He guessed he must have taken a nap and slept so soundly that all other experience was vanquished.

* * *

Rossi felt like flinging a shoe through the large screen TV he'd bought primarily for watching football. Too bad his favorite team was the fuckin' Jets. Losing again to those Goddamn Patriots.

He couldn't even enjoy the game even though they were wearing their new head-to-toe, all-green uniforms, looking football-sharp in the brilliant afternoon New Jersey sun. He wished he were there at the new Meadowlands, in his usual thirty-five-yard line lower-level seat, protected as it was from late season snow by the upper deck, the one he'd held for almost twenty-five years since back when season tickets were cheap, and no PSLs. But he'd promised Ella he'd help her move some furniture in preparation for the big family Thanksgiving dinner a little less than three weeks away. It was a quotidian task, but he had to do his part. Besides, he couldn't wait to see the grands, and that was the best part of it.

It was only the second quarter, but the outcome had already been decided. In truth it had been decided before they even kicked off, ruining a perfectly lovely Sunday afternoon.

Why he continued to torture himself with this shit, he didn't know. He didn't need the fuckin' aggravation, he thought.

The gun sounded ending the first half just as Rossi's cellphone buzzed; mercifully giving him and the Jets some relief.

"Hey, Lou," Rossi answered.

"Whatchu doin'?"

"Watching the fuckin' Jets."

"They must be losing."

"Hello? It's the Jets. Down twenty-one at the half." He sounded more petulant than a man in his fifties should over a kid's game.

"You won't mind missing the rest of it then, will you."

"What's up?"

"Our asshole struck again. Manhattan Mall. Two vics. Get over there, forthwith."

"Fuck. I'm about to get tired of this bastard."

"Then I've got a novel thought. Why don't you catch his sorry ass? I'll call Park. Have him meetchu."

"10-4. Where're the vics?"

"In a service corridor. Just follow the crowd."

"Not my first barbecue."

"Yeah, yeah, yeah. Why'd you ask, then?" They both knew that that was a throwaway comment made out of frustration with no reply necessary or expected.

* * *

Rossi pulled his unmarked Ford CVPI to the curb in front of the same entrance Grayson had entered an hour or so earlier.

"Don't give me a ticket," he said, flashing his shield at the unis guarding the wide glass doorway and tasked with denying entry to civilians. The unanointed.

The lieutenant had been right. All he had to do was follow the multitude dressed in suits, scrubs, dark blue parkas with FBI emblazoned in bright yellow, hazmat suits, and other bored-looking officialdom of various persuasions. The thought crossed his mind that, unlike some of those senior muckety-mucks, at least he looked like a real cop.

Rossi hesitatingly climbed the escalator's moving steps in a vain attempt to will it and himself to get there faster. At the top he took an appraising look around the mall and saw Park not far behind him at the bottom of the escalator. The kid had to have raced to Midtown. He wore the ever-present grin that Rossi had begun to expect. It must be nice to be young.

He waited for Park. The kid jogged up the escalator. Endless energy. Two more unis at the entrance to the service corridor. Park and Rossi flashed shields. It appeared that young Park was enjoying showing off his newly acquired detective's gold jewelry. Opened the squeaky doors. Fifty feet from the remains, the coppery smell of ripe blood, excrement, and gore, hit them.

You never get used to that sour smell.

Rossi noted the more than somewhat nervous flitter of Park's eyes. All the more reason Rossi felt he had to remain stoic, for the kid's benefit. Of course, less than a block from Broadway and with its music inspiring him, he positively knew that the sun'll come up tomorrow.

Standing over the bodies. It might have been a scene from a film noir. Except Park and Rossi didn't wear brimmed fedoras or dark suits with white shirts and dark ties like mid-century detectives, and they weren't smoking. Except it wasn't black and rainy out with electric neon lighting the puddles. Except there was no dramatic lyric-less jazz music playing. Except there was no discordant beguiling melody of Taxi Driver, Peter Gunn, or Perry Mason. It didn't look or feel like a Scorsese film. The day outside was sunny, bright, and chilly, and happy early holiday shoppers were beginning to pack the sidewalks, intent on getting a jump on their seasonal purchases. Other than those artistic contradictions it would have been perfectly noir.

Park and Rossi both took unofficial photos using their smartphones. Mostly to refresh their memories when it came time to make a case. Although the method of death was all they needed to know to decide who the killer was. The pictures the ME's office took would, as always, be the legal crime scene photos.

Park said, "I'm getting tired of seeing severed heads."

"And that's a good thing, my friend, because you'll never get used to it. Proves that you're still human," said the senior Rossi to his young charge, consolingly.

Chapter Twenty-Two
"So, what do you hear?"

The only good thing about getting called out on a Sunday afternoon was that after viewing the crime scene Detectives Rossi and Park could go home, doing their reports and follow up Monday morning. Back in his NYPD car, no parking citation on the windshield, Rossi again texted gory crime scene photos to Bookworm. His phone buzzed immediately.

Book didn't even identify himself, and offered no friendly greeting. "Son of a bitch. Didn't we just stop working?" He continued.

"Seems like it." And in truth it had only been about fourteen hours since they'd parted on Saturday night.

"Dude's getting brazen. Three kills in one weekend."

"No kidding. Something about this one feels different, though."

"Whatchu talkin' about, Sal?"

"Not sure. Hannah, Friday night, seemed like it was for his pleasure because he fains to do it. This one? I don't know. Maybe opportunity or necessity."

"Fains? That's a good word. I need to remember that one. Sounds old world. But this necessity you mention? You mean like self-defense?"

Rossi smiled at Bookworm's approval of his vocabulary. "I don't know. Maybe. I'm just spitballin' here. Or at least using that as an excuse. It's just a feeling I've got. You know how us cops are."

"I hear you. Y'all want us to think y'all got some kind of superpower, but the truth is you're just throwing shit at stuff 'til some of it ends up sticking.

"And now you know our secret. Don't tell anybody else. Anyways, I'll talk to you tomorrow. Let's huddle up then, see if we can come up with anything."

"Sounds good. Later. And hey, be careful out there."

"You, too. And not for nothing, don't get ambuscaded."

Bewildered by the word he wasn't familiar with, Bookworm looked at his smartphone as if it could help him find the answer, but Sal was gone. Then he remembered his dictionary app, looked up the word, and laughed. "Okay, Sal. I promise," he said to no one.

* * *

The precinct was a beehive of insanity. The captain, since arriving at work, had unfortunately heard from the commissioner who never called unless shit hit the fan. Usually the deputy commissioner was their go between. Kept the big man from getting his hands dirty. According to the Commish, he had already fielded calls that morning from Hizzoner; the governor; and far less pleasant than either of them, multiple worldwide news organizations.

Everyone in the solar system of officialdom was worried about the looming Christmas holiday season and whether the city would have its normal influx of out-of-town revelers — since a serial killer on the prowl tended to put a damper on peoples' Christmas festivities — and more importantly, their dollars, which the city's tax coffers were counting on.

Hizzoner had chewed out the commissioner who, although he works for the citizens of New York City, serves at the pleasure of the mayor. The commissioner chewed out the captain, who proved that shit actually does roll downhill, as he reprimanded the lieutenant. Rossi and Park had in turn been called on the worn and tired frustrated carpet tired of being used in that manner.

Back at their desks, that ass-chewing completed, Rossi said to Park, "I don't know about you, but I enjoyed the hell outta that." His voice, indeed his entire body, reeked of sarcasm.

Park looked like he was about to cry. Probably the first time he'd ever had his ass so thoroughly handed to him. Asian parents, or bosses, never had to do it, since the young people were all classic overachievers.

Rossi's cellphone buzzed. "Talk to me, Book. I hope you got some good news. I just had my ass handed to me in a McDonald's bag, and His Imminence The High Lieutenant forgot to include my Happy Meal toy."

"That's bad, dude...don't I always have your back?"

Rossi didn't know if Bookworm was talking about the ass-chewing or the McDonald's joke. "Just tell me."

"I talked to one of my boys. This is just his take, you understand. I can't vouch for his veracity, or his accuracy, but he says look for someone who isn't what they seem."

"What does that mean?"

"Don't ask me. You're the detective. Detect. I'm just saying. Think about it. Sherlock Holmes always finds the quaesitum, no matter how confounding the case."

"But that's fiction. This is real. And hey, you're the one with the city's pulse. I thought you'd have some theories."

"I get it. But you're the one getting paid. I'm getting the leftover largesse of the NYPD."

"Okay, fine. I knew you'd bring that up. Oh, and by the way. I talked to Ella. You're invited for dinner, Saturday before Thanksgiving. The invitation is for one, or a plus-one, whatever you want to do."

Truth was Rossi had told his wife about Bookworm long before, and even with her husband's assurances, she was somewhat more than a little nervous about having an informant, someone who lives and operates on the fringes of the law, in her home. Rossi had ended the discussion with "trust me". As usual, she did, and that was the end of her nervousness and the discussion.

"Great. You're the best, Sal. An early Thanksgiving dinner. I'm there. And it'll be just me. That way I get to eat more. Believe me, I'm pantophagous, so you don't have to worry about me. What time? What can I bring? Wine? Carnegie Deli cheesecake? Black and White cookies? What?"

Bookworm's mom had raised him right even in one of the Bronx's worst neighborhoods. He knew you always take something to a dinner invitation.

"Seven-ish. Wine would be perfect. And just so you know, Rosé goes good with turkey…and stuffing. Best of all, with pumpkin pie. Of course, Black and White cookies are always good. Um, let me think."

"Rosé. You got it, Sal. And Black and White cookies. Thanks, man, thanks a lot."

"De nada," said Rossi in somewhat more-than-lacking Spanish, switching from his usual more formalistic Latin.

* * *

Looking anything but circumspective, like he had nowhere else he had to be, which he didn't, Reefer hopped on the subway train number six line for the twenty-minute trip downtown. It wouldn't have taken even that long except for the frequent station stops. He'd just missed the previous train and had to wait ten minutes for this one. He stood, so that the older passengers could sit. He'd learned proper manners from his Southern grandmother, and she would be proud of him. What she'd said was "Even if you don't have anything else, you can have good manners. They don't cost nothing."

The train rocked; the sound and smell never changed. Nearing the last station on the line, it rumbled and rushed to a stop before birthing a flood of nearly all of its daily contingent of straphangers from the suddenly open doors, most, if not all, oblivious to everyone and everything going on around them while they checked the minuscule displays of their smartphones to find out what hypercritical messages of importance they missed while in the underground tunnel. Uniformed Port Authority Police officers, stationed on the platform, kept a watchful eye on everyone with evil intent, that their presence alone would discourage bad actors who frequent stations — some of the most crime-ridden settings in the city.

Out of years of habit when seeing the police, Reefer held a gasped breath and bounded fast, two at a time, up the steep steps from the underground entrance, encroaching onto the teeming cold scarred sidewalks of The Naked City before releasing the tense breath. He was fast when it came to running; would've been even faster if he didn't smoke so much. But a man has to have priorities. If it weren't for smoking dope he wouldn't have a training regimen at all, it being the key component. The soles of his worn leather lace-ups scuffed lightly on concrete worn smooth with age. The apparitional white vapor of his warm breath a reminder that the city's bitter wintertide cold, much like Sting's barking *Hounds of Winter,* was on the wind. He pulled the hoodie's tie tight around his bare head and wished he'd worn gloves, or at least thought to stick a pair in the hoodie's front pocket.

Pushcart vendors would soon be hawking steaming, hot, seasonal roasted chestnuts, vying with the mostly immigrant purveyors of fake Rolexes chasing the American dream in one of the world's most expensive cities, and Salvation Army bell-ringer sidewalk Santas lording over their ubiquitous red kettles collecting the public's dollars.

Reefer walked. There was nothing else to do. The clues encountered were at once rampant and nonexistent. Isn't that the way of life, everything and nothing? His old haunts did nothing but haunt him; or did they taunt him? Of that he wasn't sure. Nevertheless, they accepted him, if not graciously, at least no worse than gratuitously. Not into oblivion, they remembering him, just as he remembered them. He was the agonist of this story, the haunts reminding him of that wayward tale.

He thought of what had passed him by, and what he'd yet to pass.

They weren't all that different.

He wished he were more like Bookworm, but it was too late for that. Or was the wish and the fact of what he was doing proof that he was? Nearer to the man than he might have thought. Indeed, he hoped his motive was somewhat more than just a little altruistic.

Depending on the street, or neighborhood, the aroma might be that of pizza, Indian food, spicy Thai, or Middle Eastern delights. Except if one canted too far west or east, then those pleasing aromas might be overpowered by the altogether unpleasant acrid diesel odor from tugs and freighters inclining their trade on the twin rivers. The genuine organic scent of ocean salt infused river water. Even though the one to the east, which in fact used the direction as its name, wasn't a river at all, but a tidal estuary.

An easy perambulation along Mulberry Street, Reefer passed Umberto's Clam House where famed schizophrenic mobster "Crazy" Joe Gallo was gunned down, ironically while having dinner on his forty-third birthday. Reefer hadn't even been born when the hit occurred, but all New Yorkers knew about Umberto's, it a fabled part of the city's macabre crime history and lore.

The warm aroma of Italian delights evanesced as he departed Little Italy with its red, green, and white colors of the flag of Italy decorating all the restaurants, markets, bars and of course, Catholic Churches, a couple with sidewalk altars. After crossing a narrow, unmemorable, barely two-lane street to the sidewalk on the other side, the essence of Chinese food wafted on the crisp autumn air as he entered Chinatown.

Chinatown and Little Italy weren't so much amalgamating as they were coexisting, but since there were enough tourists' dollars to go around it seemed to be working for both of the ethnic nabes.

Reefer gazed curiously at the neighborhood, as if he were noticing it for the first time. Most of the buildings looked much the same as they did when they'd been raised in the middle of the nineteenth century when the denizens had been mostly Irish. Then, it had been known only as Lower Manhattan. In fact, most of the city's buildings and its grid were designed, laid out, and built in the nineteenth century by people who hadn't ambulated it in over one hundred and fifty years.

Hip-hop music bled like an unstanched ugly wound through the open doors of Chinatown shops, intruding on both tender and experienced ears. It becoming the universal sound of the city's minority neighborhoods. Reefer's head bobbed to the bangers he recognized.

Traditional oriental shops however, sold oriental fans, umbrellas, and small ornate statuary of Buddha, tigers, and elephants, artfully sculpted from Southeast Asian jade, lapis lazuli, and ivory.

Reefer chose this particular neighborhood because he knew his old crew still had the habit of plying their despicable trade on unsuspecting tourists, who, from Boise, Toledo, or Jackson, Mississippi, weren't as wary or as streetwise as native New Yorkers.

He could have walked the route blindfolded, guided as he was by the delicious smells of the various international cuisines. A native of Harlem who admittedly spent way too much time in the Stygian streets of a decaying Gotham, back when it was shuttered and shuddered before it had been returned from the edge of perdition. But the upside was it had given him a familiarity that could have served him well as a tour guide.

Of course, it was a piece of cake once you figured out that the long avenues ran north and south and the shorter streets east and west, to crisscross Manhattan all the way north to Yonkers. Addresses became unnecessary as long as one knew the avenue and cross street.

The only exception to that was the great Broadway which cambered from the northwest to the southeast for the entire reach of Manhattan island.

He felt no guilt as he walked. His hope being that what he was doing now, helping Bookworm, and in turn the NYPD, absolved him of all his sins, those past and those yet to be committed.

When thought of as a metropolis New York seemed leviathan, but when considered as discrete neighborhoods, it could have an almost small town feel to it. The feel of the wards of the Sharks and the Jets in West Side Story, and that's how Reefer saw the city many thought of as the capitol of earth.

Toward the end of the second block of Chinatown's Mulberry Street, Reefer thought he caught sight of one of his boys, name of Insane. Appeared that he was trawling, casting his net. Insane wore a black outfit that might be called either a track suit or warmups. And expensive coordinating Nike running shoes in the event he needed to. His haircut was short and neat and razored around his baby face and ears. Probably trimmed by a female cousin or sister. A shard of a thin mustache, which gave him nothing more than the image of someone trying to appear older than he was. Trying to look less epicene, even though he wouldn't know that word. He just wanted to look more grown up. Although he was almost twenty-one, a stripling, Insane looked no more than twelve. Even though he wasn't happy about it, it was his young look that put potential victims at ease and kept them from suspecting him of being the threat that he was.

If the suit had been made of soft black velour, a made man named Guido or Carmine, he of La Cosa Nostra, would wear it with a heavy gold chain around his neck.

Insane looked like he had his eye on a pigeon. He was the best pickpocket Reefer had ever known. The lightest touch in the theft universe. His legerdemain practiced and beyond compare, he was better than men twice his age and with more than double the number of years of experience. Even though he could scrap, the last thing he wanted was for the interaction to take a turn to the physical, with man or woman. An altercation in public always presented the possibility of witnesses, police being called, and the opportunity for too many things to go sideways.

Reefer spotted Insane's target. A middle-aged woman, probably on vacation with her family. He wanted to warn her. Shout: Lady! Watch your pocketbook! But didn't. Right before Insane was about to pilfer the woman's purse, he felt eyes on him, piercing him to his core. Noticing Reefer, it distracted him long enough to throw him off his mammonistic plan.

Reefer stifled a laugh and doubled over convulsively. Still had it covered when Insane turned toward him and, imbued with boundless energy and attitude, ran across the street vigorously, rage in his eyes. The skin across his cheekbones tightened. His countenance gave his nickname even more appropriateness than usual.

In an attempt to calm him before he neared, Reefer called out respectfully to his old friend, "Insane in the Membrane", using the entire nick the young man had given himself when he was but a mere juvenile, from the song by the popular classic hip hop group Old School Players.

"Don't Insane in The Membrane me, Reefer. I was getting ready to lift her Gucci bag. Even on the street, even at wholesale, I could've got five Ben Franklins for it. You ruined it for me. You owe me…again." Insane's ire could not be mistaken. He lit a cigarette, took one puff, and threw it at the street, sparks flying, like it tasted bad, putting a fine point on his anger.

Because the economy was coming around and with it an equivalent increase in tourism and business travel, likewise, the business of mugging was improving. Still snickering, and unable to take Insane seriously because he knew him too well, Reefer said flippantly, "Put it on my account." His attempt at levity fell short however, as the younger man gave him a dirty look that showed he wasn't buying it. Reefer then changed the subject. Looking around intently, he asked, "Where're the rest of the brothers?"

"Around. They're watching. Keeping an eye on things."

"I figured they were." There was something both comforting and at the same time discomforting about knowing that they were being watched. He tugged on the hood of his fleecy out of habit and glanced around with an uncertain look on his face, knowing he wouldn't see the eyes that were almost surely on him unless they wanted him to. Clearly they did not.

Until a moment later, when three brothers — two of them lighter-skinned, one darker — casually approached, one from the Little Italy direction to the west from whence Reefer had just come, and two from the east, from further into the depths of Chinatown.

"Reefer," said the one who had taken his place as the leader of the small gang. Tasting the name like it was the first time he'd ever spoken it. Not known for his bonhomie but for his grim manner, he spoke sullenly, but calmly, sounding almost disappointed to see him. Sullen was better than truculent when it came to Spike. He was cooler than the other side of the pillow; he could be disarmingly charming, but the dourness was still there.

Then there was the disposition somewhat more than a little mean. A hint of the violence of which he was capable, churning just beneath the surface, always seemed to be there, too. Imminently available if it were needed. Anyone who knew him hoped that just beneath the surface was where it would remain, no one desiring to be the one to cause it to bubble to the surface. Obstreperousness was fine, even expected from Spike, but no one wanted to see the violence he was more than capable of and happy to put on display. He was the best bad guy most people had ever known, or possibly he was the worst good guy. The difference was subtle but nonetheless it was there.

Indeed, he vacillated. He wasn't totally ignoble but he didn't mind if others believed he were. Although he preferred amity, it was always colored with deadly cunning.

"Spike," acknowledged Reefer, almost kindly, but with a flicker of disdain or maybe it was the returned scorn he thought he'd detected in

Spike's caustic unblinking gaze, and wondered if there was something in what Spike wasn't saying that he, Reefer, should have picked up on but didn't. Oh well, he'd have time to figure it out later, for the good or bad. It could be as simple as Spike feeling like Reefer coming around was figuratively stepping on his toes just as Spike was taking control, just spreading his wings.

The other two inclined their heads toward Reefer in dueful respect.

"I guess you can tell Insane has gotten insaner. Speaking of insaner, Reefer, you still smoking?"

The gravitas with which the question was directed didn't much bother Reefer. Spike always told him he smoked too much. "Not much. Only on weekdays and weekends."

"Yeah," Spike spat in the street gutter sarcastically, catching Reefer's attempt at a joke, but nonetheless not finding it amusing. "I've told you that the madness is gonna get you or the weed is gonna kill you."

Truth was Reefer *was* cutting back. Thought he was sleeping better already. "I'll take it under advisement, Spike," he said, drolly. "I need to talk to y'all. How about a cuppa coffee? Some place warm? I'm buying." Reefer had gotten paid by Bookworm, so he had money to burn. At least that's how being flush felt to him.

"Get outta this weather? That's a very good idea, Reef. Let's do it," Spike said like the smartass he was, rubbing chilled hands together briskly. He was ready. He'd been out in the cold too long already to suit him. He was a native New Yorker but winter's cold still didn't sit well with him and it was drawing too near for comfort.

Spike's natural bearing was as tall and straight as the copper Statue of Liberty as she kept watch over New York harbor in the cold. In fact, he had to tone it down to keep from being so noticeable, because being noticed isn't a good thing for someone in the business of crime. He carried his nickname with panache due to the black leather collar emblazoned with silver studs and spikes he wore practically all the time, the one that looked like it should encircle the neck of an angry German Shepherd, rightly so as his demeanor wasn't far removed from that species. In the warmer summer months when he wore a black tank top he'd wear a matching studded arm band similar to the one Freddy Mercury wore on stage at Live Aid. With his medium length Afro, his naturally pissed off attitude and spiked collar, he resembled a member of The Warriors gang, from the movie of the same name, ready to do battle with their gang rivals, the white-faced Baseball Furies. Even though the leather headband he wore made his medium length fro look a little like a muffin top. But Spike came by it natural. He was of the street born, nurtured, and raised. There was nothing fake about Spike. Like him or hate him, he didn't care. Didn't affect him. What you did was your choice.

So, in accord and on a mutually agreed upon mission, they set off east two by two, except for Reefer bringing up the rear, sundering their way through the crowd, many of whom were displaced or society's dropouts, whom even Spike thought of as deplorables, believing himself above them; along Mulberry's ancient cracked concrete through Little Italy, crossing a street and moving into Chinatown, it marked by hanging banners and signs with Chinese characters in the traditional red. The McDonald's with a red torii gate framing the entrance and Golden Arches with the namesake sign written in Chinese characters surprised most visitors. Although in this instance the gate didn't signify a sacred site like it does in Asia. Colors of gold and silver, Chinese lamps, and the smell of wonderful Chinese dishes marked the beginning of the densest population of Chinese immigrants in the Western Hemisphere.

The group continued on their mission until they found it; a pair of shabby double doors with mullioned windows, opening stridently on a characterless coffee shop; Chang's the name over the doors, occupying the first floor of a nearly two-century-old, tired, four-story building. It was accommodating, not because of its personality or architecture, but only because of its production of coffee. If truth be told, the business existed solely as a delivery system for caffeine and not so much for comfort, with none of the modern-day yuppie luxuries of a Starbucks. Unaware to most, decades before it was a coffee shop it had been a Chinese brothel, catering to Caucasian clientele wishing to sample the treasures of the Orient, and teeming with business. Two young Chinese women and a highly regarded male elder, most likely Mr. Chang himself, all dressed respectfully in clean white uniforms, were at the counter busying themselves fulfilling call-in orders.

A hand-lettered sign over the counter ordered unconditionally: *Remove hoodies and dark sunglasses before entering.* All followed strict instructions and relaxed the ties of the dark hoodies and lowered them since, no monks them, the hoodie had become the totem of street thugs and wannabes everywhere. This group fell under the category of active street thugs. The aged owner bowed hospitably, greeting them as if they were his most revered customers. Of course he wouldn't dream of treating anyone inhospitably, no matter their station or lack of legitimacy.

The chilly group of misbegotten wayfarers placed their orders at a whitish Formica-topped counter that had probably been brightly dazzling once upon a time, then decamped around a chipped and broken formica-topped round table for four of a similar color. There was something honest and comforting about the shabby and worn but, nevertheless, clean coffee emporium. In the way of Asian culture, cleanliness was above all. Even if it was old.

The elderly purveyor bowed obsequiously as Reefer settled the tab for them all, and then was the last to join the others at the crowded table. An ancient small black and white TV with poor reception and no sound hung high in a corner of the room and was tuned to CNN, whose talking head was spewing forth formally about new trouble in the Middle East. It was obvious from the story's description at the bottom of the screen what was occurring even without sound. Apparently people were growing bored with old trouble.

A chessboard of black and gray marble with traditional pieces carved from ivory of questionable legality harvested in China appeared out of place on a corner table. From the looks of the arrangement it was a game paused but in progress. An aged family heirloom, the elderly proprietor was probably playing a lifelong friend from the neighborhood in an ongoing game.

To be resumed whenever he returned.

The only other customer in the shop was a tense-looking young Asian woman. Her apparent anxiety didn't seem to be the result of the coffee. Reefer assumed she was Chinese; this was Chinatown, after all. Which meant she wasn't made in Japan. A young Chinese woman he'd met sitting at a dive bar once had told him that apparently old joke. She'd thought it hilarious.

Spike took a large gulp of the large cup of manly black coffee, sat back, and said, "That's a fine cuppa shut the hell up." Everyone looked at him curiously wondering where that unique turn of phrase came from. He said, "What? My pops used to say that. Never did know what it meant, but always liked the rhythm of it. All the way back to when I was a kid."

Reefer wasted no time in cutting to the chase. "I need some assistance," he said, as they glanced at each other wondering what was coming next. "What do you know about the Unholy Ghost?"

Without answering the question, and his voice showing no discomfort, but maybe a hint of disappointment, Spike said, "Heard you and Bookworm be helping The Man." Then almost incantatorily, "But I unnerstan. You gotta do what you gotta do. You always were too good for this life, anyway."

Surprised by Spike's unexpected praise, Reefer said, "Maybe so, maybe not, but if you and the guys help me and Bookworm help Five-0, we figure it'll be good for all of us."

"Word," said Insane, not looking up from his hot mug but nodding in agreement. Barely able to keep from laughing, Reefer took a sip of his usual medium-coffee with cream and sugar, called coffee regular in the parlance of native New Yorkers, and pounced on the opening. "See, Insane agrees."

Averting his eyes to keep from losing his composure hysterically, and at the same time not wanting to embarrass Insane, Spike angled his head left, chuckling softly under his breath. After regaining his composure and changing the direction of the convo he said, "You remember Scout."

"Scout," Reefer said, in acquiescent acknowledgment. "I should. I'm the one give him his name." Indeed, so called because that's what he was — the group's scout.

"Well, Reef, he's training a new brother. Business is so good we needed to add another scout. We just haven't given him his street name yet."

Said Reefer, "Scout One and Scout Two. Or One and Two, for conciseness, or brevity, as Bookworm would say." *I guess he's rubbing off on me — using two-dollar words like those.* Although no one would think Reefer was especially clever or long on bel-esprit, he'd always been able to think fast on his feet.

Pushing the proper dreads he sported away from his face, the new Scout grinned sheepishly, indicating he was cool with his new label. Even though it was hard to do. His facial muscles constricting because they didn't get a lot of practice smiling. Maybe he could use the new name to his advantage to advance his career. Maybe he could go on and get promoted to Scout One. He was ambitious, after all. Even when he sold dope on the street corner. Destined for greater things.

Spike, recognizing the new man's subtle enthusiasm, said, "One and Two. It's settled, then."

Taking advantage of Reefer's generosity, the scouts, obviously the strong silent types, munched on crumbly blueberry muffins and sipped super huge steaming-hot non-fat seasonal eggnog lattés with raspberry drizzles, letting Spike do their talking. Scout Two bobbed his head to a Bruno Mars banger over the shop's speakers hidden.

Scout One said, "You know what would be good with this? A Dragon Roll. Or a bento box. We are in Chinatown, you know."

Spike said, "Bento boxes are Japanese. And sushi with coffee? Dude, you sick," and shook his head pityingly.

Reefer said, "So, now that we've got the names issue settled, what do you know?"

Spike spoke frankly, "Well, it's not what we know; it's more like what we hear."

He had hoped he'd get at least a small rise out of Reefer with the somewhat more than a little smartass answer, but it didn't work. Reefer resignedly asking, "Okay, Spike, so what do you hear?"

Spike cracked his knuckles in frustration at his ploy not working, and said, "He's somebody famous." He didn't think anyone, even Reefer, who he actually liked, should win a battle of wills with him.

"Somebody famous? The hell that means?"

"Shit, I don't know. A movie star, a TV star, a singer. Maybe he's a Jet or a Giant. Something. Maybe he's Mick Fuckin' Jagger."

"Get the fuck outta here."

"You asked what we hear. That's what we be fuckin' hearing. Get Five-0 to figure it out. They're gettin' paid to do that shit. I'm not gonna do their goddamn job for them."

"I hear you, Spike. Be cool. Chill," Reefer chastised, carefully.

"I'm cold. I'm cold," he said. Insane and the two Scouts eyed Spike, nervously. They knew that his mood could turn in a second and didn't want to be anywhere near him if it did. In contrast to the chilly New York weather outside, partaking in the hot coffee and in the heat conditioned room, it had begun to warm them. But they decided they'd gotten everything done they could and stood to leave. Each going to the restroom to answer the call of nature after the large hot drinks.

Before they reached the entrance to leave, two young female workers were attacking the table they had used, clearing mugs, and wiping down the surface. Had to be perfect before anyone else could sit there.

With the group now warm and nourished, Spike opened the squeaky door to the street, then showed some of the charm he dispensed sparingly, to the proprietor, "Thank you for your kind hospitality, sir." He even raised a fragile smile when he mouthed it, but it didn't reach his eyes. Without making a sound, the older man bowed fawningly as the group exited the coffee shop into the late afternoon chill, the setting sun reflecting off the tall towers in the nearby financial district. Most notably the new World Trade Center, the replacement constructed for the matching pair demolished on 9/11, and the tallest building in the Western Hemisphere, visible from all of Manhattan, all the way to alphabet city, and the sky beginning to gray. They passed two chilled workers setting up a small sidewalk Christmas tree lot. It would be open for business soon. The sun's retreat making it even colder. By Christmas it would be full dark before five p.m.

Outside in the cold, Spike said, "Reef, why don't you send me a Facebook friend request? Make it easier to keep in touch."

"You're on Facebook?" Reefer asked, surprisingly.

"Gotcha, didn't I?" Spike said, roaring with laughter. "Hell no, I ain't even got no computer. 'Course I might get one before the night's over. If we get lucky."

"Be careful, Spike, if you're going computer hunting." What else could he say? Spike had gotten Reefer good.

"I know what time it is." Indeed, Spike was very much aware.

Chapter Twenty-Three

"If you say so."

"That's what he said," Reefer told Bookworm, like he was revealing a secret. "Somebody famous."

"I wish we had a little more to go on than that, but I'll let Rossi know."

"Cold."

"So, how was his attitude?"

"Spike's?"

"Yeah."

"Ah, you know. Spike is Spike. If he was any bigger he'd make people pay him to let 'em live."

"I was worried about that."

"Nah, it was okay. Spike and I are cool."

"Hope so."

"Don't worry about it. We're cool."

"If you say so." But Bookworm was skeptical. He knew it was best to consider Spike circumspectively and it could be at your risk if you didn't. He knew Spike was not someone with whom one could ratiocinate.

* * *

Bookworm phoned his detective friend. "Famous is what Spike said. So, what do you think? Does that mean anything?"

"Means almost nothing. This is fucking New York City, for God's sake. Forgive me. I don't mean to sound indelicate. But, just about everybody in New York is famous. If they're not yet, they're gonna be. At least in their minds." After a frustrated pause, he continued. "Think about it. John Lennon lived in the Dakota before that asshole shot him back in 1980. Bruce Willis, Denzel No Last Name Needed, Howard Stern, Keanu Reeves — fuckin' John Wick himself, lives here, for God's sake."

Rossi ended the call with Book and walked determinedly to Lou's office where his boss hammered rhythmically on a keyboard. The office was typical for a mid-level public servant—average size, beige paint, cheap desk, gray metal file cabinet and bare walls, except for the nail holes left by the previous office holder. The only personal effect— a brass and wood plaque marking the lieutenant's twenty years of meritorious service to the NYPD and the city of New York.

"What's up?" the lieutenant asked without looking up. He recognized Rossi's aftershave.

"I need you to do me a solid. I need a powwow with all the detectives in the unit to see if anybody can think of something I might've overlooked."

"That's all you need, huh?" was his rhetorical response that didn't take him mentally away from what he was doing. The lieutenant wasn't really ineffectual. It just seemed that he had his own agenda. An agenda different from Rossi's. He wasn't as old but thought he was more experienced than his charge, and smarter, and there, in a nutshell, was the rub and the root of most of their problems. Not grousing, but nevertheless looking somewhat more than a little put out, the boss capped a pen theatrically that he wasn't even using, sighed, and pushed himself up slowly from his desk, and muttered, "Let's do it, then."

Don't knock yourself out, Rossi thought, and wondered what was eating him. Besides the Unholy Ghost. *Good, now he knows how my life is.*

On the way into the conference room, the lieutenant sent the first person he passed in the hall to the Dunkin' for two huge boxes of donuts. Told them to put it on the department's "standing account". The precinct didn't really have a standing account, but they probably should have. The lieutenant didn't know who had thought to put a Dunkin' next door to a police precinct, but whoever it was was a genius. The lieutenant was glad they did. It was an old joke, but truth was, cops had to have their caffeine and sugar to maintain energy during a long shift. Coffee and donuts— the two most important food groups for cops everywhere.

Fortunately, it was a slow day and all of the detectives were happy to have something to divert attention from paperwork, especially with Thanksgiving less than ten days away. Many were already thinking about roast turkey, baked ham, and stuffing. Not given exactly to indolence, but looking for anything to entertain them, but at the same time, not too taxing. Trying to hurry the special day along.

* * *

About thirty detectives entered, with all of the sounds, moaning, sideways glances, and complaints one would expect. Not because they minded the interruption, but because they thought that's what was expected of them. Once seated, the lieutenant said dourly, "Detective Rossi needs our assistance. So, I'll turn the floor over to him." The bored looking assemblage and the medium-sized briefing room smelled of stale coffee, inexpensive aftershave, subtle perfume, unfiltered cigarettes, and cheap hair tonic.

Rossi stepped to the desktop walnut-colored wooden lectern casually placed on a six-foot-long cheap wood laminate folding table, to hoots, catcalls, and wolf whistles of male and female detectives of different races. Most detectives are surprisingly risible.

At least more so than one might think.

"Friends, Romans, Countrymen," he said, playing along, hands raised like a deified Caesar speaking to the throngs in the plaza, glanced at his Seiko dive watch, and checked the time to make sure he didn't get verbose and run too long. "I've gotten word that the Ghost is somebody famous. My question to you geniuses is: What could that mean?"

"A TV star? Or A Jet?" Speaking up first, said a young detective sheepishly.

"Yeah, remember? Flash Gordon's secret identity was the quarterback of the Jets," said a senior detective who knew more trivia than anyone else in the department. "A serial killer could be doing the same thing. Hiding as somebody famous in front of our faces."

The young detective, truly befuddled, and showing his youth, asked, "Who's Flash Gordon?"

The senior trivia expert just shook his head plaintively, feeling genuinely sorry for the young man.

"A Jet? Their own mamas don't even think those bums are famous," said another.

The hoots began again.

"Let's stay on track," said Rossi, his near-terminal case of moral outrage on display for everyone to see, as he mimed banging his head in frustration against the top of the lectern, as it shifted unevenly on the table. An act he considered a display of great forbearance. After pausing to take a large gulp of tepid coffee from his dark blue ceramic mug adorned with the official NYPD shield logo, he continued, "Come on now. Help me out here. Who else?"

"Musicians."

"Soap stars. This is New York, you know."

"Politicians."

In response to that, someone said, "We're up shit-creek if that's it."

"Everybody on YouTube," said a still wet behind the ears detective, speaking of that which was his entire world.

"Well, hell, that's everybody in the goddamn city," said an aged, jaded detective who was trying to hold on until retirement. Just trying to make it across the finish line. It would suck to screw it up at this point.

After a few minutes more of the detectives throwing shit at the wall and some of it even sticking, Rossi said, sarcastically, "Thank you ladies...and gentlemen. You've given me more shit to consider. Like I didn't have enough already. I appreciate it. Really. Thanks a lot."

"You can count on us," said a bored vacuous voice from the rear.

Proud of himself for not letting them hector him into ending before he was done, Rossi cleared his throat and said, "Thank you all for your ideas."

"You killed it, Rossi," said a smartass disembodied voice, not supportively. "No pun intended."

Then, turning to Park for support and another set of ears, Rossi said, "Well, that wasn't worth a shit."

"I'm not sure, Sal. It gave me some new things to think about."

"Maybe so. But we need something more substantial to go on; something solid to work with right now.

"I hear you, partner."

Rossi, too, was ready for Thanksgiving, and hoped with all his heart that maybe, just maybe, the Unholy Ghost might take a holiday break. But if he were able to augur through his years of experience, it would be just that — hope. Because he'd typically found that psychopaths weren't moved by such prosaic thoughts. But it was always possible the killer might have family he needed to visit which could fetter his intent. Even psychopaths had loved ones. Besides, one could always hope. Indeed, the season of hope was just about here. Even so, he had a premonitory feeling that hope was all it would be.

Chapter Twenty-Four
"Is it sharp?"

Gordon awoke and decided he simply had to go see the most famous department store windows in the city at Christmas time. He thought he remembered seeing them before, but couldn't be sure. Although there were others, everybody knew the festive decorations at Bloomingdale's, Tiffany's, and Bergdorf Goodman's were must-sees, and convenient for walking since they were all within two or three blocks of each other on Fifth Avenue. The Bergdorf store famous for being on the site of the original Cornelius Vanderbilt II mansion, built in 1883. Tiffany's celebrated for being immortalized in the Audrey Hepburn vehicle *Breakfast At Tiffany's* and the famous tune *Moon River* from the same film by the inimitable American crooner, the late Andy Williams.

The three blocks of Fifth Avenue that encompassed the famous shopping sites were enveloped with travelers from all fifty states and many countries during the expansive New York City Christmas season, known throughout the world as New York's most wonderful time of the year; it started early, right after Halloween, with the erecting of the huge cheerfully lighted tree at Rockefeller Center overlooking the wintry ice-skating rink and The Empire State Building bathed in red and green light.

Cars, limousines, and cabs honking, Gordon exited the taxi he'd taken from the Upper West Side and stepped onto the sidewalk into the crisp morning air. He wore expensive brown leather driving gloves to ward off the cold. They and the wool muffler looped around his neck were the only additions he donned to fight the chill.

Breakfast at Tiffany's sounded like a good idea and, although he somehow knew they now had a café in the store for that very purpose, like Holly Golightly in the movie, he bought a pastry and a cuppa from a sidewalk vendor and began his leisurely morning by gazing at the multi-carat diamond engagement rings in the capacious windows at the world's most famous jewelry store.

He didn't know if he would ever have need for one; even if he did and, if he would have the means to purchase one, he could still enjoy the seasonal scene. A few minutes later, done with the tasty red fruit danish, and after licking off the leftover cherry filling, he insouciantly made his jump shot by tossing the wax paper wrapper in a wastebasket and began the short but brisk stroll to Bergdorf Goodman's.

With Christmas nearing, the more he felt like young Holden Caufield in the famous novel *Catcher In The Rye* by the great J.D. Salinger.

Everyone had heard of Bergdorf Goodman's. Four floors of the classiest and most expensive clothes that the city had to offer, and that was no small feat. Their Christmas decorations were as classy as one would expect. Gordon wasn't the only one participating in the no-cost Christmas window shopping on the beautiful, crisp November morning — maybe the only activity in the city that didn't have an expense associated with it — however, as the sidewalk had a thick red velvet rope dividing it for the busy season, one had to follow the line in the right direction, which this year, was south to north on the wide sidewalk. Santa's diminutive elves were hard at work toiling away on the displays, cobbling toys, hanging garland, and decorating trees.

An extremely attractive woman of near his age, in line afore him, turned and smiled as he couldn't help but staring. Gordon thought attractive women would be his downfall. *If only there weren't so many hot women in the world it's possible that I might be normal. That's what I'm going to choose to believe, at least.* If so, then his situation wouldn't be so abstruse. He took a brief moment away from the hordes on the sidewalk to stare into his soul and saw no one was there. At least no one he recognized, anyway. What he saw was rancor. A manifestation of evil. And the sunny day grew dark.

A short visit at BG's, as the locals christened it, since New Yorkers were always in a hurry and couldn't take the time needed to say the whole name, and he was seeking entertainment, at least to him, of a life affirming but depraved sort.

A cab ride to the northernmost reaches of Manhattan to Fort Tryon Park and the internationally famed Cloisters Museum would hopefully for him fill his sick needs. The less famous northern park also designed by Frederick Law Olmstead, he of Central Park fame. Gordon couldn't believe he'd only heard about the museum famous for its collection of medieval and Byzantine art but as far as he could remember, he'd never visited it.

Gordon climbed out of the taxi at the 82nd Street main entrance into the Great Hall where he picked up a floor plan map and description of exhibits. One somber-faced elderly woman, of the type who work only at museums or other tourist spots in the city requiring little drive or ambition, wore a despondent gray cardigan sweater for warmth in the huge chilly abbey. Gordon bought an admittance ticket from her.

Like many old women, she wore too much perfume; and not a pleasant one. Smelled like something from the middle of the last century. Shalimar or Chanel No. 5. Her demeanor and dress made her a perfect first contact for the aged monastery, it filled with ancient relics of which she was an equal peer. Gordon thought he might have to come back on his way out and pick up an inexpensive keepsake as a reminder of his visit, that is if he weren't in too big of a hurry to escape, *and* if he could stand the scent of her perfume again. Recognizing that he didn't have a particularly strong stomach, that might just be more than he could take.

He turned right out of the museum store into the silent Great Hall and, except for his own, lacking even the hollow echo of light footsteps on the polished dark tile or hushed voices extolling praise or delight over some particularly moving artifact. Although lighting was illuminated, the Hall remained somber.

Out of range of the greeter's perfume, the moldy smell of ancient stone walls was overpowered by the scent of cleaners and scrubs and the paint they were using for a remodeling job. Most fortunate for Gordon if the day worked out as he hoped, since the museum's strategically placed security cameras hadn't been returned to their assigned duty. He passed through the Hall, reaching a corridor that traversed through the center of ten small display rooms, five to a side, toward the Greek and Roman Art Gallery. It filled with statuary and busts carved in marble and bronze of generals, Caesars, and philosophers. After a half hour spent in the first gallery and twenty more to go along with over a hundred additional rooms in the massive museum, Gordon knew that if he had any hope at all of getting no more than a cursory glance at everything, he realized he would need to step up his pace, and took a staircase downward from the main level to the first.

There, the many mirific artifacts from all the stretches of Europe; art, tapestries, and reliquaries, satisfied and piqued the curiosities of all who entered. The internationally renowned yet graphically violent Unicorn Tapestries depicting a bloody hunt of the mythical beast, created by an unknown artist five hundred years ago in Western Europe, were the main draw of the lower level and led people into the following room with various artifacts from different environs of Europe.

Emerging through the stairwell's strident metal door, he began his journey through multiple centuries of European art and history that he hoped to traverse in a mere couple of hours, unless he were delayed by any unexpected but nevertheless welcome opportunities.

The stairwell door opened into Gallery 16 with its collection of medieval paintings and small sculptures from Spain and Eastern Europe. Though not from the medieval era, a collection of Picassos from the renowned Spaniard were housed there as well. Gordon couldn't understand the why of it, but he nevertheless thought of Picasso as a personal favorite artist.

Quieter there, since a huge oriental rug, threadbare from decades of weary tourists' shuffling footsteps, covered most of the unforgiving hard tile floor, the centuries old heavy wool fabric softening footfalls and muffling voices. The antediluvian stone of the lower level smelled even more ancient and damper than that of the main level.

The artifacts gently commanded quiet respect, and so he was, quietly respectful. The vast collection asked the same questions of everyone. Why are you here? For what and from where did you come? Gordon was there to honor them, but if he were honest with them, and himself, it was also to in turn nefariously honor himself. For his own heinous satisfaction.

Through Gallery 16, a display of narwhal tusks in the following space beckoned. Gordon could recall reading in *The Daily News*, how an intruder had murdered a museum curator who was working late one night by running him through with the nearly ten-foot-long tusk from the sea animal many thought of as legend or fairytale. Would if only he had the opportunity. He gazed longingly and wishfully at the tooths of a living fable that many thought of as the unicorn of the sea and just as unbelievable. The scientific name for narwhal, Monodon monoceros, meant one tooth, one horn.

"Mr. Cole...Grayson Cole?" A male voice broke the dreadful quiet.

"Excuse me?" said Gordon hesitatingly, and unsure if it was he to whom the stranger was speaking since he was the only other one in the room. It was the second time he'd been referred to by that name recently, but it didn't enable him to understand it any more.

"You're Grayson Cole, aren't you? I met you at your book signing at the Barnes & Noble on the Upper West Side about three weeks ago."

"I'm sorry. You must be mistaken." *Book signing? What the hell is he talking about?*

"It's okay. I just thought you'd remember me since you signed three books for me, for family, you know. But I guess when you're an important author you can't remember the little people," he said sourly.

"No, no, it's not that. Just too much rye, or small batch bourbon. Please forgive me for not remembering." *I still have no idea what he's talking about.*

"No problem. We're good. I'm James, by the way."

Gordon lifted a narwhal tusk the color of aged bone from the ceramic Japanese umbrella stand where it was displayed with its brethren. Caressed the knurls sensuously and fingered the point. No skueomorphs, these. They were the real thing, the ivory tooth from the unicorn of the sea.

Without looking in his direction or turning to face him, he said, "Don't worry about it. I'm Grayson. Pleased to meet you." *I might as well play along.*

"I've always wondered about those. Is it sharp?" James asked, watching Gordon finger the tip.

"You're going to have to tell me," hissed Gordon spinning around, a demonic snarl suddenly morphing on his face, as he lowered the tapered staff to waist high and ran it through James' torso, center mass, piercing the solar plexus. *The pain must be exquisite.*

Six feet away, the knurled tusk exiting his back, James' body enervated as its soul left its earthly reliquary in a torrent of hot anguished blood.

"I'm guessing it was pretty sharp," said Gordon, softly, sarcastically. He put his foot on James' chest and pressed his full weight onto the man and aided by the twists in the beautiful staff of ivory, harshly pulled the artistic tusk free, to a loud sucking sound. He glanced around to make sure he was alone still — fortunately for him it was Monday, the slowest day of the week at the museum — before withdrawing to the nearest exit which led him out through a cloistered garden, in an attempt to avoid seeing anyone, or even worse, being seen by anyone.

He made his way as quickly as he could toward Broadway to the east before feeling comfortable enough to hail a taxi. Then walked briskly a block or two south before attempting to wave one down, when he found himself in front of a shop that sold New York City trinkets and bibelots. Two classic tunes by the Beatles, *Come Together* followed by *Blackbird*, playing loudly from a cheap Eighties-era stereo, emerged through the open double glass doors, and although Gordon thought they were cool songs, he didn't recognize them, a blatant indication to anyone else of his recent creation, for lack of a better word, deepening the conundrum enveloping the enigma that was his personal dichotomy.

Gordon stepped through the open door, locating the Middle Eastern shopkeeper, who was restocking the I Love New York section, and asked him if he knew who the last two songs were by. The middle-aged man gaped open-mouthed as if Gordon most certainly had to be certifiably insane, maybe even an escapee of the Bellevue Psychiatric Hospital way downtown on First Avenue, or if it were still in existence, The New York Lunatic Hospital for The Criminally Insane on the then called Blackwell's Island before its name was changed to Roosevelt Island, but it hadn't been in operation since closing in 1894 back when Theodore Roosevelt was still the NYPD Police Commissioner, and he said, "Hello? The Beatles?"

Gordon could see the stunned look on the man's face and hear the surprise in his voice, so, trying to cover for his lack of knowledge, said, "I'm not really into music that much. Are they new?"

That didn't help his perception so much as hurt it, though, and the man asked somewhat more than hesitantly, "Sir, are you okay? Can I call someone for you?"

Deciding in retrospect that his question had been a mistake, Gordon said, "I'll be fine," and departed. Himself confused by what he thought was the man's overreaction to a simple question of little import. Gordon waved down a yellow taxi, this one a small Toyota SUV, and after returning to the psychological warmth of the townhouse he thought of as his home, he decided to Google The Beatles on the iPad he hardly ever used to see if he could find out anything about them. He hoped they weren't just an innocuous culturally insignificant band with little information available.

Good thing that he'd noticed a billboard in Times Square promoting Google and asked a homeless beggar what it was. The dirty, cold man was surprised that a professionally dressed, fairly youngish man didn't know about Google, but he was kind enough to explain it to him and Gordon bought him a venti latté at the nearest Starbucks to thank him for his time and the helpful information.

After setting a blaze in the big fireplace, Gordon sat down in his huge leather chair letting the warmth envelop him. With the iPad in his lap and, after figuring out how to use the program, he found out that The

Beatles were considered by many to be among the most, if not *the* most, influential musicians of all time and virtually all bands to follow thought the four mop-top Liverpudlians had been as important as Elvis.

What is a mop-top Liverpudlian? And this Elvis, who the hell was he? And what the hell kind of name is Elvis, anyway?

The oddest macabre tidbit of all, however, was that the acknowledged leader of the band, a long-haired young man named John Lennon, had been murdered, shot to death, a couple of weeks before Christmas, 1980, at the entrance to the superstar's apartment at the world-famous Dakota, the location now believed to be haunted, and it was no more than three blocks from where Gordon lived. He guessed rightly that that caused quite a stir, not just on the Upper West Side, or even in New York, but if these Beatles were that big, the world over.

Gordon swiped through the information. Shot in the back four times. By a young man named Mark David Chapman who had been raised in Decatur, Georgia. Now sixty-seven, still in prison. Constantly denied parole. Was an unemployed security guard who sat down and read *The Catcher In The Rye*, a world famous novel by J.D. Salinger, set in New York City at Christmas time, and waited for police to come and arrest him. He was a born-again Christian. Pled guilty. Killed Lennon because of his un-Christian lifestyle, not out of any hostility toward the superstar.

Sitting around waiting on the police after just one kill? That was just stupid. What kind of a nut does that?

But after his mentally and physically exhausting encounter at The Cloisters, Gordon's time spent reading by the warm fire made him drowsy and soon he was asleep, swaddled comfortably in the soft leather of the old chair.

Chapter Twenty-Five

"Do we have an ID?"

"Dammit," yelled the lieutenant from his office. "Rossi! Front and center. On the double."

"Sir?" Rossi halted in front of his desk, his shadow Park fast on his heels, doing his best to keep up, trying not to bump into him after the sudden stop.

"The Unholy Ghost."

"Fuck."

"Couldn't have said it better myself," Lou said, running his big hands over his tired face.

"Where? How?"

"The Cloisters. Get your asses in gear forthwith. You don't want to know how. You'll find out soon enough."

Asses in gear and forthwith. Rossi knew that that meant double double-fast. So much for that asshole slowing down for the holidays, he thought. He'd come to think of the suspect as male because most serial killers are and because he usually uses a blade of some sort. Or at least a sharp piercing weapon as a priapic substitute. Most female serial killers got straight down to business with a gun.

Rossi raced up West Side Highway as fast as the aging but well-maintained V-8 would take them. Even setting the portable blue bubble light in the dash and giving the siren a short burst when needed to warn citizens to get their asses the hell out of the way.

Past the site of the late 1800s era Charles Schwab mansion, he transitioned to the Henry Hudson Parkway before taking the single lane Cloisters Drive exit to the famous museum's main entrance. A marked patrol car and matching crime scene van were already parked outside the lower-level front door, nearest one to the park and responsible for its protection, probably from the 34th precinct.

Rossi and Park flashed their shields at a still wet-behind-the-ears uni guarding the door, charged with denying entrance to anyone who wasn't a LEO, and right now that was mostly tourists from out of town.

The Cloisters seemed to be a little more than somewhat off the literal map for most New Yorkers.

It had been years, but when they were little Rossi had brought his kids to The Cloisters because he thought history was important. Even back then they seemed to be drawn to it. He guessed they just liked old shit. The smell and the scene returned him to those days; he'd have to work hard not to let this scene ruin that happy family memory.

Detective Park just thought it old. He didn't like the smell. His mom had always said he got her sensitive nose. If it was true, he didn't like her for that.

Another uni, this one a little older than the one at the door, escorted them to the lower level to what had been a crime of opportunity.

"I'm sure you've seen bad scenes before, detectives, but youse oughta prepare yourselves."

Although the manner of death was surprising even for the Ghost, the uni had not seen any of his previous work with which he could compare it. This scene didn't measure up to the worst this invisible perp had already done. Not nearly as gory as past scenes, certainly not like the headless body hanging from a wash line in the severe moonlight, but that was most likely due to the fact that it happened in a public place with little privacy and so he didn't have the time needed to wreak his usual havoc. What the scene lacked in gore however was more than made up for in presentation, positioning the large bloody tusk artistically across the gaping wound in the victim's torso.

After glancing around sickly, Rossi said, "Murder by narwhal; not one of his worst but nonetheless done with flair."

Although the scene wasn't that bad, Rossi would never get used to it, especially how bad the smell could be. He hoped Park wouldn't either, but it was too early to tell. Keeping your humanity was what made the job difficult, but it was also what made it bearable. So you could still live with yourself.

Park gulped audibly and began convulsive dry heaves.

"Go get some water, detective," said Rossi, not unkindly.

Park really would have liked to put on a brave face, but couldn't. "Thank you, sir," he mumbled and left hastily, still convulsing as he went.

"Do we have an ID?" Rossi asked the senior officer on scene.

Looking at his driver's license, he read, "James Elmore Rankin. From New Rochelle. Probably just wrong place wrong time."

"No kidding," said Rossi. "Running into the Unholy Ghost will fuck up anybody's day."

"You think that's who did this?"

Rossi nodded emphatically. "Nobody but."

"That sucks," he said, looking at his feet so he didn't have to look at the victim.

"I'll say. I've wasted the last fifteen months of my life chasing that son of a bitch's sorry ass."

Rossi did his best to keep his emotions under control. Getting vexed wouldn't do any good. Might hurt the investigation if he got too emotional, in fact. Harm his interpretation of the evidence, or lack of, or cause him to miss something. With little to be gathered from his standpoint, Rossi turned the crime scene crew loose. Three mature veterans worked efficiently, each on different tasks, with no backtracking or repetitious work.

After awhile and talking to himself and Rossi as he worked, the team lead, with a strained look on his pulpy red face, said, "No friction ridges on the tusk. This chilly weather, probably was wearing gloves. Even if the attack wasn't planned. What I'm saying is," explaining like he was talking to a kid, "my guess is it was likely a crime of opportunity. Only thing we can hang our hats on is for there to be two blood types. If so, we run DNA, hope our guy's in the system."

The National Crime Database spanned the country and every law enforcement agency. If he was in there they'd find him. If. But he hadn't showed yet in fifteen months.

"Shit," said Rossi, "This guy is too good. We won't find anything."

* * *

Rossi and Park returned to headquarters; both wearing hangdog looks.

"And?" said the lieutenant.

"And fuckin' what?" asked Rossi.

"Was it *our* son of a bitch?"

"What do you think?"

"From the sadsack looks on your faces, I'd say it was."

"Then you'd be right," Rossi said glumly and with his usual hint of attitude.

* * *

Feeling older than his years, Rossi groaned as he dropped into his squeaky desk chair, then decided to call Bookworm. "We got another vic. What's up with you guys?"

"Shit. He's determined to fuck up the holidays for the whole city."

"Sure looks like it. Anything happening on your end?"

"After talking to Spike and the gang, Reefer's still pounding the pavement. Literally. He says he's going to stay in the street, whithersoever, hounding contacts 'til he finds out who the son of a bitch is. I've never seen Reefer this pissed off...or motivated." Bookworm grinned, pleased with himself for using the fancy word. He hoped Rossi appreciated it.

"Great word, Book. Whithersoever. Your nickname is well-deserved. I for one am glad to hear he's out there. We can use the help. Maybe he can get around to where almost forty thousand New York City police officers in the world's biggest and best police force, can't get to." The forty thousand doubling their number in 1980. The main reason The Naked City was safer than ever. Whether he truly believed one young man with no investigative experience could really help was doubtful, but his intent was to sound hopeful to Book.

Bookworm didn't respond, only hoping his main man wasn't on a fool's errand. Even if he were, Bookworm was proud of him. Like a father of a son or perhaps more like an older brother of a younger following in his huge unfillable footsteps.

Chapter Twenty-Six
"Happy Holidays"

An annual holiday tradition for the Rossi family was dinner at the world-famous Plaza Hotel. This year, the family dinner was held a little over a week before Thanksgiving. Salvatoré and Ella got there early and waited for the rest of the family to arrive in the large lobby of the magnificent hotel popular for being known as the setting of *Home Alone 2: Lost In New York*. The family, children, their spouses and, most importantly, the grandkids, began to arrive in the mid-twentieth century high-ceilinged lobby. Salvatoré the Younger spotted Pop Pop and Nonna and came running, throwing his arms around his grandparents. A toddler in a stroller remembered Salvatoré, and the baby seemed to recognize his voice. Salvatoré the Elder was sure they would soon be BFFs.

Salvatoré knew the evening would cost him several hundred dollars, probably more than a grand, but wasn't that what a grandfather was for? Indeed, wasn't that his responsibility? What else was a grandfather good for, anyway? Anything for the grands.

"Happy Holidays" rang out as everyone arrived. They had just come from the Museum of Natural History a short walk away on the lower west side of the park. They usually did when they met there. Young Sal liked the gigantic dinosaur skeleton, more popular than ever due to it coming alive in the Ben Stiller movie *Night at the Museum*. Rossi knew their path took them past the New York City DEA offices in Columbus Circle, just down the block.

"Happy Holidays, Mom and Dad."

"Happy Holidays, Pop-Pop."

"Happy Holidays, Nonna."

"I sure am hungry," said Sal, III.

"What do you want?" asked his namesake grandfather.

"A *Home Alone* banana split," he said, his cherubic round face lighting up. He was referring to the eighteen-dollar treat the hotel created reminiscent of the one Macaulay Culkin ate while lying in bed in the movie of the same name.

"Maybe for dessert," was the answer Sal the Elder gave him, same as previous times. He'd only asked because it was a game they played.

The elder knew what his grandson would say even before he asked. A family tradition. Always the same when they came here: The Banana Split!

They entered the Palm Court, the hotel's iconic elegant dining room, to be led to their large, white cloth-covered reserved table. Actually three pushed together to accommodate their number. The hotel purchased flowers in bulk from a local floral wholesaler who had them flown in from around the world on a daily basis thus allowing some of those fresh-cut flowers — it's always spring somewhere — to now adorn the center of their table. The server passed around menus to them all. Rossi asked for six bottles of a moderately priced red wine, slightly chilled, as he insisted all wine should be, agreeing with the best sommeliers. Of course, nothing at The Plaza was moderately priced.

A moment later, another server, a consummate professional Rossi remembered from previous visits, unbouchoned the first bottle with a loud pop as the cork released and, with the Italian in his soul rearing its head, Rossi said, "My favorite sound in the world except for the sweet resonance of a grandchild's delighted laugh." The entire family loved it because, after all, they knew that under the gruff, crusty exterior what a kind-hearted soul he really was.

The longtime employee poured Sal a taste to see if it met with his approval. Examining the pour under the lights, Sal said, "Don't mind if I do." A tired *shibboleth*, but one he enjoyed using, nonetheless.

Then, all the while sipping from long-stemmed glasses of Italy's favorite white wine — a charming Pinot Grigio Salvatoré had requested — they perused the menus before placing food orders.

French onion soup was ordered by the adults to start and Salvatoré ordered pan-seared diver scallops and East Coast raw-oyster appetizers for everyone to share. Two sirloin steaks, apple-brined Cornish hen, a prime veal chop, the two-pound lobster, and the Dover sole were ordered, each getting their favorites. Sal ordered big bowls of glazed seasonal vegetables, mushroom ragout, and butter whipped potatoes, to be served family-style from which everyone could choose their sides.

Young Sal chose a hot dog with French fries and mac and cheese from the children's menu, known as the Eloise menu, so named because of the popular with generations of kids, Eloise children's books about the little girl who lives at The Plaza, by Kay Thompson.

Everyone dined in style, having looked forward to it and begun talking about it since August before the seasonally hot weather of summer had taken its leave.

Before the dishes arrived Rossi blessed the sumptuous meal with a silent prayer that ironically, he asked that it not be interrupted by The Unholy Ghost. Sal made the sign of the cross and recited the accompanying words and felt uneasy saying Holy Ghost in the same breath. He looked around at his family. This was the accomplishment of his life he most cherished. A wife he still loved, and even liked, lo these many years. She had proven many times over that his instincts about how she would be as a wife had been good almost thirty-five years before. Children that were capable, productive adults with happy marriages and beautiful grandchildren that he adored.

Yes, this was it. Even if he caught the Unholy Ghost, he would never be this proud.

Two and a half hours later, and barely able to move after stuffing themselves, they walked through The Plaza lobby, disappointed not to bump into the former owner of the famous hotel, Donald Trump, or Macauley Culkin himself, he the godfather of Michael Jackson's kids. If indeed they had, it would have topped off a perfectly jocund evening. Hugs and kisses were exchanged all around, and see-you-Thanksgivings, too, now just a little over a week away.

Standing on the aging, fading, red-carpeted steps in the even chillier than normal weather for a late November night, the water in the Pulitzer Fountain, named for the famous newspaperman who donated the money to build it and the centerpiece of The Grand Army Plaza in the center of the broad boulevard, appeared frigid and ready to freeze solid.

Chapter Twenty-Seven
"Mind if I sit down?"

Grayson woke late, during the eleven o'clock news. He didn't understand how he had slept so deeply yet dreamed of narwhals and unicorns. He decided it must have had something to do with the animals' tusks. And the glass of wine he'd had. Always the wine. Unless it was the rye. Creating in his mind's eye a creature existent and one of fable. But at least he wasn't using it for gargling…yet.

Then he went back to sleep and slept through the night.

* * *

Gordon didn't sleep through the night as he got up just long enough to pee…twice. Gordon of the distorted reality when awake. Grayson of the distorted reality when asleep. So they both went back to sleep, each unaware of the other, but unwittingly cooperating to sleep. Each willing reality to sleep with them. But reality wasn't usually all that cooperative. Reality tended to be an asshole of biblical proportions. Much like when the sea turned to blood, or global earthquakes occurred, or even the hundred-pound hailstones. Getting pounded by one of those would mess up one's day, no doubt about it.

* * *

Grayson needed exercise after a long night's sleep and decided a brisk walk on the new Manhattan High Line would be a great place to get it.

The High Line was a walkway created on the now-defunct bed of an almost one-and-a-half-mile spur of the New York Central Railroad on the Midtown westside and elevated thirty feet off the ground. Dismantled in the '60s, that was the last time anyone in New York had heard the loneliest sound in the world: the sound of a train's horn at four o'clock in the morning. The High Line was popular with locals and tourists for spectacular views of the city while getting fresh air and exercise. Though some might undeniably question New Yorkers' version of fresh air.

Grayson caught a cab to the High Line 34th street entrance to begin his walk, run, jog.

* * *

The High Line was thick with colorful seasonal flowers in garden areas spaced between occasional sections of trees heavily shading the walkways only offering brief glimpses of nearby tall buildings, but also giving protection from prying eyes of office workers from windowed and mini-blinded aeries. Important, at least, for those who weren't using the High Line for exercise during lunch breaks.

Benches situated under trees offered brief respites from the runs and diversions from his physical and mental exertion. The nervous sun did nothing to warm the afternoon. Gordon picked a bench in a nice shady spot in a manmade garden and began slicing an apple with a traditional red Swiss Army Knife. He looked up when a shadow was cast over the apple he carved.

"Do you mind if I sit down?" asked a confident young woman who nevertheless wished she were prettier.

"Not at all," said Gordon with all the charm he could muster, his face scrunched up from the bright sun blinding him as he gazed upward.

She sat and said, "Thank you. Lovely day."

"Isn't it? Even with the cold," Gordon agreed.

"Yeah, but this sun is certainly pleasant."

"But this is New York. Stick around awhile. It will change. I'm Gordon, by the way."

"Don't say that. It might be snowing tomorrow. I'm Neely."

Then, suddenly remembering his manners, Gordon said, "Pleased to make your acquaintance, Neely. Please pardon my behavior; my sainted mother would be horrified. Would you like a slice of apple?" *Do I even have a mother? I amuse myself sometimes.*

"No, thank you. I have a sandwich here for my lunch," she said, digging in the large bag that Gordon thought was only a purse but was apparently a tote, or a carryall, a place of safekeeping for all of her treasures.

"I usually take my lunch here. It's my favorite spot on The Line," as she called it, being a regular. "I work in that building right there," she said pointing to a nearby mid-sized, red brick, mid-century building. "Tenth floor. You can see my office right through that window. Well, not an office so much as a cubicle, to tell the truth. But it's home," she said shrugging *c'est la vie.*

Gordon and Neely made small talk for the better part of an hour. Then she simply had to be getting back to work. She returned half of her sandwich to her bag and when she looked back to Gordon, he wielded the small red Swiss Army knife, the corkscrew protruding, like a thrusting weapon, and then he did, thrust it. Burying it and twisting it jaggedly into the hollow of her throat. Gordon had to jump out of the way to dodge the blood that gushed as she gurgled and rasped from the wetness and dearth of air. She had not even had time to register surprise. Gordon left the corkscrew there, buried up to its red handle, since he was quite sure no law enforcement agency had a record of his fingerprints, even though it was kind of risky.

Oh well, I didn't plan this one.

She died quickly, in a gasping, gurgling, vain attempt to breathe. He gently lay her on the bench, and straightened her heavy coat around her in an ill-fated attempt to keep her warm. He thought that was how she would like it. Providing her comfort against the afternoon's chill.

Instead of continuing his walk on the concrete High Line, unseen by anyone, energy renewed by the pleasant diversion, Gordon made his way through the tangled jungle of a garden to exit into an almost-deserted park area. Once again, killing made him feel more than alive, eudaemonic even. He felt confident that some ancient philosopher, Greek, British, Chinese, or someone, somewhere, had made manifest that which he was sure was an undeniable connection between life and death.

Still on a high from his surprisingly successful afternoon, since it wasn't his plan when he left, Gordon arrived home.

* * *

Rossi and Park were about to call it a day and were saying their goodbyes to the rest of the detectives and thanking them again for their ideas about what famous could mean.

Before they could leave, though, the lieutenant said, "Not so fast. You need to get over to the High Line, 34th street entrance.

Rossi was afraid to ask, but he knew the answer, though. "Our asshole?"

"Looks like it. Swiss Army knife buried in a woman's throat on a park bench."

"That certainly isn't salutary."

"I hear you. Fucked up our day. Now we got to put in some

overtime."

The lieutenant really didn't mean to sound like an insensitive jerk. It was just that the Unholy Ghost was getting to everybody and not everyone expressed it well. Everybody understood that.

* * *

The crime scene was what they expected, as gruesome as the others. And like others, leaving the weapon. Like he was teasing the police.

The chief investigator said, "We got prints."

Rossi was head down, examining the garden's plants where the killer had made his exit, but snapped upright at that. "Usable?" he said, hopefully.

"Yep. Enough. We just have to pray our man's in the system."

"I guarantee you he's not," said Rossi. "We couldn't get that lucky."

"We'll see."

The investigator was of a mind that all criminals are stupid or they wouldn't be criminals, and they were just waiting for the opportunity to screw up. Rossi wished that that were true but too many years on Gotham's violent front line had taught him that you couldn't count on it. The Unholy Ghost seemed particularly clever. That trait being how he'd been able to elude law enforcement for the better part of a year and a half.

After taking pictures of the scene and, so as not to disturb the fingerprints in blood, the begloved investigator did not remove the weapon from the latest victim's raggedly wounded throat, waiting instead for the medical examiner to remove it on the table and bag it for safekeeping with all of her other effects before signing them over to the officer in charge of the evidence locker. The team was careful to protect the weapon when they bagged the body.

Park and Rossi were silent on the drive back to the precinct. There was nothing for them to discuss. The Unholy Ghost was wearing on them both. Park was genuinely wondering if he should make a career change. Truth be told, Rossi would seriously consider putting in his retirement papers if he didn't think it would feel like running. He was tired of this shit and would rather spend his time playing with his beloved grandchildren. He knew they were growing up fast.

Chapter Twenty-Eight
"That's him!"

On the Saturday before the family came over on Turkey Day, Salvatoré volunteered to go to the market for a few last-minute items so Ella could continue preparing for their early Thanksgiving dinner with Book as their sole guest. He was looking forward to Bookworm coming to their home and enjoying a visit — hopefully not just talking about the Unholy Ghost.

When he returned, Ella was busying herself straightening the living room, kitchen, and the dining room, where they would spend the most delicious part of the evening. Earlier she had put up and decorated their green artificial Christmas tree, strung matching garland around the gas fireplace, and been to the nearest Barnes & Noble where she'd bought three hardbacks, stacking them on the antique coffee table in front of the sofa, although Salvatoré referred to it as a wine table since it was rarely used for coffee. Indeed, considering the amount of wine they drank, he thought it a desideratum, and since it was rarely used for coffee. The apartment was abundant with traditional holiday aromas of roast turkey, stuffing, green beans, and mashed and sweet potatoes, and already looked ready for Christmas.

At six o'clock the door buzzer sounded. Rossi hurried across the room to let his friend in. "Book. Come in. Come in. Welcome to our home."

"Thanks, Detective. Happy to be here," he said, handing Sal two sacks, one containing two bottles of Hampton Water French Rosé, owned and made by rock icon Jon "Bon Jovi" Bongiovi and Jesse, his second child and first son, the other filled with the famous Black and White cookies.

"Wine and cookies. You outdid yourself. By the way, we're not working tonight. Call me Sal."

"Sal it is."

Sal called to the kitchen. "Ella, come meet Bookworm…er…John Campbell. Say hello to our guest errant of the delightful wine and the classic cookies."

The old kitchen was modest, designed for someone with far fewer culinary skills than Ella and who didn't cook as often or for as large a family. But she'd long ago adapted to its limitations.

Ella entered drying her hands on a dish towel, and said, "Pleased to meet you, John."

"Please, call me Bookworm. My grandmother is the only one who still calls me John."

"All right then, Bookworm."

She took the wine sack and looked inside. "Oh, my goodness. We've been meaning to try this. Thank you so much."

Rossi said, "Why don't we have a glass before dinner and watch some football."

"I'm in," said Book.

Rossi got three glasses from an antique China cabinet handed down from Italy and poured them each a modest amount to get started, only because the night was young. After a small toast all around, Ella returned to the kitchen to put finishing touches on the dinner. Rossi turned to the Alabama-Florida game where both teams were unenthusiastically playing out their schedules waiting for their respective bowl games. But hey, it was football. Stretching from his chair to where Bookworm sat on the sofa, Rossi said, "To preprandial."

Book shrugged and said, "You got me on that one."

"Preprandial — before dinner."

"All right. I'll drink to that," said Bookworm.

Rossi said, "Always remember the popular Italian wish, *dolce far niente*. It's sweet doing nothing."

They touched glasses and, after a conservative sip, Bookworm set down his glass and picked up the top book from the stack Ella had placed on the table. *Rapacious* was the newest by author Grayson Cole. Book didn't like the way the tome smelled; it smelled new. He liked the aroma of old books; it was life affirming. But even old books started out as new ones. The Cole book was sitting on top of the latest offerings by John Connolly and Ace Atkins' newest Spenser novel who, in agreement with the late author's estate and publisher, was continuing the popular series begun by the great Robert B. Parker.

"I haven't read anything by Grayson Cole. What do you think of him?" Book said, looking at the cover art.

"I haven't read him yet, either. You'll have to ask Ella."

Bookworm flipped the book over to read the synopsis on the rear jacket cover, then turned whiter than pale. Startled and almost shouting, he said, "That's him! That's him!" Then all but threw the book back on the table.

"That's who?" said, Rossi.

Pointing at the picture of Grayson Cole, he said, "Gordon, the dude at the bar with Hannah right before she was murdered."

"Get the fuck out of here," Rossi whispered.

"His hair was a little longer; and he had a weekend stubble and he wasn't wearing professional makeup like he is here, but that's him. I swear. As God is my witness," Book said holding up one hand in an oath and the other flat against his heart.

"Spike said word was he was famous."

"God dammit. That's him. I swear," Book said, hand still raised.

Rossi reached for the book excitedly and studied it a moment. "Okay, sorry to interrupt our dinner, but I'm calling Lou right now. I'm sure the boring son of a bitch isn't doing anything on Saturday night but sleeping. Get him to run down an address. We'll send some unis over there to sit on his sorry ass, keep any eye on him, make sure he doesn't do anything he shouldn't. But even though we have your ID of him, fingerprints matching the ones on the Swiss Army Knife would seal it. But how do we get them? I'm just thinking out loud, by the way; I don't expect an answer."

"Can't somebody follow him if he goes anywhere and get his fingerprints somehow? Undercover guys don't usually look very bright, but surely they can do that?"

"Our undercovers are good. One looks like he could play linebacker for the Jets. The other looks like Al Pacino when he played Serpico in the movie. Which means he looks like Serpico. But let me get Lou to do his part first, secure an addy, and get the unis over there forthwith to make sure he's locked down. We'll figure out the rest."

"Sounds good. It appears we're working now, so I'm back to calling you by your first name...Detective," Bookworm said with a chuckle. "But first, I got a question. Did you know him?"

"Know who?" he said, punching the buttons on his phone to call the lieutenant.

"Serpico."

Rossi thought Book was serious until he saw the shit-eating grin on his face. After he figured out that Book was just throwing shade, he said, "We're definitely working now, smartass. But I forgot to ask. You don't have anything better to do right now, do you?"

"I'm all yours."

Chapter Twenty-Nine

"From your lips to God's ears"

Using the power of a warrant, the lieutenant got Grayson Cole's address from ConEd and would have a car with two officers at the man's Upper West Side residence within thirty minutes. The lieutenant called Rossi back to let him know.

"We're cooking," Rossi hung up and told Book. "Unis will keep him locked down until we get the undercover guys on site."

"Cool. I should probably let Reefer know what's going on. Since he's been instrumental in all of this. 'Course, it is Saturday night. No telling where he is. This is Reefer I'm talking about, you know. In fact, I hope he'll be able to hear his phone over the music."

"That's fine. What I'm thinking is if we get the undercover guys there Monday morning, we're good. We can switch out unis 'til then."

Bookworm spoke with Reefer who was happy to be in the loop again. "He was glad to hear from me," Bookworm said after hanging up. "And can help out if we need him for anything."

After their unexpectedly exciting yet absolutely delicious evening, Bookworm decided not to stay late and called it a night.

"I'll see you down to the ground level," Rossi told him.

Bookworm knew him well enough to know there was no sense in arguing. On the sidewalk below, the light snow that had begun to fall earlier had now turned heavier and blanketed every surface making the city look like a beautiful swirling snow globe. Typical for Gotham, two hours and you might have six to eight inches. The hush from the shroud of white was overpowering.

It had been a good decision Bookworm made to take the subway since having pre-, mid-, and post-dinner glasses of wine and one last glass of chilled grappa he would have been in no condition to drive.

Not drunk enough to miss his subway stop, though he still wouldn't have wanted to end up in the drunk tank with the boys of the NYPD drunk tank choir singing their inebriated hearts out like The Pogues' *The Fairytale of New York,* ironically about the boys in the NYPD drunk tank choir singing carols on Christmas night, the absolute last place anyone wanted to be during the city's extended Christmas season.

Even with the light pollution from the brightest city on the planet, the brumal poetic sky was reminiscent of Vincent Willem van Gogh's world-famous nocturne *Starry Night*, it hanging a little more than a mile away in New York's MoMA, the Museum of Modern Art, where it had been the centerpiece of the museum's permanent collection for over three-quarters of a century. The icy dark night looked like the Trans-Siberian Orchestra opus *A Mad Russian's Christmas* sounded, maybe the winter artists' most recognized musical composition.

Too bad Rossi and Book were too occupied by evil to fully enjoy the beautiful night with its gentle layer of thick snow beginning to muffle the late-night sounds of the city like nothing else was able to, coupled as it was with angry dark shadows piercing fresh glistening white.

"I think you, my friend, will probably get a special commendation from Hizzoner, the very mayor himself, for this," Rossi said to Bookworm.

"I don't need no fuckin' commendation. I just want to nail the bastard."

"From your lips to God's ears," a favorite saying of Rossi's and one all Italianos were familiar with.

Chapter Thirty

"I'll be back"

Seven o'clock Monday morning, two undercovers arrived at the no-name diner across the street from Grayson Cole's building. Even though the sun was barely up, the linebacker wore sunglasses. Serpico didn't, not solely because the sun wasn't bright enough yet, but also because he didn't think he looked as much like Serpico when wearing shades. The diamond stud earring he wore was chosen because it was exactly the same size and cut as the one Pacino wore in the film. He alternated with the season between a straw bucket hat and a loose- fitting black watch cap for the same reason. He didn't like having a beard — it itched too much — but it completed the Serpico costume. Only three other customers at that early hour on a Monday which, like all restaurants in all cities, was likely its slowest day of the week. Faded posters of NYC sites — The Empire State Building, Statue of Liberty, and Yankee Stadium — in cheap plastic frames decorated tired, beige walls. Probably bought at a nearby New York City souvenir shop years before. A mini jukebox sat on the table of the booth they occupied. From the songs listed, not a banger on it. The music box had probably been there since the '50s. In the front window overlooking the sidewalk, they could keep an eye on both the entry drive to Cole's building, the center courtyard used for parking, and the door to his townhome two doors down.

They had no more than sat when their cellphones vibrated almost simultaneously where they had placed them on the mid-century modern Formica tabletop. Rossi texted them several pictures of Cole downloaded from the Internet, just to be sure they knew what he looked like. They were ready to go, except for coffee. As if she read their minds, an elderly Caucasian woman scurried over with a round glass Bunn carafe, wearing an old-style uniform she'd probably been wearing since she was young.

"I'm guessing you want caffeinated?"

Serpico said, "You're joking, right. Does anybody drink decaf?"

"You'd be surprised," she said, unamused at his attempt at being clever. She'd heard that so many times it often made her want to scream.

But on a Monday morning, screaming just took too much energy, so she filled cups and walked away with no more comment.

In the event they needed to make a hasty exit, Serpico paid in advance for a pot's worth and a tip, all in cash. And maybe if they returned soon enough they'd have some breakfast — maybe a Spanish omelet or banana waffles, unless the no-frills diner couldn't make anything so fancy, in which case they'd have eggs over medium, bacon, whole wheat toast, and more coffee. Two large cups each and a little more than two hours later, the man in the pics exited the townhome that was adorned with his street number in shiny yellow brass above the door. He was bundled up for the cold, but without a balaclava. So even from across the narrow street they were able to recognize their quarry.

Serpico hopped up, and said to the cashier apologetically as he passed her sentry behind the counter. "I'll be back," not knowing when or even if it were true or not.

He paralleled Cole on his side of the street until the dude crossed over at the intersection to merge with him. Serpico bent over, peering in a display window containing the latest and greatest Nikes until his target passed, then fell in behind him. He felt both a little bit nervous and anguished by being that close to the asshole who had killed double the number of people as Son of Sam. That thought made him wonder if, like the previous killer, they'd make a movie about The Unholy Ghost, and if so, who would play him. Probably a younger looking Pacino. That fleeting thought, lost in the moment, caused him to grin slightly and lightened his mood.

Just over a block south, not a care in the world, Cole ducked into his regular coffee shop.

A clever plan was immediately crystallizing for Serpico. All he needed to do was nick the man's empty coffee cup before the workers cleaned his table. Easy for a professional undercover detective. Mission accomplished. Case closed. Serpico followed Cole in through the annoyingly strident door. Found him sitting at a scarred two-top on the way to the restroom. That would make it even easier.

First problem: they brought Cole his drink in a to-go cup. Although he knew that it would still work somewhat for the transfer of fingerprints, those wouldn't be nearly as good and complete as on a ceramic mug. He was disappointed. So Serpico sat and enjoyed a comforting hot latté on a cold morning, and tried to relax. Having his third large coffee of the morning, good thing he was still youngish, he should be able to hold it, no problem.

It wasn't long before Cole finished his hot drink, but one of the workers cleared his table before he even left, wadding up the paper cup and tossing it in a huge trash can behind the counter filled to the brim with its other compatriots, smashed and twisted look-alike cups. When Cole did leave he continued south in the direction he'd been walking. Disappointed at being unable to get the cup, Serpico followed him out. Next stop: dry cleaners. After picking up an armful of clothes, Serpico calculated Cole most likely would return home.

Serpico was right.

It was a short outing this time and so, after following him at a distance back to his plush townhome, Serpico returned to his window post across from his partner. Cole stayed in the rest of the day. It was a long Monday; Serpico and the linebacker had breakfast, lunch, and dinner at the diner. Two eggs, over medium and a side of bacon, for each, the real stuff, none of that turkey bacon crap for either one of them, for the first meal; the midday meal was a BLT with mayo and mustard for Serpico, tuna on whole wheat for the linebacker; and New York City's favorite cold weather staple, meatloaf and mashed potatoes for an early dinner for both.

After a while, an NYPD squad car pulled to the curb half a block away to take over the night watch. Serpico and the linebacker would return to relieve them, or their replacements, at seven the next morning. But before they reached the door Serpico's phone buzzed with a call. He saw the name. "Detective Rossi, how's it going?"

"Just fine. You got time to debrief?"

"Course. Where at?"

"How about The Dive Bar. That's it's name by the way, not a value judgment. Right around the corner from you guys on Amsterdam. 732."

"Be there as soon as we can."

"I'll be sitting at the bar in the Dive Bar." Rossi thought that was clever.

Serpico didn't think it was as funny as Rossi did, but he wouldn't hurt his feelings. Because Rossi believed he was very clever even if no one else did. All you had to do was ask him. He'd tell you.

The sign over the entry door read "Dive Bar." It was a dark sports bar with copious amounts of pub grub just down the block from The Cathedral Church of Saint John The Divine, The Episcopal Diocese of New York, one of the largest churches in the world. Close enough for parishioners to drop by after mass on Sunday for some hearty fare and a cold one or two.

A slate sandwich board sign holding the door ajar read in chalk: *We Have Beer As Cold As Your Ex's Heart*. That was always good for a laugh for first-timers and repeat customers alike. Especially after a couple of cold ones — beers not relationships.

From his perch at the long, scruffy, dark bar packed shoulder-to-shoulder with the afterwork crowd and neighborhood residents, Rossi waved down the undercovers.

"Welcome, gentlemen, welcome. You ever been here?" Rossi said. The truth was it was Rossi's favorite sports bar in the city.

They shook their heads silently as they took in the sensory overload of all of its sights and smells. Some pleasantly affirming, some not so much. Given his childlike love of the holiday, the linebacker particularly liked the white Christmas tree lights that hung above the bar year 'round.

Serpico got the impression that Rossi was more interested in hanging out and talking shop than talking about the day's events, but after a couple of those cold ones that were indeed as cold as an ex's heart had loosened their tongues, they got around to talking about their day.

Rossi agreed with Serpico that getting Cole's prints would be all they'd need to make a case against their primary suspect, convinced as he was that the pictures he'd seen were of the dude Bookworm had seen with the victim shortly before she was killed. Then they talked about the logistics of their watch. Rossi thought the detectives had set up in the perfect spot to surveil their suspect.

Showing that they took their job responsibility seriously, after his second cold one the linebacker stood and said, "That's enough for me. We've got to be back at the diner by seven in the morning. And five-thirty is going to come early. The sun is barely up at seven, and it's not happy about it either."

"Good man. Save your receipts and I'll get Lou to reimburse you ASAP."

"Cool."

They fist bumped and he was on his way. Serpico left soon after.

* * *

At seven the next morning, the undercovers were in their previous day's spot in front of the large picture window. The linebacker wore a nondescript plain gray hoodie with a hand warmer pouch in front. In the event Cole went for coffee again and he was able to make off with his cup, he'd have a place to store it until he could get out of sight of the store and the perp.

They settled in with a pot of coffee the same elderly waitress in the same old-style uniform brought them, anticipating another good tip. Better than her usual. Serpico hoped she had more than one of the uniforms, or at least washed it between wearings. The things one thinks about.

At nine-fifteen, like the day before, Cole's door opened and he was on his way. Apparently he kept on a schedule and was going to the coffee shop again. The linebacker rushed to get out, but this time, guessing where he was going, lagged behind just a bit. A block later, his guess had been right when Cole entered the coffee shop again. A couple of moments later the linebacker followed him in where the owners greeted him warmly. He wished they'd ignored him, not wanting to draw attention to himself, or even be noticed.

Cole went to the same table as the previous morning. A creature of habit, it seems, so it must be his favorite. This morning they served Cole his drink in a logoed ceramic mug. Things were looking up for the linebacker as long as he kept close and in control. Cole was in no hurry, rising slightly and reaching over to a nearby table to get a previously read newspaper. Apparently, when one is a wealthy author one can enjoy their morning coffee more leisurely than working stiffs. Besides, there's no reason to pay for the newspaper when a perfectly readable used one was within one's grasp. It looked like the *Post*.

Even from across the room the linebacker could see the large print headlines were about The Unholy Ghost. Even the linebacker thought that was ironic, the perp reading about his own murderous ways. By this point, he was even more convinced that Cole and the Ghost were one and the same. Since it was beginning to look like he might be there for a while, the linebacker went to the counter and asked for an everything bagel — toasted, with real butter; none of that margarine shit for him. He'd long thought you could tell how old someone was, and how uncool they were, if they called any spread — butter or any of the multitude of margarines — oleo.

He knew it wasn't possible to get a bad bagel in New York. Same for pizza. The worst you ever had was still good. Like all real New Yorkers, he ate it the way you were supposed to — a slice folded in half, from side to side. The worker passed him the two halves of the bagel right out of the toaster, still too hot to touch.

He picked them up with a paper napkin and, along with a white plastic serrated edge knife and two tiny tubs of butter, returned to his table.

While looking down to make sure he covered every centimeter of the surfaces in the glorious rich butter, he surreptitiously kept an eye on Cole, now involved in the sports section. Checking on the Jets. There was the answer for him being a killer. Being a Jets fan would drive you to kill — either yourself or someone else, but someone was going to die. The linebacker was able to enjoy his bagel and coffee regular before Cole popped the paper and set it aside. A sure sign he was readying to leave. A large gulp followed and he rose. Told the workers goodbye, and sauntered slowly to the door.

The pair of workers were busy — one with a customer, the second clearing other tables. This was the linebacker's chance. Walking toward the restroom like it was urgent, he surreptitiously picked up the telling mug with a paper napkin, using only his thumb and index finger on the lip to be sure of not smudging any fingerprint evidence. Slipped it in the large front pocket of his hoodie before appearing to change his mind about the restroom need and double-timing it to the shop's door. Picked up Cole before the next corner and continued to tail him. A thirty-minute brisk walk south and he entered a large two-story Barnes & Noble.

The linebacker followed him in. His destination was a huge display of Grayson Cole books. Recognized by the store's staff, they all gathered around their famous guest. It left the linebacker ignored, which was the way he preferred it.

Grayson spent the next hour signing their stock and chatting with a few customers who thought it was their lucky day to visit the store while the world-renowned author was there. While Cole was occupied, the linebacker texted Serpico and Rossi. Mission accomplished, they decided Rossi should replace the undercovers with a couple of unis. Rossi would meet him back at the diner to get the mug.

The linebacker then asked a cashier for a small B & N sack he could carry the cup in. Finished with his signings, Cole left, and the linebacker followed him home. He took up residence back in the diner with his partner. It wasn't long before Rossi showed up, a huge, satisfied grin on his face, believing the case was almost over. The linebacker passed him the sack, somewhat relieved to turn its responsibility over to someone else. Rossi returned to the precinct and handed the mug over to the lab tech on duty.

"How long to find out if we have a match to the Swiss Army Knife?"

"Normally, I'd say three hours, but I know how bad we all want this guy, so stick around. Shouldn't take long."

"Sounds like the second-best news I've gotten all day. If it's a match, it jumps to first best."

Chapter Thirty-One

"Certainly took y'all long enough"

The troops arrived outside Cole's Upper West Side townhome complex forthwith and almost at the same time. Marked and unmarked cars, lights flashing, but no sirens.

Wearing heavy lace up ECCO winter boots, with a warm parka replacing his thin suit jacket, and following the muzzle of the serious looking .40 Glock gripped comfortably in his right hand, Rossi crept sure-footedly up the snow-crusted steps of the stoop, the rubber lug soles of his boots securing his way. Holding his breath in the hope that the Unholy Ghost's reign of terror was about to be over. Ten unis, two of them female—showing the largest police department in the world's diversity, plus the two undercover dicks, brandished weapons in backup, Rossi and Park, plus Bookworm and Reefer because they'd earned the right to be there, shuffled around in the snow behind him, some stamping their feet to keep warm, but Detective Rossi had the honor of banging on the door loudly, and shouting "NYPD, open the door."

Rossi readied to pound again, but then came the soft sounds of weary footsteps and a TV playing from inside and a minute later the bright stoop light came on. Keeping the chain engaged, Grayson Cole timidly cracked the door and peered through the narrow space. After all, it was late at night in New York City.

Rossi glanced at Bookworm to see his reaction to the suspect's face. Book didn't need a better look. A big grin lit up his face and he nodded confidently. Then, just to make sure Rossi got it, he mouthed broadly, "That's him."

Detective Rossi showed his shield, then withdrew handcuffs, and said loudly, "Detective Sal Rossi, NYPD Homicide. Open the goddamn door." The man did so, hesitantly, and Rossi said, "Grayson Cole?"

Grayson nodded in the affirmative.

"You're under arrest for murder."

Cole turned red with what appeared to be genuine confusion. "Under arrest? Murder? I don't understand. Is this some kind of joke?"

Aggressively locking the cuffs tightly on him, Rossi said, "I assure you it is not a joke."

"Who am I supposed to have murdered?"

"Believe me," Rossi said sarcastically. "We got a list of names. You'll see it when you're arraigned. Speaking of being arraigned. Park."

Park recited the Miranda warning by heart. "You have the right to remain silent. Anything you say can be used against you in court. You have the right to talk to a lawyer for advice before we ask you any questions. You have the right to have a lawyer with you during questioning. If you cannot afford a lawyer, one will be appointed for you before any questioning if you wish. If you decide to answer questions now without a lawyer present, you have the right to stop answering at any time."

Rossi continued. "You understand? You probably shouldn't say anything else without a lawyer present...unless, of course, you want to. Speak or not. Your choice. Get it?"

Cole was embarrassed and confused, but it was that embarrassment which triggered a rage inside him. His facial features transformed, something tight around the eyes changed, and he said sarcastically, "Well, it certainly took y'all long enough. You're close but, uh...no cigar. That pussy couldn't kill anybody if his life depended on it. All he can do is write about it. I killed all those worthless pieces of shit."

"He? What do you mean 'he'? And who are you?" Rossi said.

"I'm Gordon," he said paradoxically.

Rossi, along with everyone else, stared at him in stunned disbelief. But Rossi only for a moment. He smiled cheerfully and said, "Well, Gordon, you're under arrest too."

Many novelists began their career with a stroke of the pen. In my case, it was just a stroke. A near fatal stroke at fifty years old and searching for ways to improve my brain function after, led me to writing fiction. I had no other goal than to help to heal my brain. But as a voracious reader a funny thing happened. A dozen pages into *Bottom Dwellers*, my first, I knew it was good enough to be published. And the day I finished it I knew what was to follow. Two more Dwellers books and God only knew how many more novels after those. The next two, *Mind Dwellers* and *Trail Dwellers*, along with the first all set in historic areas of north Georgia, set me on my new career path. Writing fiction—far more interesting and fun than the high-tech sales I'd been doing for more than twenty years.

A Brain in Third Person, the title of my next, alluded to the way I always spoke of my brain, like a separate entity from the rest of me, and is about a man who becomes a serial killer after a brain injury, and is set in my home of Atlanta. *A War in The Bronx* followed, about rival drug gangs in—you guessed it—New York City, before returning to *A Brain In Third Person, II The Return Of The Bad Penny*. *Devil's Sympathy* comes next and changes continents but follows the serial killer theme with a writing professor at Oxford University in England who has been killing people for forty years with a sword concealed in his gentleman's walking stick. *World of Rage* is a postapocalyptic dystopian thriller about two small groups of survivors of a virus intent on killing everyone on earth. And I started it a year before anyone had heard of COVID-19.

Eleven years after starting writing to improve my brain I feel cleverer than ever. Notice what I just did there? And feel that my creativity continues to grow.